EMERALD SECRETS

Book 3 – Seattle Trilogy
A Contemporary Christian Novel

Dawn V. Cahill

EMERALD SECRETS

Book 3 – Seattle Trilogy
A Christian Contemporary Novel

"I will lift up mine eyes unto the hills, from whence cometh my help. My help cometh from the Lord, which made heaven and earth." Psalm 121:1-2

All Scripture is taken from the King James Version of the Bible.

Cover design by Dineen Miller
Edited by Brilliant Cut Editing
Formatting by Rik, Wild Seas Formatting
(http://WildSeasFormatting.com)

To my Lord and Savior, Jesus Christ, and my Heavenly Father. Of all the talents you could have bestowed on me, you chose the gift of writing. And for that, I'm deeply grateful.

Prologue

"Hey, Risky. It's me."

"Yeah, Bro?"

"Got the info yet?"

His voice rasped into her ear, and she jerked the phone away. She glanced down the corridor and, seeing only a vacant hallway, closed the door of the tiny office. "Not yet."

"I need it today."

She paced from the desk to the window and back again, already regretting this. "I — Are you sure you want to go through with this? Think about who you'll be dealing with. You could get caught."

"I won't get caught. It's what Dad would want."

"Where he is, he isn't going to know."

"Don't say that!"

She clenched her teeth and stared out the small window at an expanse of pavement. "Well, I could get caught. You want me to lose my job?"

He cursed. "Once we get what should've been Dad's, you won't ever have to work again."

She closed her eyes. Numbers pressed into the back of her eyelids. Enormous, six-figure numbers. Enough to pay off debts. Buy some property on the island. Crossing her fingers, she nodded her head. She'd better not regret this.

"All right." Her feet carried her to the computer,

booted up and ready for her password. "I'll do it right now." Before she changed her mind. "Got a pen?"

"Yep."

After a few clicks of the keys, she found it. "Ready? Here it is." She gripped the phone as if to steel herself from what she was about to do. "Six four four five Southwest Elliott Drive," she whispered. "Seattle, Washington."

Chapter One

Howard McCreary wasn't expecting the doorbell to ring that damp June day in Seattle. He was looking at the dwindling balances in his trust accounts while he waited for a phone call from an LA agent he was considering. After a messy, expensive firing of his former agent, Morton, he needed another gig like his next breath.

It's not easy being a has-been rocker. When the gigs dry up, so does the money.

Another ring echoed, pulling him from his brooding thoughts, and he swiveled his chair around. "Dominic! Get the door."

He stayed where he was, listening. A faint click of the front door was followed by low murmurs. He touched the groove behind his ear. Oops, he hadn't put his hearing aid in yet.

"Dad?" Dominic appeared at the door, his long red hair screwed up in an irritating man bun. "Someone's here with a package for you."

Howard hadn't ordered anything. The person could be a fan, here on a pretext. On the other hand, nobody but Livy and DeeDee knew his new address. And he trusted his daughters not to share it. "Well, get it and bring it in."

"He said you need to sign for it."

He sighed and rose. This better be legitimate. He went to the front door, where a youngish man with a full beard stood holding a clipboard. Green embroidery on his shirt and matching cap looped out the words Emerald City Couriers. "Mr. McCreary?"

A fan would never call him that. A fan would address him by his stage name, Declan Decker. "Yes?"

The delivery guy thrust out a manila envelope. "A package here for you."

After taking the envelope, Howard skimmed over the packing slip. "Who's it from?"

The man pointed a black-painted fingernail. "Here's the sender's info."

"There's no name here." Howard looked up. "Just a box number."

The guy shrugged. "Sorry, can't tell you. I just deliver stuff."

Maybe it was a legal document that needed his signature. He slid his finger under the flap and opened it. Peering inside, he gave a whistle. Empty!

Not willing to give up, he dug to the bottom, and his fingers brushed against something. He pulled it out.

A photograph.

What? He lurched at the faded image of his late wife. Luna had been dead for over twenty years. Yet here she was in living color, in mid-laugh, her hair blowing. A dark-haired man stood behind her, but his cheek rested on top of Luna's head, hiding his face. The man's arms wrapped like an octopus around her middle. Staking his claim.

No way for Howard to identify him. Clever move.

In the background, GasWorks Park.

On the photo's flip side, a single penned line mocked him. "Your wife was cheating on you."

A knife pierced his gut, and he dropped the photo. How could this be true? During their seven years of marriage, he'd never once suspected, or even feared, that Luna cheated on him.

A throat clearing drew his attention to the open doorway, where the delivery guy waited, watching him. He held out the clipboard. "Can I get your signature, please?"

Howard signed, pushed the clipboard practically into the man's belly, said goodbye, and slammed the door. Breathing hard, he bent and picked up the photo, amazed by how much the accusation stung, even twenty-plus years after the fact.

Who could've sent this? And why? Nobody but his family knew his address. He rushed to the living room window to spot a small white car disappearing down the street. Then searched his phone for Emerald City Couriers. "When you needed it delivered yesterday!" shouted the website. He dialed the number.

"Hello," he replied to the female voice. "I need some information about a package that was just delivered to me."

"I'm happy to help you. What's the name of your business?"

"This isn't a business. It was delivered to my home and I need to know who sent it."

"Oh." Voices floated from the background. "I see. Wasn't there a name on the order?"

"No." He rattled off his address. "Can you check your records?"

"Let me check." Muzak waltzed into his ear for a minute. Then a click. "I'm not finding a request for that address."

"A young guy with a beard delivered it. Thirty-five or so, I'd guess." He gave a brief description, including the black fingernail.

"That sounds like Julius. He's still out on deliveries, but I'll ask him about it when he gets in. Can you call back tomorrow?"

He paced to the fireplace, then landed a swift kick on the bricks as though they were to blame. "I already asked him. He didn't know."

"If it was a self-serve order, we won't have any record of it."

Another kick, followed by a punch to the defenseless armchair cushion. "Why is that?"

"Some clients come in and prepare their own parcels. It's ideal for simple orders and much cheaper if we don't have to pick it up."

"Were there any walk-ins this morning?"

"There were quite a few around lunchtime. It's been busy today, and with the manager on vacation, we're a little short-handed. Anyway, I suggest you call back tomorrow. You never know, Julius might remember something."

With the fight drained out of him, he plopped into the armchair. "Will do. Thank you for your time."

~~~

Worship band rehearsal only lasted an hour, but Livy Lorenzo might as well have danced an Irish jig. Pregnancy made even simple things like singing difficult. Even while sitting on a stool. She sought DeeDee's gaze, noting the strained lines on her pregnant twin's face. She rubbed DeeDee's shoulder, needing connection.

There was no one she'd rather go through pregnancy and childbirth with than Deeds. She scooted forward and nestled the mic into the stand, then looked up to see Melodie Lansing heading her way.

Slinging her red Epiphone guitar off her shoulder,

Ravenna Chapel's guitarist stepped around bandleader Alan and planted herself in front of them. "Did you guys see today's column in StarSights?"

"That silly blog? No." DeeDee Rush massaged her bulging belly. "By the look in your eyes, it must be juicy."

"It was about your dad."

Dad again. The downside of having a famous parent? People assumed she and Deeds wanted to talk about him as much as they did. She scrunched her face and glanced at DeeDee, who raised her brows. What was Melodie talking about? Dad hadn't been in the news in years.

Mel's tone turned defensive. "When you have a famous dad, you shouldn't be surprised when his name hits the tabloids." She fisted her free hand on her hip and studied first Livy, then DeeDee, her dark eyes aglow.

"Mel, I'm glad you waited until practice ended." Livy absently rubbed her own pregnant belly, not the first time she and her twin subconsciously moved in sync with each other. Mel couldn't have known how she really felt about the subject of Declan Decker. "What did it say about our dad?"

"They called him a has-been." Melodie shifted the guitar to her left hand. "And hinted at a secret love interest."

Livy had to laugh. "People can say what they like. He'll always be Dad to us."

Melodie flipped her wavy hair behind her back. "But is it true?"

"The secret love interest?" DeeDee shook her head, her platinum Katie Perry pixie cut as gleaming as her husband Nick's new Fender bass. "Not true." She grinned as doe-eyed as Katie Perry. "He enjoys his freedom. It would take a special woman to make him give up his single status."

"In fact," Livy added, "he broke up with his latest girlfriend just before he moved up here. She happens to be the widow of Nils Nelsson, his best friend. You remember him?"

"Of course! Lead singer for Free the Defendants." Melodie raised her brows. "Why did they break up?"

"After a year together, they realized their feelings for each other would never blossom into love. They'll always be great friends, but nothing more."

"Ah." Graceful as a dancer, Melodie swiveled, then set the guitar carefully in its case and snapped the decal-covered case closed. Straightening to her full height, she jammed her hands in the pockets of her red sweater. "I remember so well when your dad released his first album — 1991, right? I was only fifteen, but my friends and I all had such crushes on him. It was Declan-Decker-mania in my middle school, man. Posters, magazines, the whole nine." She laughed and nudged Livy's leg with her red leather boot. "Bet you didn't know that, did you?"

Livy gripped the mic stand, childhood memories flooding her mind as vivid as if they'd happened yesterday. "Of course, we did. We were only five, but we remember the screaming crowds outside our house all the time. It drove our parents crazy."

Melodie adjusted her tortoiseshell glasses firmly on the bridge of her nose. "I was probably one of them."

Two feet away at the other mic, DeeDee grinned. "So how would you like to meet him?"

"Serious?" Melodie widened her eyes. "The very idea makes me twitchy."

Placing a calming hand on Mel's arm, Livy laughed. "No need to twitch. He doesn't come across as a rock star. Honestly, he's just a regular guy."

Her whole body seemed to melt as Melodie sighed.

"To be honest, it would be fabulous to meet him. As long as it's casual."

DeeDee met Livy's eyes as if to say, Time to do some planning! "Would a Sunday morning worship service be casual and low-pressure enough?"

"Probably." Their friend shrugged as if persuading herself that meeting Declan Decker were no big deal. "Anyway, you should check out the article."

Chapter Two

Howard's heart rate slowed, settling into its normal cadence as he opened his email. Someone was playing a sick joke on him. Luna had never, would never, cheat on him. Any more than he would've cheated on her. He scanned his inbox, and the top one hit him between the eyes.

From: #1fireantsfan78
Subject: Your wife Luna

Luna again? He wrestled with himself for a moment, unsure if he should open it. Yet the sender claimed to be the number one fan of his former band. Was this connected to the photo or a mere coincidence?

So he opened it.

> Declan Decker, or should I call you Howard Mccreary? I have two old vhs recordings of your wife Luna. Ive attached a digital sample so you can see for yourself, and a photo of the tapes. These recordings could fetch me thousands $$ in the adult entertainmet market, but Im gonna give you first dibs. If you want them you can have them for 250 grand apeice.

He'd seen painfully bad writing in his life, but this was atrocious. Had this person even graduated from high school? Morbid curiosity boiling over, Howard clicked the link, then mentally kicked himself. Idiot. That could've been a virus.

But no. Not a virus. He would've taken the virus over this…this travesty. This mockery of his late wife. His stomach churned as the one-minute segment unfolded before his eyes. His beautiful wife, degrading herself in a video she surely would never have wanted anyone to see.

Unfortunately, he couldn't unsee what he'd just seen.

His fists clenched. This could not get out. Luna—love of his life, mother of his daughters—must be dying all over again.

Nostrils flaring, he opened the attached photo. Sure enough, two bulky VHS tapes were set on a wooden backdrop, probably a table. *Me and Luna* was scrawled on the white labels.

After a glance over his shoulder to make sure Dominic was nowhere in sight, he searched the email for any identifying information. Nothing. He forced himself to finish reading.

Tex me at this number or send an email.

By now, his head burned as if he sat under a heat lamp. He drummed his fingers on the table and pondered his next move.

He poised his hands over the keyboard. "Did you send that photo?" If typed words could snap, these would've popped off the screen.

He waited five minutes for a response, then tried again.

"Who are you," he wrote, "and how did you get this tape?" He hit send so hard it sent shock waves up his arm.

The reply only increased his confusion.

11

My freinds call me Bro.

"That tells me nothing," he wrote back. "I want to know your real name and how you knew Luna before I agree to do business with you."

More finger drumming. Restless, he stood and paced the spare room of his rented house, then checked the screen again.

Don't matter who I am. You want the tapes
or not?

He pounded his fist on the desk, jostling the laptop.

A muffled voice reached him from the doorway. "Da…?"

"Yeah?" He squinted at his son's lips as they formed words.

"What's going on?"

"Nothing. Why do you ask?" He moved his chair so Dom couldn't see the screen.

"You were yelling and s…" More mumbling.

"I was what?" Dom's bad teenage habit of talking under his breath made communication difficult sometimes. And his own partial hearing loss didn't help.

"You were yelling and swearing."

"Sorry. It's nothing. Just the usual crap in my inbox. People are always asking for money." Howard emphasized his exasperation, and Dom nodded, blissfully ignorant of the sorry state of his dad's finances. And emotions.

Once Dominic disappeared, Howard replied to Bro. "Of course, I want the tapes. But how do I know you don't have ten more copies?"

He paced and clutched his head in both hands, waiting for a reply.

You just need to trust me when I say I just
have two.

He shook his head. Trust him? He had to be joking.
"I'll consider your offer," Howard wrote, "if you agree to
reveal your identity to me."

While he gave Bro time to think about it, his brain
hammered him with all the things that could go wrong.
Whatever Bro did, it would be in his own best interests.
Not Howard's.

After ten minutes with no reply, Howard hurried into
the kitchen for a beer to calm him down. Dom leaned his
elbow on the counter as he munched a chocolate chip
cookie and frowned out the window. Howard grabbed a
cold bottle of Coors from the fridge and popped it open.

Dom mumbled again.

"Enunciate, please." Howard emphasized each
syllable with a tap of his finger. "You're having a
conversation, not singing a rock song."

Dom rolled his eyes. "It's always raining here." His
whine scraped Howard's nerves.

"Look, I'm busy right now. I need to…"

"When are we going back to LA?" The raised voice
needed no repetition.

"We're not," he snapped. "Margo, my Realtor, is
trying to sell our house. We're staying here." Dom didn't
need to know his dad pinned his hopes on this transaction
netting him several hundred thousand, in hopes of
recouping some of what he lost in the settlement with
Morton. But if the house didn't sell anytime soon, he was
screwed. With Southern California home sales slowing,
but prices rising, he wasn't optimistic. And now he had
Bro's demands to deal with. The half million he was
asking for would pretty much clean out Howard's funds.

He started back to the study to see if Bro replied, but stopped when Dom called out, "Mom said I could live with her."

Shoulders stiffening, Howard turned. "We've already had this discussion, son. The court awarded me custody. You know that." His feet tapped. He needed to get back to his computer, yet his son needed him. A swig of beer eased his paternal concern fighting with his haste to settle things with Bro. "Besides, aren't you looking forward to being an uncle in a couple months?"

"Yeah, I guess." Dom stuffed the last piece of cookie in his mouth.

Howard's mouth watered. "Where'd the cookies come from?"

Dom remembered his manners long enough to swallow before speaking and to look at him. "Livy and DeeDee brought 'em over last night. You were gone."

"Really? If I'd known they were going to drop by, I would've stayed home. So how are your sisters?"

"Huge." Grinning, Dom held his hand in front. "Like, their bellies are this big."

"So how can I even think about moving back with my first grandbabies due to arrive?" Howard kept his tone casual so Dom wouldn't pick up on his agitation. "Man, I want to see them grow up. Spoil them." The anticipation of being a first-time grandpa was the only bright spot left in his life. "Look, Seattle is a nice place to live, with a great music scene. You'll get used to the rain," he told his son, then grabbed two cookies before hastening back to the computer.

Bro's garbled message waited.

> You can have one tape for 250 grand. Make sure the cash is in unmarked bills, if you

prove to be a man who can follow simple
instrutions I'll set up a second meeting for
the other one. Take it or leave it.

Howard dropped his head into his hands and
kneaded his scalp as if doing so would make his decision
clear. If he took the offer, he only had the man's word that
his wife's images would not end up on some sleazy
website. If he didn't...well, the result was unthinkable.
Embarrassment for his daughters. Besmirching of the
woman he loved. Degradation of her memory.

Not acceptable.

He clenched, then relaxed his fists a couple of times,
swallowed beer, and poised his shaking fingers over the
keyboard. "And I have to have your word that none of
this will go public."

Two long minutes elapsed.

Deal. You have two days, meet me at
waterfront park Wenesday at midnight
with the cash. Come alone or the deal is off.

~~~

Livy kicked her shoes off on Nick and DeeDee's
porch as Nick unlocked the door and held it for her. Inside
the red house on Laurel Court, the familiar piney scent
and comfortable furnishings still reminded her of the six
years she and DeeDee had shared this home. Their last six
years of premarriage, prepregnancy, single-girl life.

Livy turned and smiled at DeeDee, who tailed her,
holding her husband's hand. "I miss this little cottage.
Still, I'm impressed with how you and Nick have
transformed the place into your own romantic love nest."
She glanced around at the deep purple throws and
pillows dominating the black leather sofa.

DeeDee, still skinny even with a protruding belly, tossed her a grin. "Back atcha. Talk about transformations. You sure put the charm back into Scott's man cave."

"I tried." Livy followed her sister to their old favorite hangout, the sunroom, relishing the balmy 70 degree evening. "After he removed all his ex-wife's décor, it looked awfully bland. But now with a few extra sofa pillows and some pretty plants, I feel right at home." She couldn't help a soft smile at how much she looked forward to returning home to Scott and their own love nest.

Nick strode toward the kitchen with a wave. "You two go do your sister thing. I'm going to start the barbecue."

"Thank you, Mr. Deeds." DeeDee blew him a kiss.

Livy sat on the wicker loveseat beside DeeDee's big tabby, Miss Piggy, sprawled out as usual in a perfect crescent. She opened her iPad as DeeDee plopped beside her, cradling her baby bump in one hand, stroking the cat's orange fur with the other. "Okay, I'm dying of curiosity. Let's take a look at what StarSights is saying now."

" 'Good morning, Seattle!' " Livy read, flinging out a dramatic hand. " 'Greetings from the Emerald City. Has-been local rocker Declan Decker moved back to town. According to Decker's Twitter feed, he's loving his new semiretired life back in his hometown and looking forward to spending more time with his daughters and soon-to-arrive grandbabies. Was it really him our source spotted at Pike Place? And who was the pretty young brunette with him? A secret love interest? We'll keep an eye on him and let you in on what we find out!'"

"This is ridiculous." DeeDee snorted out a laugh, and

Miss Piggy opened her eyes.

"I know, right?" Laughter bubbled out of Livy. "I don't see any photos to prove it."

"A secret love interest." DeeDee's chuckles tickled her neck. "How dramatic."

"How cliché." Livy copied the link and opened a new browser. "I'm sending this to him. He'll laugh so hard."

"Good." After patting the awakened cat, DeeDee pulled her onto her lap. "And we can tell him about Mel."

With a chipper trill, Livy's phone rang. "Dad?"

"What is this BS?" He barked his words the way he used to do when they got into trouble.

She swiveled to DeeDee. Not the response they'd expected. She put him on speaker. "It's just a gossip column that tracks local celebrities."

"Rock stars, for instance," DeeDee cut in. "Like you. Sometimes they'll target the Seahawks or one of the Mariners. Or Amazon bigwigs."

"Not that we ever read this piece-of-trash column." Livy tossed her hair behind her shoulders. "A friend of ours tipped us off. Hilarious, isn't it?"

Why was Dad acting so strange? This wasn't the worst thing anyone had ever written about him. Not even close.

Silence vibrated before Dad broke it. "Someone is making stuff up. There's no secret woman in my life."

"Well, we know that, Dad. We just thought you'd be amused."

"Do you hear me laughing?"

As Livy flinched at the uncharacteristically harsh reply, DeeDee leaned in, her fingers tap-tapping the cat's fuzzy back. "Dad, you've been a target for the tabloids since the nineties. You should be used to this."

"Didn't mean to snap at you, kiddos," he said. "But

I'm sick of people poking their noses into my business. And it's only getting worse."

Livy pursed her lips. "Getting worse? What do you mean?"

"Forget I said that," he ground out. "I'm not in the best of moods today."

"Um, Dad?" DeeDee kneaded her scalp. "Is everything okay?"

Long silence. "Look, I need to go. I'll call you later, okay?"

He clicked off, and Livy eyed her twin. "We forgot to invite him to church to meet Melodie."

"Melodie can wait. Something's going on with Dad. Something he evidently doesn't plan to tell us."

Chapter Three

"It's a beautiful day at Emerald City Couriers," chirped the ridiculously upbeat female voice.

"Hello. This is Howard McCreary again, calling about a delivery to my house yesterday."

"Hello, Mr. McCreary. How can I help you?"

"Is Julius available?"

"No, he's out on deliveries. Can I take a message?"

"What time do you expect him back?"

"Anytime after four. Depends on how long his deliveries take. Can he call you back?"

"No, that's okay. I'll catch him later."

In person.

~~~

He found Emerald City Couriers in an old distressed-brick building located, coincidentally, a few blocks from his former home, the little rental he and Luna had called their own before he signed his first record deal and moved to a mansion on Lake Washington. Visions of the twins as little girls in matching pajamas, practicing ballet steps, brought a smile to his face. Beyond the roofline of elderly brick offices, the Space Needle soared into a clear cerulean sky. Three cracked cement steps brought him to the door he sought. Emerald City Couriers, proclaimed the gold-plated letters on the beveled glass door.

After a glance at the time on his phone—4:36—he

flung open the door, accompanied by a chime, and breathed in the odor of old mold and fresh paper. A few people mingled about, none of whom looked like Julius. The main counter had a new layer of shiny Formica, but nobody anywhere near it.

He might as well sit and play games on his phone like a millennial while he waited.

"May I help you?" The sweet voice belonged to a heavyset young woman peering at him from behind the counter.

"No." He shook his head. "Just waiting for someone."

One brow rising, she gave him a quizzical look as though such a thing just wasn't done around here. "Well, just let me know if you need anything."

"Will do." Blocking out the constant sounds of commercial activity, he turned back to his phone. Twenty minutes of Pac-Man Doodle brought the eighties flooding back…memories of a bittersweet era. The decade he'd met Luna, had twin daughters, found fame and fortune.

He was deep into the memories when the front door chimed and Julius breezed in, his light brown beard splayed over his chest.

Howard stood. "Hey. Julius?"

The other man visibly jolted. "Hey. Don't I know you?"

"Yes, you delivered a package to me yesterday." Howard thrust his hands in his pocket, fingers jostling keys. "I need to know who sent it."

Julius tipped his head. Was that a flash of irritation in his narrowed eyes? But his professional mask stayed intact. "The West Seattle address?"

Howard nodded.

"I don't have that information, sorry."

"Don't you even remember what the person looked

like?"

The guy's feet turned toward the counter like he couldn't wait to get away. Over his shoulder, he said, "It was a woman."

A woman? "What'd she look like?"

"Nothing special. Old, blonde. It was a cash order, so I didn't really pay attention." He stopped at a doorway labeled Employees Only, saluted, then disappeared.

Howard drove home, racking his brain for any older blonde women he might know. He wasn't sure what Julius had meant by "old." Such a relative term. Julius might consider Howard himself old.

So, a blonde woman of any age over fifty. Someone who must have known Luna. Someone who possibly also knew Bro.

In other words, a crapshoot.

Chapter Four

Howard fingered his jacket where the paper bag filled with 250 grand in cold, hard bills lodged beneath his armpit. He glanced around Waterfront Park, careful to zero in on the area between the fountain and the Aquarium. Descending a short set of stairs, he checked the time on his phone—11:53 p.m. Nobody dared hang around here this time of night except the homeless, evidenced by the dark lumps of blankets and scattered debris.

For the hundredth time, he reread the text he'd received today with instructions—no, demands—for tonight's exchange. He needed to get every detail right. The ominous words flashed like a beacon into the night. Earlier today, Bro had actually called him. "If you involve the cops," he had told Howard, "and I get arrested, I have someone on standby prepared to release the other tape." Despite the electronic distortion of the voice, the threatening tone came through loud and clear.

He had to do this. For Luna. For his daughters. How embarrassing for them if they ever learned such a tape of their mother existed. He'd had many years' practice shaking off the press's attempts to publicly humiliate him. But he drew the line firmly in front of his family.

Twenty yards before him, the black waters of Elliott Bay whispered, and somewhere, a siren wailed. He tensed, and the hair on his arms prickled. It would be just his luck if any cops roamed this place.

The silence deepened as the siren faded. Movement to his left made Howard turn his head. Two bums shuffled along the wooden platform, heads and shoulders drooped. Their voices reached him, but he couldn't decipher their conversation.

Midnight. And here came a black-clad figure hurrying toward him, the face hidden in the shadow of a hoodie. No way to tell his age, race, or other distinguishing traits. Tall. Long arms. Like Slenderman. A brisk, no-nonsense stride. Not an aimless shuffle like the homeless folks, or furtive glances like a drug deal going down. No, this person had business here.

His walk was springy, like a young person's, not like someone old enough to have had a fling with Luna.

When Howard spotted the dark scarf wrapped around the bottom of the person's face, his heart rate quickened. It was time.

Without a word, the man held out a photo, their prearranged identifier. Howard took the photo, equally silent, and shone his phone on it. He flinched at the smiling image of Luna in her sunflower bikini, on a beach somewhere, posing on one leg. He remembered that bikini. He slipped the photo in his jacket pocket while pulling out the money bag with his other hand. "The tape?" He held out his palm.

Bro produced an old VHS video and let Howard shine his phone on it. *Me and Luna* was scrawled on the label. He opened the bag and showed Bro the cash.

The tape and the money changed hands. And just like that, it was over. Bro hadn't said a word for the entire minute. He'd hid his face so successfully, Howard would never be able to identify him in a lineup. It would be futile to ask Bro any more questions about his identity or his connection to Luna.

After Bro turned to leave, Howard let him have the five-minute window he'd insisted on. He listened to the distant voices of the homeless, to the music of the fountain while he clutched the tape in the possessive way he would clutch anything for which he'd paid 250 grand.

How was he going to come up with another 250 grand in a week when he and Bro would meet again for Part Two of the transaction? Especially if his house didn't sell.

Only one of his accounts had enough to cover the second payment. But he couldn't touch it. Yet if he didn't, Bro might put the other tape out there. And the backlash from his fans, much less his daughters, would be worse than losing 250 grand.

His feet jostled in time with his careening thoughts. He needed to get home and see just how despicable this tape really was. Weariness washed over him.

Suddenly, he longed for his comfortable bed. He longed to close his eyes and escape reality, if only for a few hours.

Chapter Five

Livy's shoulders relaxed, and she breathed in the calm aura of the maternity clinic. The designers of Evergreen Birthing Center had hit upon a sensory combination that surely never failed to soothe anxious mothers-to-be. Kudos to Melodie for recommending this place. Soft mint-green walls, photos of smiling mothers and babes. All of it overlaid with a subtle lavender scent. She and DeeDee approached the young receptionist whose blue hair matched the counter.

"You're early today," said Melodie's friend, Crissy Collins. Even after ten years on the West Coast, her Brooklyn accent turned it into *You're oily today*. "I have your prenatal tea. Enough for two weeks."

"Great." Livy took two twenties from her purse and handed them to Crissy.

DeeDee did the same. "How's your tea business doing? Got many customers yet?"

"Not yet. Just you two and a few other preggie ladies. And Mel, of course. It's been tough getting customers. Most people turn me down."

Maybe because her tea cost twice as much as store-bought tea.

"If you know anyone who might be interested, tell them about this." Crissy lifted two small boxes adorned with sketches of women sitting among paisley and flowers. Expectance-T, said the label. "I wish I'd known about this stuff when I was carrying Amanda." She handed one box to Livy and one to DeeDee. "Here you are. Enjoy."

Despite the tea's price, Livy and DeeDee were happy to help the young family. According to Melodie, Crissy and her husband, Drew, an entry-level accountant, struggled financially to support themselves and their little girl. No secret how tough it was for many young families in Seattle to make ends meet, even on two incomes, with rising rents and property values a constant reality. The two of them had never had to struggle the way so many young couples did, and they knew the Lord wanted them to help simply because they could.

DeeDee thanked Crissy and stowed the tea in her purse. "Is Dani ready for us?"

"Yes, she's in the Blue Room. Livy, you're first."

You're foist, you're foist ran through Livy's mind as she made her way back. She enjoyed Crissy's East Coast accent almost as much as she enjoyed her husband's Texas one.

The midwife, Dani, was peering at her laptop when Livy walked in. She brushed a lock of short black hair from her forehead. "How's Mom today?"

"Not too bad considering I look like a hippo."

Dani chuckled. "You look beautiful. How have you been feeling overall?"

"The tiredness is getting better. DeeDee and I did as you suggested and stopped teaching at our dance school. We hired a couple of friends to teach, and we just pop in to keep an eye on the place."

"Tell me again what the name is?"

"Saffire School of Dance." Sidestepping the rolling stool she'd nearly kicked, Livy dug through her purse for a business card.

"I'm glad you're taking it easy." Dani put the card in her slacks pocket. "And how's Baby?"

"Rocking and rolling." Livy leaned a hand on the floral wallpaper as if she'd been knocked off-balance.

Laughing, Dani handed her a gown. "Go ahead and get changed. I'll be back in five minutes."

When Dani returned, Livy lay back on the crinkly paper and focused on the ceiling mural, a peaceful meadow scene, while the midwife felt around Livy's abdominal area. Dani's eyes narrowed in concentration as her fingers explored around, up, and over the developing baby. Livy held perfectly still, closed her eyes, and soaked in the lavender scent, the ethereal music piping into the room. Warmth enveloped her as though Dani had wrapped her in heated towels.

"Hmm," Dani muttered.

Hmm? Livy's eyes flew open. What was that supposed to mean?

Dani, frowning, retrieved a tape measure, then placed it around the base of Livy's bulge. She repeated the same for the circumference. Now a furrow had appeared between the midwife's brows.

Livy forced out the question she didn't want to ask. "Does everything look okay?"

Thin paper crackled beneath her.

But Dani didn't reply, merely remeasured. Finally, she said, "Just double-checking for accuracy." Her usual good cheer had disappeared. No pep talk or upbeat patter today. Something was wrong—something the midwife didn't want to tell her.

Was the baby dying?

Surging adrenaline shook Livy. Dani listened through her stethoscope, then nodded. "Heartbeat's good. One hundred fifty-one beats per minute. Nice and strong. But I'm going to send you for another ultrasound."

"Another one?" Livy's own heartbeat stuttered. "Why?"

Concern loaded the look Dani cast her. "Well, your uterus isn't as expanded as it should be by thirty-two weeks. Now" — she held up a hand when Livy opened her mouth to speak — "don't let that worry you yet. There may be nothing wrong. But see this?" She showed Livy one of the many diagrams she used to explain the technicalities of pregnancy.

Her temple throbbing, Livy studied the chart she'd seen a dozen times already, an outline of a pregnant woman with abdominal lines indicating the different stages of pregnancy. What fun she and DeeDee had poring over all the developmental charts and diagrams.

But now a pall cast a shadow over a time that should be joyful.

Dani indicated the thirty-two-week line. "Assuming your due date is accurate, you should be here. Instead, you're here." Her finger moved to the thirty-week line.

With a gasp, Livy grabbed the table edge. "Isn't that the same as my last exam two weeks ago?"

"That's what your chart says."

"You mean my baby has stopped growing?"

"I don't know. That's what the ultrasound should show." Dani cocked her head and searched Livy's face. "Please don't worry. It's possible we miscalculated the due date. But just to be sure, have Crissy set you up with an ultrasound tomorrow."

They talked for a few more minutes. Then Livy returned to the waiting room on shaky legs. "I need another ultrasound," she whispered to Crissy, avoiding DeeDee's questioning eyes. She'd share the news when she felt up to it.

But DeeDee was already hurrying to Room 2 as if she meant to ask Dani herself.

"How did the exam go?" asked Crissy when she'd finished setting up Livy's ultrasound appointment for the following day at Northwest Hospital. She studied Livy's face. "Everything looks good?"

"Not really. Apparently, my baby isn't as big as it should be."

"Oh no. Well, that may not be a bad thing."

"How so?"

"Smaller baby, easier delivery. You'd think, anyway."

"I hope you're right."

"Need any more prenatals?"

Livy glanced at the display of vitamin bottles behind the desk. "No, I'm good. Not sure about DeeDee."

With her hands cradling her baby bump as if shielding it from an unseen danger, Livy meandered to the chair vacated by DeeDee. A couple came in, the woman in skinny jeans with a slight bulge in her abdomen. Not far along enough to need maternity clothes.

Low murmurs in the hallway pulled her focus away. DeeDee and Dani stood there, identical frowns etched on both foreheads, DeeDee's jaw dropped in stunned surprise.

"Livy, can you come in here for a minute?" Dani motioned her in.

As Livy tried to question DeeDee with her eyes during her approach, DeeDee pinned her with a wide-eyed, you're-not-going-to-believe-this stare.

What? Livy mouthed.

DeeDee shook her head and followed Dani back into the exam room.

"Have a seat, girls." Dani leaned against the exam table. "Okay, the same thing is happening with both your babies. Maybe it has to do with the fact that you two are twins. I've seen identical twins deal with issues similar to each other when they've been pregnant. But what's going on with you two is a first for me."

Livy clutched the hand that DeeDee gripped her with. "What, Dani? What's a first?"

"Both of your babies measured the same size as at your last visit. It's baffling." She shifted one ankle over the other. "If I didn't know you better, I'd wonder if you'd both taken up a two-pack-a-day smoking habit."

"Wow." DeeDee's fingers pawed at her shoulder where her long hair used to hang, as if she'd forgotten she cut it.

"I'm only half-joking," said Dani. "You're both taking your multivitamins? Drinking your tea?"

They nodded in unison.

"Good. Keep doing that. You and your babies need those herbs and minerals. And both of you will need growth scans to see what's going on and ultrasounds to check your placentas and the amniotic sacs."

Livy's breath caught at the earnest concern on Dani's face. "Does — does this mean our babies might..." She couldn't voice her fears.

"I don't know yet what it means. I'll know more when I see the results of your tests. I suggest you get them done tomorrow."

"Mine's already set," Livy said.

"Great. In the meantime, rest as much as you can." Dani placed a warm hand on Livy's shoulder and the other on DeeDee's. "I'm staying optimistic that we miscalculated your cycle dates."

Easy for Dani to say. The clench in Livy's gut and her

elevated heart rate said otherwise.

Dani hugged both of them and wished them the best. Then they staggered to the lobby where Livy paced while DeeDee set up her own ultrasound appointment for the next day. Outside, a light spring rain fell on the pedestrians, sending them rushing under awnings or covering their heads with bags or backpacks. Inside Livy's black Jaguar, rain dampened the driver's seat through the cracked-open window. Livy fumbled her way behind the wheel, heedless of the moisture on the backside of her maternity jeans, and let loose with her emotions. Her cries, and DeeDee's wails, bounced off the windshield and echoed back into their ears like an ambulance in distress.

Wiping her tears, Livy sucked in a breath. "I'm pretty sure we didn't miscalculate our last cycles."

"I'm positive I didn't. I've been tracking it ever since my wedding day."

"Dani's just trying to think positive."

"How are we going to tell our husbands!"

Chapter Six

Livy picked up a *Parents* magazine off the waiting room table and tried to read it. It wasn't as if she hadn't already had two or three ultrasounds. But none of them had the portent this one did. Last night, over Scott's favorite dinner of minced beef cannelloni, she'd finally told him of Dani's discovery and the purpose of this appointment. He'd embraced her and assured her he'd take the day off work to be with her. Then he suggested they pray. What a guy. God had blessed her and DeeDee with the world's best husbands. In fact, DeeDee and Nick should be walking through the door any minute.

"Nervous?" Scott's worried eyes searched hers. He was getting better at reading her with each passing month of marriage.

"Yeah, but trying not to be."

The hallway door sprang open, and in walked DeeDee and Nick. As they sat, tension marred DeeDee's face, and deep lines creased Nick's forehead. She and Scott probably mirrored them.

"Here come Mr. and Mrs. Deeds." Her attempt at levity fell flat when nobody laughed. An aching silence shrouded them as though they feared if they hoped for the best, life would throw them a curveball. Best to expect the worst, to soften its blow. Scott pulled Livy tighter against him and stroked her hair. She leaned her head on his shoulder and felt her heart rate decelerate. Sitting here like this, in the shelter of her husband's reassuring arm, she could almost believe she was overreacting.

To her right, Nick squeezed DeeDee's hand and peered at her. DeeDee's face relaxed, and she cast him a weary smile.

"Olivia?" A nurse armed with a sunny smile, her eyes brightly innocent, stood ready to do battle with the gloom. "Come on back."

She and Scott followed the cheery woman to a windowless X-ray room where Livy changed into a gown. Veronica, the stocky young female technician, came in a few minutes later. Another smiler. Was smiling a requirement for graduation from medical school? *How To Disarm Your Patients 101: The Art of Getting Them To Believe All Is Well.* A skeptical smile on her own face twisted her lips, and Veronica glanced away.

Livy lay back and opened her gown. She gritted her teeth while the woman dripped cool gel all over her belly and began to move the probe around and over the unborn baby. Her skin itched where the gel tickled it, and her fingers twitched with the need to scratch it. Her full bladder didn't help. A loud pulsing noise, like a snare drum underwater, filled the room. Her spirits surged at the sound of her baby's healthy heartbeat.

"Are you ready to find out the sex of your baby?"

Scott shook his head. "No, we want to be surprised," he said, drawing out the last word. Her husband's drawl always intensified when his emotions got in his way. She suspected Scott deep down hoped for a boy, but would never admit it. He already had two girls from his first marriage. If this baby was daughter number three for him, he'd rather wait to find out. He'd adore their baby no matter the gender, but Livy secretly wanted her husband to have that experience of a son. If not this time, then eventually.

Nick and DeeDee, at DeeDee's insistence, already knew they were having a girl. One of the rare occasions in all of her and DeeDee's thirty years they didn't sync with each other. Nick already had one biological daughter, whom he saw only occasionally. Yet he, like Scott, just wanted a robust, healthy baby, whether boy or girl.

Veronica angled the screen so they could see their child. The ghost-like curves of baby arms and legs stayed busy, as they did at each ultrasound. "No abnormalities. All the organs are where they belong. The brain looks the way it should. You've got a normal, healthy child."

"I assume Dani sent over the records from my last appointment?"

"She did, and I've reviewed them. It's a bit of a puzzler. I've got some good measurements here. We'll compare them to the last sonogram to see if the growth pattern looks normal. But there doesn't appear to be anything wrong with your baby."

Scott gave Livy's hand a reassuring squeeze. "I know you need to check the measurements before you can say for sure, but just tell us your impression. Does it look like the baby has grown?"

While Veronica glanced at the still photo of their child on the screen, she kept her expression neutral. "It's hard to say. It isn't obvious just from the photos." She turned to Livy, then Scott, this time with eyes laced with compassion. "But I'm sure it's all good. Sometimes babies don't grow as fast as we'd like, yet they're normal in every other way." She patted Livy's shoulder. "The worst thing you can do for yourselves and your baby is to worry. I promise we'll get some answers for you."

Chapter Seven

Livy, leaning against the kitchen counter, soaked in the house's stillness. No sounds emerged from Kinzie and Lacie's room. Scott's daughters usually slept till nine on weekends, whereas Scott always woke at six, no matter the day. His weekend routine rarely varied. First, coffee. Then devotions. After he spent time in God's word, he'd shower and dress. The shower's distant hum enhanced the morning's serenity. The perfect time for a cup of tea. She poured hot water over the tea bag, letting it steep for a minute. The herbal scent tickled her nose as she stirred in a spoonful of raw honey to take the bitter edge off. She rubbed her belly, following the contours of the baby's limbs—an elbow, maybe. Or a foot. Whatever it was, it enjoyed the spot just under her rib cage, unaware of the pain it inflicted. Had the baby started growing again? Impossible to tell. Wavering between hope and dread, she swallowed a couple of mineral pills. B vitamins, magnesium, and iron for her and the baby. She took a sip of Expectance-T—rich with healthy herbs like red rooibos and ginger, steam wafting from it like a miniature hot tub. She breathed in the intoxicating scent. Delicious.

Her phone buzzed from its place in the breakfast nook table. She hurried over, nearly tripping over an expectant Murf, who waved his fluffy white tail. "Murf, baby, I'll feed you and Felix after I take this call."

She snatched up the phone. Evergreen Birthing

Center. The test results!

"Hello?" She glanced toward the door, listening for evidence that Scott was still showering. This conversation required privacy.

"Livy? This is Dani."

"Dani!"

"I have your sonogram results here."

"What did it show?"

A two-second pause. "The results show an issue that could be of possible concern."

Livy braced herself against the table. "What issue?"

"They measured your baby's head, and it's the same size as your last sonogram two weeks ago. This doesn't mean anything is wrong with the baby. As a matter of fact, everything else looked totally normal. Ten fingers, ten toes. No brain fluid or shrinkage."

She clutched her chest as if to soothe her thudding heart rate. "If nothing is wrong, why would my baby suddenly stop growing?"

"The most common reason is oxygen deprivation. If the baby isn't getting oxygen, we would've seen signs of brain damage. But we didn't. Still, I'd like to continue monitoring the baby for a couple weeks to be on the safe side."

With a shuddering breath, Livy plopped to the seat. "What…what about DeeDee's results? Did her baby stop growing, too?"

"I plan to call her next. I'd appreciate it if you don't discuss this with her until I've talked to her."

"Sure."

"And I want to see you first thing Monday morning."

"Okay." Livy swallowed hard around the lump in her throat, nearly choking. Alarm bells banged in her head as she set her phone down. Dani had assured her they hadn't spotted any abnormalities. What if her baby had some hidden damage that didn't show up until birth? Would God really do that to her and Scott? They'd been faithful to the Lord and had even saved themselves for marriage. Wouldn't God honor that?

She dug a bag of dog food from the cupboard. Murf and Felix clambered across the floor when they heard the telltale clatter of KibblesNBits. Focused on the bowls' contents, the dogs ignored Scott, who chose that moment to wander in, casting Livy that crooked grin he reserved for only her. He loved her even when she had bedhead and wore his old gray Nike tank top, which only made him more amorous on lazy Saturday mornings like today. Her long hair stuck out every which way, and she looked like something dragged off the street. She didn't get why Scott found this look so enticing, baby bulge and all. Not that she was complaining. Even after a year of marriage, his eyes still lit at the sight of her.

"Good morning, handsome." She forced a smile, relishing his freshly showered scent when he bent to kiss her. She couldn't ruin his day with bad news. At least, not until she talked to DeeDee.

~~~

Livy winced at the sorrow in DeeDee's voice when DeeDee sniffed on the other end of the line. "It must be genetic."

"I know, right?" Holed up in the bathroom where Scott couldn't hear, Livy pressed the phone closer to her ear as DeeDee softened her voice.

"I can't think of any other reason why both our babies have stopped growing."

Living apart from her twin had its drawbacks. Until last year, Livy only had to cross the hall to her sister's room when she needed her. And even though Scott's shoulder was strong enough for her to cry on, he wasn't Deeds. Nobody understood her like her twin.

"Maybe we have a family history of small babies," DeeDee went on.

Livy studied her disheveled reflection in the gilt-edged mirror over the sink. Wide blue eyes stared back at her, frozen in place. A knock tapped on the door. Scott? Her thoughts must have summoned him. "Deeds," she whispered, "let's call Grandma. Maybe she'll know if this is a family thing."

"Good idea. Why don't you come on over?"

"Be right there."

When she opened the door, Scott stood there. "Done in there?"

She rearranged her features to smooth over the distress. "Yes. Are the girls still asleep?"

His grin widened. "They are." His arm snaked around her waist.

Caressing the hair on his chest, she stepped back. "Honey, I need to go see DeeDee. I'll be back in a while."

He stepped closer, his eyes still lit. "I can drive you."

"Thanks, but I'll walk. It's just a few blocks."

As she hastened into the bedroom, Scott followed her. He leaned against the doorjamb, watching her don shorts and a tee shirt. "Any news on the ultrasound?"

She hitched her breath. She wasn't ready to tell him, but how could she get out of it? She and Deeds wanted to tell their husbands together. She grappled for an excuse.

"Um… I need to get over there. DeeDee said it's urgent." She stood on tiptoe and kissed him goodbye. "Let's talk about it when I get back."

Before he could protest, she was at the door, despite Murf's questioning bark. "We'll walk later, Murf, okay?"

Fifteen minutes later, she knocked on her sister's door and entered her former home. "Deeds!"

Her sister still wore her black-with-pink-hearts shortie pajamas, the dark fabric only accentuating her tense white face.

Livy hugged her. "Is Nick here?"

"No, he's doing a recording session downtown. We've got the place to ourselves." DeeDee gestured at the sunroom, and Livy shuffled behind her.

They sat on the wicker loveseat, the tinted wall of glass protecting them from the summer glare. While Miss Piggy pranced toward them and hopped up, Livy folded her feet underneath her and pulled up Grandma Gaia's number.

"Hello, lambkin." Grandma's upbeat, all-is-well-with-the-world manner never failed to settle Livy's nerves. She set the phone on speaker as Miss Piggy head-butted her thigh and purred.

She rubbed the cat's velvety head. "Hi, Grandma. How's life in Portland?"

"Weird and amazing. Alistair and I marched in the Roe v. Wade parade last weekend. Wish you could've been here. Oh, but you had one up there too. Did you participate?"

Livy recoiled. What an odd question to ask two pregnant women. "No, we didn't." The question grated on her nerves as much as quizzing Grandma on her church attendance would grate on hers. Before she and DeeDee had become Christians, they considered such events positive signs of progress. But now...how their hearts had changed since coming to know Christ.

If only Grandma would attend church instead of events that dishonored God. She allowed herself a moment to luxuriate in the hope she and DeeDee shared — that God would save Grandma. Because, if God could transform her and her twin from unbelief to faith, no reason to believe He couldn't do likewise for their Wiccan grandma.

"Speaking of weird, Grandma," she began, "we have a weird question for you."

DeeDee took over, pouring out the details of their babies' mysterious lack of growth. "So we want to know if this is something that runs in the family."

"Did the same thing happen to Mom when she was pregnant with us?" Livy jumped up and paced, hope in every stride.

Miss Piggy circled the vacated spot and meowed.

"Or to you?" DeeDee cocked her head, her eyes bright.

Livy could picture the crease between Grandma's brows deepen, could see her wrap a long gray strand around her finger while she thought. "I've never heard of such a thing. Why would a fetus stop growing?"

It's a baby, Grandma. But now was not the time to argue terminology. She sat back down. "The midwife thinks we may have miscalculated our conception dates." She latched onto DeeDee's eyes while she talked. "But we're pretty sure we didn't. I was thinking maybe we're just following a family pattern."

"Well, you know the two of you were low birth weight, but that's typical with twins. You were both around four pounds at birth. As far as my pregnancy with your mother, ultrasounds weren't as common back in the day. If she stopped growing in the womb, I don't think it would have been detected like it is today."

"Yeah, good point. So it's possible."

"Sure. You know, I can recommend some good minerals and herbs."

DeeDee held up a hand in a Stop gesture as if Grandma were sitting right there. "We're already doing that."

"Of course, you are," said Grandma. "What are you taking?"

Livy folded her bottom lip in thought, then released it. "A multivitamin pill…"

"One that contains folic acid…"

"And minerals." Livy swung one leg onto the ottoman. "And we drink pregnancy tea every day."

"What does the tea contain?" A note of concern crept into Grandma's voice.

"Well, it's not actual tea.…"

Livy cut in. "It's an herbal tisane, looks like stuff you find in the woods, like twigs and bark. It has ginger, for settling the stomach.…"

"Dandelion leaf, to help with water retention."

"A super herb from South Africa called red rooibos."

DeeDee clucked her tongue. "Our midwife vouches for them. We buy both the pills and the tea at her office."

"I'm sure you can trust her judgment," Grandma said. "But be sure to get a second opinion."

"We plan to."

"In the meantime, if you'd like, I can do some research on those minerals and herbs just to be sure. Will you send me photos of the ingredients lists for the pills and the tea?"

"We will," said DeeDee. "We've done quite a bit of online research ourselves, but feel free to check for yourself. Good idea, Grandma."

"Well, it sounds like you're doing everything right. In fact, I bet those babies will start growing again real soon."

Livy's baby kicked her rib. "Ow!" she gasped,

doubling over. "At least they're healthy. Mine kicks so hard, he's aiming to be the next David Beckham."

"Or Mia Hamm." DeeDee grinned at her as they ended the call.

Livy managed a matching grin to cover up the quaking inside. Grandma had always been a teacup-half-full kind of person who would cling to a sunny outlook until the bitter last sip if she had to. But Grandma had no way to know for sure that her baby would develop normally. The child might have stopped growing for good.

In that case, she and Scott would need to prepare themselves for the worst.

Chapter Eight

"**N**ote to selves." Livy stopped at the coffee shop entrance across the street from Ravenna Chapel and turned to DeeDee. "Don't let Dad know anything is wrong." As if to confirm her statement, her baby chose that moment to sock her a good one.

DeeDee gave a nod as vigorous as Livy's baby. "Since he's so bent on keeping secrets from us, we can darn well keep secrets from him, too. So if he asks how the babies are, we say, 'Fine, Dad. And how is life treating *you*?'" DeeDee's hand, placed strategically on her bulge, jumped and danced along with her baby's movements.

"And then we make *him* tell *us* what he was so upset about last week." Livy pulled open the door, relishing the aroma of fresh roast permeating the place. Dad, waiting for them inside, waved them over, scrutinizing their bellies. Lucky for them, nobody could discern the babies' lack of growth with the naked eye.

"Look at my grandchildren, growing like weeds." He grinned, the irony lost on him, hugged their necks, then stared at DeeDee. "What happened to all your red hair?"

DeeDee laughed. "It was time for a change."

He nodded, tipped his head, and reached a finger under his hair as if he were scratching his ear. "I like it. Anyway, this was a very good idea, meeting here for a little prechurch caffeine injection. Should keep me awake for the entire hour."

Leave it to Dad to make light of church. Livy forced a smile in response. "We're just glad you'll finally get to see our band play."

"You won't need coffee to stay awake, Dad. We play loud enough to wake the dead."

Livy winked. "You might want to substitute earplugs for those hearing aids."

At the counter, the plump barista did a double take when Dad stepped up, her eyes wide, then rearranged her face. Livy smirked at DeeDee. Apparently, the young woman recognized him, but was trying to stay cool about it.

"Iced coffee with milk and a breakfast sandwich," he told her, casting her a grin.

The barista refused to respond to his charm. She kept her eyes on the register and punched in numbers. "Will that be cash or card?"

"Cash." Dad opened his wallet. "And I'm paying for my daughters too." He indicated Livy and DeeDee behind him. "What're you having, kiddos?"

Livy's face flamed. *Don't call us kiddos in public, Dad.* "Cinnamon latte. Decaf."

"Hazelnut cappuccino."

The barista eyed their bulging middles, then nodded, her face even stiffer. At least she didn't get all gushy like some people did when they recognized Dad.

He paid, and they found a table in the corner. "I wonder if that girl thinks her face will crack if she dares to smile at customers."

"Dad!"

He chuckled. "Well, did you see her?"

DeeDee smirked. "Yep, she was all Poker Face."

"Oh, our order's up." Dad stood. "Be right back." He returned with a tray and passed out the drinks, then sat and sipped his coffee. "Now, tell me about your band. Personnel, style of music, et cetera."

Livy swirled sweet, spice-laden coffee around her mouth and eyed the fiftyish couple across the room staring at Dad. "Our lead singer and keyboardist is Alan. He's about forty-five and has been a music pastor in the past. Now he works at Amazon."

The denim-clad woman stood, still looking their way. She nudged her companion and tipped her head in their direction.

"Don't look now, Dad, but someone's coming over here."

In ten seconds, the woman reached their table and thrust a napkin at Dad. "Eddie Vedder?"

DeeDee snorted, then covered her mouth. A laugh burst from Livy. Poor Dad, trying, but failing, to cover his annoyance.

"I'm not Eddie."

"Oh, oh." As the woman wagged her finger, her voice rose to a near squeak like a game show contestant trying to think of the answer. "You're Declan Decker, right?"

Dad shrugged. "That's what everybody tells me. Must be true." He forced a grin and signed her napkin.

The woman, her eyes glowing like a child's on Christmas morning, stuffed the napkin in her purse. "Thank you so much! I was a big fan of yours back in the day."

"And apparently, of Pearl Jam, too," DeeDee muttered after she left.

His grin was a shadow of itself. "Maybe I really am a washed-up old has-been, if my fans don't even know who I am anymore."

His light teasing tone didn't fool Livy. "Stop it." She gripped her cup. "You can still rock with the best of them."

He shook his head, examining the contents of his cup. The furrows in his face seemed deeper, older, carved in granite, even in the misty morning light. He'd aged five years since last summer.

Livy thrust through the opening he left them. "Is that what you were so upset about last week? You see yourself as a has-been?"

DeeDee swallowed a sip of cappuccino. "Something was obviously bothering you."

"Oh, that." Another headshake. "Still dealing with all the crap I thought I left behind in LA."

"You mean, the fallout from Morton?" DeeDee leaned on her elbow.

"Or the house sale?" Livy asked.

"Yes, and yes. The house hasn't sold. I still don't have a manager, nor any gigs. Not only that…"

His clamped-shut mouth only heightened Livy's suspicions that he was keeping something to himself—something important.

"Not only what?"

His face cleared, and he waved a hand. "Enough about me. You were telling me about your band?"

Frustrated, Livy sighed. Fine. They'd wrangle it out of him eventually.

"Right." DeeDee's resigned reply brought her back to the conversation. "Livy and I are backup singers, and Nick, of course, plays bass."

Livy stirred her latte. "Our guitarist is a woman named Melodie Lansing.…"

"We like to call her Mel Can Sing."

Dad chuckled as Livy went on. "She's had an interesting life. She grew up around here, but her family formed a Christian country-western band, so she got to tour the world, just like we did."

"Oh, and in case you're wondering"—DeeDee's eyes gleamed—"she's in her early forties and widowed. No kids."

"And she used to have a crush on you, Dad. A long time ago. She had posters of you on her wall. Owned all your albums." Livy shared a grin with DeeDee at Dad's suddenly frozen face. Like the barista, he was desperate not to let anything mess with his cool factor. "Plus, she writes songs. Like you."

"Has she recorded anything?"

"No," Livy said. "She hasn't been active in the music biz for a while. Now she teaches music at a middle school."

"Well." He cleared his throat, coughed once. "Since you're all pros, I'm sure yours is the best worship band in town."

~~~

Howard braced his elbows on his knees near the back. His daughters' band started the Sunday morning service with a rousing, hand-clapping number. The bandleader whipped up the crowd's energy with shouts of praise. Good thing he'd removed his hearing aid. With his LA Dodgers cap low over his eyes, he didn't think anyone had recognized him. No way was he sitting up front where he'd be conspicuous, so his daughters told him to sit wherever he'd feel most comfortable.

Most comfortable, indeed. More like, least uncomfortable. He couldn't remember the last time he'd stepped foot into a church. If not for his daughters, he'd be at home, putting his feet up on the coffee table, sipping fresh roast and watching the Mariners with Dom.

He lifted his head and eyed the stage where lyrics

were projected on the wall. His daughters' voices blended well with the leader's...not too overpowering, not too wimpy. A proud feeling welled up in his chest. Their years of experience in Nils's band was obvious. He could do this. He could sit here for an hour and listen to his daughters sing again and forget the issues plaguing him.

The good-looking lady guitarist wore a Western-style outfit: fringed vest, flowing skirt, cowboy boots as ebony as her eyes and her long hair. With her dark-rimmed glasses, she channeled an oddly appealing librarian vibe. Hmm, interesting combination. Semi-nerdy bookworm, or free-spirited rock chick? He had to find out. After the service, he'd finagle an introduction.

Occasionally, she harmonized into the mic, but otherwise, she strummed like a banshee on her shiny red Epiphone that had to have cost at least fifteen hundred bucks. He wrestled his gaze away but found himself drawn back to watch her technique. She played like a guy — fierce, confident, bending and moving with the music — but looked every inch a girl.

She must have felt his eyes on her. For one still moment, she caught him staring. And then recognition played over her face, shifting to astonishment.

Apparently, the girls hadn't told her Declan Decker would be here today.

He smiled at her. Rather than return his smile, she forced her attention back to her Epiphone, smoothing over her momentary falter as professionally as the barista across the street.

For the rest of the set, her gaze traveled everywhere but at him as if she were remembering her schoolgirl crush against her will.

When the band exited the stage, his eyes followed Country Girl to see where she was sitting. He kept his posture casual but noted from the corner of his eye that she sat down with an older couple. A platinum-blonde woman and a gray-haired man. The musical parents, perhaps?

The second older blonde woman he'd seen today. He only noticed the one at the coffee shop because she kept glancing over, then away when he caught her staring. His mind circled over and over to the same unanswerable question: Out of the thousands of older blonde women in the state, which one sent him that photo? Would he ever find the answer?

For the next half hour, he heard only snatches of the pastor's sermon as his mind wandered. The dilemma of his severely dwindled funds pressed in on him. Worse, Bro might contact him any day now, wanting more. Demanding more.

Or Howard might never hear from him again.

Uncertainty clawed at him. Bro's identity nagged him. Memories of Luna kept intruding, dragging him thirty-five years into the past.

And something else was trying to get his attention.

That beach photo. She already owned that sunflower bikini when he met her. It had been her favorite.

And in the photo with the man, her hair looked exactly like it did the day they met.

What if the two photos—and the vile videos—were taken before he met her? And not during their marriage? It would mean Bro, or whoever made the accusation, was lying.

But why?

In that detestable video, the man's face stayed off camera. Someone didn't want to be identified, apparently.

But Luna didn't look any older than the day they met. She'd been dating that violent creep. What if he'd filmed

Luna?

He filed it away in his mind as a possible link to Bro, remembering how big the guy was, how threatening. How blessed he was that Luna had left that goon for him. The goon's name escaped him, but he'd never forget the moment he first saw his Luna Tunes.

Chapter Nine

May 1983

From the moment Howard McCreary spotted the Stevie Nicks lookalike, song lyrics materialized in his head.

She's a white cobra lady —

She sat across the vast marketplace, frowning at something in front of her.

Slitherin' in my brain —

He tried to resist her draw, but an unseen force drove him on. He was going over there to see what she found so all-fired compelling.

He gestured to his friend, Nils Nelsson, who squinted in her direction.

Hissing to me softly —

"Where you going now?" Nils protested. "I think we ought to get out of here before that dude catches up to you."

Drivin' me insane —

Howard glanced behind him as they meandered among chattering browsers at Seattle's Pike Place Market, past booths filled with rainbows of jewelry, colorful heaps of handmade clothing, walls of handcrafted knickknacks. A bushy-bearded guy in suspenders tooted his flute next to a man hawking rugs.

No sign of the shopkeeper whose one remaining Jimi Hendrix tee was tucked securely under Howard's jacket.

His feet pivoted toward his prey. Nils followed with agitated steps. Beyond the westward windows, the sun hid behind a blanket of industrial gray clouds. The pristine Olympic Mountains sliced through the horizon like sails.

The blonde woman's booth consisted of a simple rustic table, with an equally rustic chair, set near a corner of the vast space. Howard's gaze roamed the area for a clue as to what her special craft might be. A calligraphy sign dangled from scotch tape at the front of her table: Personalized limericks. In fifteen minutes or less. By Luna Rickles. $20.

He stopped, shifting from one leg to the other. The young woman didn't look up as she plied her craft. Her delicate hand fluttered over a five-by-seven piece of white construction paper. Lines of calligraphy flowed in bright blue ink. Several wooden calligraphy pens sat in a row to her right, and a pile of steel nibs glinted by her left. Three bottles of ink—blue, black, and red—rested open in front of her. Her tongue peeked out of the corner of her mouth as she worked, a furrow pinching her brow.

When she finished the last line, she pulled up a small glue gun and deftly glued the finished product to a sturdy black cardboard frame. Setting aside her makeshift canvas, she tilted her head, golden hair spilling over her shoulder.

"Oh, hey there." Her voice trilled as sweet as Suspender Man's flute. "You want a limerick?"

"Uh, sure. Fifteen minutes, huh? How can you think up a limerick in fifteen minutes?"

"It must be the Irish in me." Her eyes... They reminded him of the swirly, shimmering blue marbles he played with as a kid.

"Takes me longer than that to write decent song

lyrics." He fingered the cardboard frame. "Mind if I check this out?"

"Go for it." She nodded. "The customer isn't back yet."

He picked it up and read the fancy lettering aloud. Nils craned his neck and strained to see.

> "Who was he that caught the fine pass?
> Why, it was my son, Michael Tass.
> Although a beginner,
> He's always a winner,
> And always the head of his class."

Howard chuckled, but jumped when a sharp movement caught his peripheral vision. A large man frowned down at him. With a guilty jolt, Howard set the canvas in place.

"Hey, Mr. Tass." The poetess blinked up at the big man. "Your son's limerick is done. I hope he likes it."

Mr. Tass studied the canvas, and a grin broke across his face. "This is right on. If this doesn't motivate him to keep his grades up, I don't know what will. He loves his football, you know, but he won't get to play if he lets his grades slip."

She smiled. "I hear you, Dad."

He handed her two twenties. "Here you go. Good work. Here's a little extra for you." He turned and, clutching his prize, disappeared into the crowd.

She slipped the bills into her pocket and pivoted toward Howard and Nils. "Ready?"

Nils shook his head and pointed to Howard. "Not me."

Howard nodded.

"Okay. Name?" Her mesmerizing eyes captured him. "Uh, Declan. D-E-C, um, L-A-N."

Nils snorted. She scribbled on a pad of paper in front of her.

"Last name?"

"Uh, Decker."

"Deck-er." Her pen formed quick loops. "Your name is Irish."

"Yeah."

She appraised him, nodding as if she approved of what she saw. "You have that Black Irish look about you." She dropped her gaze again. "What is your most favorite thing in all the world?"

"Music. Rock music."

"And you're a songwriter —"

"Trying to be." He shifted and cracked his knuckles.

"Why do you write songs?"

"Because I have to. Why do you write limericks?"

"Because I can." A dimple peeked through her mask of concentration. "What kinds of songs do you write?"

"Songs nobody else has come up with." He swayed side to side. "Songs that'll make me famous."

"Everybody wants to be famous."

"Yeah, but not everyone has the key."

She raised a brow. "Which is?"

"Like I said, do something no one else has ever done."

"And your key to fame will be…?"

"My music." He cracked his knuckles again. "It's unique. It's messy."

"Messy?"

"My songs are an organized, structured mess. Grungy, you know."

"Grungy." She pursed her mouth. "An organized, structured mess. That's an oxymoron, my friend."

"You calling me a moron?" When she rolled her eyes, he blurted, "Kidding. I know what the word means. I'm not a moron."

Nils guffawed.

Luna surveyed Howard, her lips twitching, and then focused on the paper. "Okay, moving on. What's your favorite color?"

"Yellow." Like her hair.

"Second favorite?"

"Red."

"Age?"

He caught a twinkle in her eye. "Twenty-two. Why do you need to know?"

"You never know." She shrugged. "Be back here in fifteen minutes." She set the pen down and smiled. With a start, he smiled back and waved as he and Nils sauntered off.

"Declan Decker." Nils scoffed. "Haha. I bet she thinks it's your real name."

"Of course she does."

"Are you gonna ask her out?"

Howard stared straight ahead. "Maybe."

"She's gonna be mad when she finds out Declan Decker ain't your real name."

"Maybe." He rolled his shoulders. "Do you have a twenty?"

"You gotta be kidding. You make more money than I do."

Howard punched Nils. "I spent all my cash on them Motley Crue tickets."

"You expect me to give you a twenty so you can go check out that blonde babe some more?" Nils shot him an outraged glare. "Go bum it off someone else."

"Okay." Howard rubbed his hands down his face and arranged his features in forlorn lines. With Nils in tow, he went in search of young mothers and senior citizens to wrangle up the twenty. Likely prospects were everywhere—gazing in merchandise-laden windows, emerging from shops with bags of souvenirs, picking their way down the slippery cobblestoned hill. He trotted out his standard spiel as he approached each one, taking care to avoid the tee-shirt shop where he'd pilfered merchandise.

"Excuse me, ma'am, I lost my wallet. Can you spare a couple bucks so I can buy a birthday present for my mom?" He scored five from a young mom and another two from a kind-looking middle-aged couple.

"Excuse me, sir, I lost my wallet, and I need a present for my sister. Could you by any chance spare a couple bucks?" He got three out of an elderly gentleman and three from a younger gentleman with a shiny leather briefcase, who acted like he was only shelling it out to get the panhandler out of his hair.

At one point, Howard thought he glimpsed the angry shopkeeper in the crowd, and he grabbed Nils's sleeve. "Let's get out of here." They hurried out of the market toward the street.

The fish-and-diesel smell of Seattle's waterfront hovered thick. Howard checked his watch and quickened his pace. He and Nils neared the fish tossers and stopped to observe the spectacle of sea creatures sailing through the air. Silver projectiles flew over and back, up and down, like a well-choreographed dance. He had all of fifteen dollars, including the two he came with. Already forty-five minutes had passed since he left the blue-eyed poetess, and his watch showed five thirty. Six o'clock, quitting time, fast approached, and he still needed five bucks.

A quivering fish launched high as he crossed his fingers in hopes Luna would wait for him. The creature landed, wriggling and dancing, in the other merchant's arms. Tourists always hung around this sidewalk with their cameras aimed at the flying fish. He scanned the nearby faces, and then nodded and approached a plump middle-aged woman clad in short slacks, a camera slung around her neck. Her shirt proclaimed she'd left her heart in San Francisco.

"Hi, ma'am," he said in his smoothest voice, trying to keep the desperation from showing. Nils stood by, smirk intact. "I was wondering if you could help me out."

The tourist cast him an annoyed glance.

"I lost my wallet, and I need some help getting something to eat and a bus ticket home."

She stared hard at him. "Young man, does your mother know you're doing this?"

"Uh—"

"My son is about your age, and I would be appalled if he had to beg like you're doing."

Nils stepped up. "You'll have to excuse my friend. He's just been laid off."

She huffed. "I thought he lost his wallet."

"Well, that too."

The woman shook her head and dug in her pocket, jowls shaking. "I'm going to give you something, but only if you promise you'll go home right now and never do this again."

"I promise. I can't tell you how much I appreciate this."

"Oh, stop." She handed him a crisp new twenty. "Now, go home."

Howard snatched the bill. "Thanks, ma'am. Enjoy your stay in the Emerald City."

As they raced into the marketplace, Nils laughed. "Way to sound like a tour guide."

Howard checked his watch again. "It's five forty-five. She better still be there."

They neared her corner. No blonde poetess. He craned his head to the right, then to the left, before frowning at Nils. "Do you see her, buddy?"

"You know I can't see that far," said Nils. "Didn't bring my glasses."

Howard's heart did a free-fall. "Man, she must've left already." Merchants bustled, busily packing up their goods, disassembling their displays, counting their take for the day.

He ambled toward her corner, kicking himself. Idiot. Why'd he take so long to round up twenty bucks? He probably could have talked her down to ten or fifteen.

"Looking for me?" a sweet voice to his left called out. He lurched and nearly tilted off-balance. The gleaming-haired poetess, brows in a frown, stood there, holding a box under her arm. "What took you so long?"

"Uh, sorry." His tongue tripped. "I was unaccountably delayed. I apologize."

"Well, here's your limerick." She set the box on the floor and reached in. The look she gave him held a good measure of reproach as she passed him a framed cardboard canvas covered in fancy red lettering. Nils squinted over his shoulder, and Howard muttered the words,

> "I'm Irish and Declan's my name,
> A seeker of fortune and fame.
> I'll write you a song,
> It's messy and long—
> For life without music is lame."

A funny feeling crept over him. There he was on paper, all five-foot-ten of him, in a red-ink, five-line nutshell.

She smiled, looking pleased with herself.

"You nailed me." He grinned and gave her the twenty he'd finagled off the San Francisco-loving lady.

"Thank you." She pocketed the twenty.

He couldn't stop staring.

She tilted her head. "What?"

"What are you doing tomorrow?"

She didn't blink. "My boyfriend and I are going to see *Return Of The Jedi*."

He wouldn't let that deter him. "How about next weekend?"

Nils snickered.

Luna rolled her eyes. "You know the Pacific Northwest Jazz Dance Competition?"

Howard shook his head.

"I'm competing in it. So I won't be here."

"Where is it?"

She smiled at him the way mothers smile at their toddlers who keep asking why. "Seattle Center. Why do you ask?"

"Maybe I'll drop by and watch. Can I walk you out?"

"If you don't mind a punch in the nose from my boyfriend."

He stood rooted to the spot, already looking forward to next weekend, as she glided away.

A hand clamped onto his shoulder, and he whirled.

"Hands in the air, young man." When Howard reared back and raised his hands, a uniformed officer patted him down, then reached under Howard's jacket, and pulled out the stolen tee shirt. Another cop grabbed his arms and pinned them behind his back.

Pain slashed his shoulders like a switchblade. Howard gasped.

"You're under arrest. You have the right to remain silent."

Panic threatened to erupt. He tuned out and glared at the scowling shopkeeper behind the cop, then at Nils, making a swift getaway toward the exit.

He cursed as the officer snapped handcuffs around his wrist with a decisive click. More curses spewed off his tongue as the cop hustled him past gawking shoppers, and again when the officer jammed him into the back of a patrol car. He shrank down in his seat while the car passed the blonde poetess strolling along the sidewalk hand-in-hand with some dude. And he cursed all the way to jail.

Chapter Ten

Ah, Luna. If you'd lived, you'd be a new grandma in a couple months. I still miss you, you know. You were my muse.

With a loud riff from the brunette's red guitar, the band reminded Howard where he was. The animation on her face drew his attention back to her as though she expected every eye, especially his, to land on her. Everyone around him was standing, and the brunette — Melodie? — was singing a country-flavored tune. Nice, sultry voice. Polished, confident. Much like the rest of her.

The song ended, and he sat while someone made announcements. He'd never been a fan of pickin'-and-grinnin' music. So why were country-western lyrics suddenly running through his head?

I traded in my rock and roll
For a little country soul;
Threw away my leather suits
Bought five pairs of cowboy boots.

What if he were to release a country album? Sure, he could figure out how to sing with a twang and teach himself to play the banjo. But what would his fans think? Much less the media? He could only imagine the headlines. *Declan Decker abandons rock and roll, turns country.*

He shook away the image. The odds that he'd ever don pointy-toed cowboy boots were about as likely as moving to the Bible Belt.

~~~

DeeDee finished coiling the microphone cord and checked the others' progress. Livy had one more mic to put away. Nick winked at her as he hauled the last music stand to the storage room behind the stage. She responded with an exaggerated wink of her own. Alan lugged the keyboard away, and, DeeDee noted, Melodie had disappeared. She always stayed to help, so where did she go?

Only a few parishioners remained in the sanctuary, one of them Dad, stabbing at his phone in the front pew as he waited. Scott lounged next to him, watching Livy's every move with that newly-married-man smile.

When the stage was clear, Livy and DeeDee visited the ladies' room, where they found Melodie staring at herself in the mirror like a deer caught in headlights. DeeDee rushed to her side. "Mel. Everything okay?"

Melodie slid her gaze to them and nodded. Then shook her head, her bright eyes latching onto DeeDee.

"Yes?" DeeDee nodded along. "No? Which is it?"

"You…" Melodie burst out. "You didn't tell me your father was going to be here!" She turned and scurried out the door. The clang of her boot heels grew fainter, then faded away.

DeeDee sensed, more than saw, Livy's chin drop, surely mirroring her own. Then the laughter bubbled out.

"She never got over her crush on him, apparently." Livy snickered.

"Poor girl." DeeDee managed between giggles. "She's so painfully shy. Well, we're just going to have to do something about this." She placed a finger on her chin, an idea brewing. "In fact, maybe Dad just needs a new woman in his life. Maybe then he wouldn't look so unhappy all the time." She waggled her brows at Livy, and they returned to the auditorium.

Scott, Dad, and Nick stood there, watching their approach.

A smile tugged at Dad's mouth. "What's so funny?"

"Nothing." Livy tightened her lips against the grin pulling at them. "Just having a sister moment."

He gave them a doubtful stare, then went on. "Anyway, I was just telling your husbands, lunch is on me today. Ian Cutler's on Shilshole Bay has the best seafood in town. Sound good?"

"Sure, Dad." An idea tickled DeeDee's mind. "But wouldn't it be nice if you had a date, too?"

He shrugged. "I'm fine with just the five of us. I don't need a date."

As she and Livy followed Dad out of church, DeeDee met Livy's eyes, recalling Melodie's hasty retreat. Despite her ease on stage, her comfort with performing, Melodie had once confessed that she still battled social awkwardness in one-on-one interactions, especially with attractive men. She hadn't dated much since her husband died.

DeeDee could see a long stretch of dateless years ahead for Melodie. All because she let her nerves get the best of her. Too bad. She'd just missed a chance for an invitation to lunch with the fabulous Declan Decker.

Unless she and Livy intervened.

~~~

After several texts back and forth between Melodie and DeeDee, Melodie finally agreed to meet them for lunch at Cutler's. "It's not a date, girlfriend," DeeDee insisted. "It's just a chance for you to meet him. He's totally cool, really nice. C'mon, you may not have another opportunity."

From their booth, DeeDee gazed past the cars packing the lot, to the peaceful bay. Gulls soared and played in the cloud-studded sky, its horizon dotted with sailboats. They'd waited twenty minutes, and Melodie still hadn't shown. DeeDee pinched off another piece of sourdough bread from the loaf and slathered butter on it, but it couldn't quiet her growling stomach. "Our babies must be *very* hungry by now," she whispered to Livy beside her, who was mouthing something across the table to Scott.

"Is your friend going to be here soon?" Dad's measured patience only heightened her annoyance. "If not, we should probably go ahead and order."

Nick's eyes started to glaze over as he took sip after sip of coffee and downed appetizers. "I think that's a good idea. I, for one, could use some food real soon."

DeeDee looked out the window to see Melodie emerging from her silver Jetta. She'd changed out of her church clothes into a simple blue sundress and flip-flops. Tossing her windblown hair out of her face, Melodie stepped gingerly onto an island of fresh bark dust, ducked under the frail branches of a newly planted tree.

"Here she comes."

Melodie strode inside and made her way to their table. She plopped into the vacant seat beside DeeDee, trailing sun-scented air behind her. "Sorry I'm late. I had to run home first."

Dad stood and held out his hand. "Hi, I'm Howard McCreary. You must be Melodie. You sounded great this morning."

"Thanks. Glad to meet you." Melodie gave a stiff smile, returned his shake, then shook hands with Scott and Nick. The vinyl-backed menu trembled in her hands, and she studied it like she had final exams in an hour. Dad opened his mouth to say something, but must have thought better of it when he saw Melodie's focused expression.

DeeDee nudged her. "Lighten up," she whispered when the men started talking again. "This is your chance to make a good impression."

Melodie merely flashed that tight smile again and recited the mantra she used whenever she was nervous. "I'll be fine."

Directly across from Melodie, Dad surveyed her with narrowed lids. DeeDee could halfway imagine what must be going through his head. *Most women fall all over me, but this one acts like I'm the last person she wants to talk to.* Melodie, meanwhile, made comments under her breath about the menu items, studiously avoiding Dad's gaze. DeeDee wanted to wring her neck and tell her to stop being such a cold fish. And she would, if not for the other restaurant patrons who kept looking over at their table.

Dad was rarely able to go anywhere in public without attracting attention. The downside of fame. But after years of practice, he no longer seemed to notice unless someone got right in his face, like the lady at the coffee shop. She sighed and listened to Melodie with half an ear, nodding and replying in all the right places.

"So, Melodie." Dad's stage voice commanded attention. "How many guitarists does it take to change a lightbulb?" His mouth twitched. Ha. He was going to get her attention, whatever it took.

Melodie's head shot up as her limbs visibly loosened. "Ten." She flashed brilliant white teeth. "One to change the bulb, and nine to say, 'Not bad, but I could've done it better.'"

Groans and laughter all around, Dad's most of all.

"How about this one." Nick winked at DeeDee, then grinned at Melodie. "What's the difference between a savings bond and a bass guitarist?"

"That's easy." Melodie cast him a knowing smile. "The savings bond eventually matures and earns money."

More laughs, plus a sheepish one from Nick. Dad nodded in Melodie's direction. "She knows her stuff."

Her face crinkled with mirth as she looked across the table. "My dad raised me on guitar jokes." Her smile widened before she tossed her hair back and returned to the menu.

DeeDee peeked at Dad, his gaze on Melodie, a glint in those famous dark eyes.

His phone rang, loud and intrusive, and the sparkle vanished. He squinted at the screen, and his face transformed. DeeDee blinked. It was like watching Belle's prince transform into an angry Beast.

As Dad rose, excused himself, and strode to the exit, DeeDee turned to Livy and saw her thoughts echoed in her twin's eyes. Whoever was on the other end of that call, she was convinced, held the answer to Dad's secret.

Chapter Eleven

Howard clamped the phone against his good ear. "Bro," he snapped behind the restaurant, the only unoccupied area except for two seagulls playing with a piece of bread. "I was right in the middle of a family dinner."

"Meet me Wednesday night at Freeway Park if you want the second tape," rasped the distorted voice. "On the sidewalk above the pond."

Howard bared his teeth at his unseen caller. "Midnight again?"

"Nine forty-five." The call clicked off before he could ask why such an odd time. Yet he couldn't question it. Bro held all the cards.

The same question stared him in the face again. Which fund should he deplete? He jabbed his Realtor's phone number on the keypad. He didn't care if she was getting tired of hearing from him. "Hard to believe she came so highly recommended," he mumbled. "If she isn't going to do her job, I'll find someone who will."

Voice mail again. He ended the call, then stopped by the men's room on his way back in, neutralized his expression in the mirror, and strode to the table as though he hadn't a care. Ignoring his daughters' questioning faces, he sat and ordered a pitcher of beer from the passing waiter.

"Who was that, Dad?" DeeDee asked.

"A business partner." He avoided her eyes and

picked up a fish cutlet, making a show of dipping into the special sauce and taking a huge bite. He needed to keep his mouth full so they'd stop asking questions.

Livy didn't buy it. "You sure looked mad. Everything okay?"

"Yep." He didn't meet her eye as he savored the perfect, deep-fried morsel. The waiter set a pitcher of dark beer in front of them. Howard filled chilled mugs for himself and the guys. "Would you like some?" He looked up to see Melodie watching him, her eyes like deer in the headlights.

"Sure."

Despite the ensuing shallow, meaningless conversation, his daughters kept casting worried glances at him. He couldn't blame them. Bro's impossible demands had turned a pleasant meal into a morbid scene from "Hotel California." No matter how many times he stabbed it, he just couldn't rid himself of that beast. He only half-listened to Nick on the other side of him, reminiscing on some childhood memory.

Howard jolted to attention when he heard, "I think we're going to head home." Scott stood. Then Livy followed suit. "My wife needs to rest. Thanks for the lunch, Howard."

He nodded in his usual nonchalant way. "My pleasure. Thanks for joining me."

Nick and DeeDee also stood. Nick helped DeeDee with her sweater, his proprietary manner endearing.

"Melodie, aren't you sticking around?" Howard asked when she got up, taking a quick peek at her slim, tanned legs. "I don't want to drink half a pitcher of beer by myself."

DeeDee smirked at Melodie. "Go on. Have a beer with Declan Decker. Sheesh!"

Melodie, all shy librarian, cast him a half-smile — her version of flirtatious? — and sat back down. The other four hugged his neck, and moments later, he was alone with Melodie, who gazed at him as if expecting he'd start the conversational ball rolling.

Okay, then, he would.

"So." He topped off her mug of beer, then his own. "My daughters tell me your family was in the music business."

She lifted her mug with a quivering hand. Either from the full mug or from nervousness.

Or both. Too bad he couldn't ask her exactly how old she was. Early forties, according to DeeDee. But she didn't look forty.

Like DeeDee had said last year after he hooked up with Brittany, each woman he'd dated was younger than the last. If he and Melodie started going out, she wouldn't be the youngest woman he'd ever dated. That honor still went to thirty-seven-year-old Brittany.

Melodie took a sip, then set it down. "We called ourselves The Mighty Quinns. That was our family name. Remember that old song?"

"'Quinn the Eskimo'? I liked that song."

"I did too. Anyway, we were a Southern Gospel quintet."

"I bet you were a mighty good quintet."

"Ha! Thanks. Mom and Dad, my two older brothers, and me. Our sound often got compared to the McKameys. Do you know them?"

"Doesn't ring a bell."

"They're a family gospel group from Tennessee. My mom grew up outside Knoxville, so she had the Southern twang thing goin' on. Just like Mama McKamey. But in our early years, we were based here, where there's not much demand for our sound. We were way more welcome down South. That's where we did most of our touring."

"But you grew up here?"

"Until high school. We relocated to Nashville for a while but came back here when my parents retired from music. My dad had developed heart problems and" — she shrugged — "wanted to be near his family for his final days."

Howard opened his mouth to ask the obvious question but didn't know how to present it in a sensitive way.

She answered it for him. "He passed away about ten years ago."

"He must have been pretty young."

"Yes. Only fifty-one."

Younger than Howard's current age. "And the rest of your family? Are they still around?"

"One of my brothers lives here, the other stayed in Nashville. My mom is still here, and now she's not-quite-happily remarried."

"What does that mean?"

"It means, my stepdad is a wonderful Christian man who treats my mom well, but he isn't the grand love of her life."

An image of Luna popped into his mind. "I get that. Her soulmate is gone, yet she didn't want to be alone."

The cloudy light from the window cast ripples on her dark hair. "Absolutely. I decided not to do it the way Mom did after my own husband died."

"What did you do different?"

"My husband, Thomas, died in a plane crash five years ago." She broke eye contact, gazed at the beverage in front of her. "It was the hardest thing I've ever had to endure. After I got through the grieving process, I realized I didn't want to remarry the first nice man who came along just to be with someone."

"I totally get that. Any kids?"

She looked up, her eyes dark with grief. "No, even though we tried for five years." Still the skittish deer, she ducked her head, her cheeks tinged with pink as though she regretted the TMI.

What a refreshing change from the brash, aggressive women he'd grown used to. "I'm sorry. Life sucks sometimes. I lost my wife when the girls were only six."

While they talked about lost spouses and childhood dreams, Melodie visibly relaxed, laughing at his feeble humor attempts. The beer gone, Howard flagged down the waiter and requested the bill. Yet he didn't want their conversation to end.

"Would you like to go somewhere to listen to live music?" He winked. "Assuming you're brave enough to be seen with me in public."

"Let's give the paparazzi something to gossip about."

What a good sport. With her history, she must be used to the limelight. Albeit not on the same scale as himself.

"I know the perfect place." He stood and picked up the bill. "Do you like jazz?"

"I do." She tilted her head, regarding him. "Although I wouldn't have guessed you were a jazz aficionado."

"Shh." He put a finger to his lips. "Don't tell anyone. I have a reputation at stake."

Laughing, she stood and took his arm. "It just means you have good taste." She followed him to the counter where he paid, then strode beside him to his car. He ushered her into the passenger seat.

"Which club are we going to?" she asked after he

backed out.

"A very special one."

"What makes it so special?"

"Yours truly used to own it."

"Really?" Her voice rose to a near squeak. "You owned a jazz club?"

He turned left onto the boulevard toward downtown. "Well, it wasn't a jazz club then. It was a dance club. My late best friend — Nils Nelsson — and I bought it sometime around 1998 and sold it a few years later when I moved to LA."

He felt her scrutiny, relished the attention, and tossed her a grin. She flashed her flawless smile back. He could actually fall in like with this multi-faceted woman. And if she didn't mind the ten-plus-year age gap, neither did he.

Big fluffy clouds decorated the cheery blue sky, and he could almost hear robins chirping in each tree they passed.

"When we first opened up, Nils and I wanted to share a little of our success. Artists and bands would come in and audition to play on live music night, usually Saturdays."

"How many of them made the cut?"

"I'd say we accepted about seven artists out of every ten that auditioned. A few of them actually went on to land recording contracts."

"Like who?"

He reeled off a string of names. From her nod, she recognized them. "I'm impressed."

"The hardest part was when we had to tell them no. Either they didn't have the talent, or they were just missing that edge. We would encourage them to polish their craft and work on getting better. Most of them were good sports about it. But I remember one guy. After I gave him the brutal truth about his musical ability, he pitched a fit, called me names, the works."

From the side of his vision, he saw her head shake. "He sounds immature."

"Funny thing was, I thought I recognized him. Pretty sure he was the guy my wife was going out with when I met her."

"One of those small-world moments."

"He was one mean dude back then. He assaulted both her and me so, at his audition, I wasn't inclined to do him any favors, even if he had possessed talent. Which he didn't."

"Do you think he recognized you?"

"I don't think he made the connection. I looked quite a bit different, and I was using my stage name. I gave him constructive feedback, hoping he'd take it to heart." His pulse quickened as the memory rotated in his mind. "But his true nature apparently hadn't changed. Anyway, the place is much different now. It's quiet, and we'll be able to talk without shouting."

"You never told me the name."

"It's called French Quarter. Near Fifth and Pine."

"Oh, I know the place. It's been ages since I've been to a jazz club. Thank you for doing this."

A beep resounded from somewhere in Melodie's vicinity, and she pulled a smartphone from her purse.

He glanced over. "Do you need to answer that?"

"No, it's Crissy, one of my besties. Nothing urgent." She held the phone in her lap, gazing not at him but out his window. "It's kind of cool how she and I met. You'll like this."

"I will?"

Her eyes moved back and forth as they passed office buildings and apartment complexes. "Mm-hmm. We met because of you."

He made a whatchu-talkin-about face at her, unsure what to think. "Because of moi?"

"Oui." She chuckled. "I met her on Twitter about a year ago. We were both followers of yours, and one day she sent me a message. She'd noticed my comments on your tweets and wondered…" She dropped her gaze to the phone, rubbing it with her thumb.

"Wondered what?"

Her cheeks glowed, and a half-smile curved her pretty mouth. "She asked me if I was as big a fan of yours as she was."

From anyone else, such a remark might sound creepy. But coming from this classy, elegant woman, it felt like a compliment. "And what did you tell her?"

"I told her I bought all your albums and saw you in concert exactly twice. And she said, 'Yeah, you're a megafan like me.' "

At least she didn't gush like some megafans.

"She noticed I live in Seattle, like her, and it turns out we're only a few miles apart. We just clicked, and we've been friends ever since." Her grin widened. "So thank you for doing your part to help me meet my new bestie."

"Can't take credit, but you're welcome." He turned right onto Fifth. "Look, we're almost there."

He found a parking garage around the corner, and they strode the broad sidewalk to the entrance of French Quarter. A young homeless guy held up a battered cardboard sign reading, Anything Helps. The man avoided eye contact when they passed.

As Howard escorted her into the dim lounge, she looked around with an awed expression at the gleaming bronze and glass interior and smiled at the tastefully offbeat artwork. She stopped to scrutinize a jumbo-sized, framed photo of the original French Quarter in New Orleans, and he found his hand brushing against her slim waist. Her dress felt soft to the touch. A few patrons noticed them walk by, and he grinned inside. He and Melodie would give the gossip columnists something to talk about, all right. The paparazzi wouldn't have to make up a "pretty, young brunette."

He ordered them coffee and took advantage of a lull to voice the question he'd been dying to ask. "Which of my concerts did you see?"

She ran her pink-painted fingertip along the edge of the beverage menu. "The first one was in 1995, at the Kingdome."

He nodded, remembering. "Which no longer exists."

She echoed his nod. "Then a few years later, the time you played at the Tacoma Dome."

"The one with the bomb threat? That's one I'd rather forget."

She tilted her head, and the years fell from her face as if she were reliving that day. "At least it was a false alarm, and we got to see you play the following night."

The memory stirred up long-forgotten anger at some folks' idea of kicks. "There are some really sick people out there. Nobody ever found out who it was, but I always figured it was some twisted dude—or dudes—who thought it would be fun to mess with me." His voice tightened. "And inconvenience fifty thousand people at the same time."

Empathy shone from her dark eyes, and she shook her head as if amazed by the lengths someone would go to for attention. Something stirred inside him.

"By the way"—he leaned forward, capturing her gaze and holding it—"I'm really enjoying spending time with you. If you don't mind, I'd like to take you out again next week."

Her eyes widened, but only for a split second. She raised her perfect brows at him. "I don't mind at all, Declan Decker."

Chapter Twelve

As Livy trailed DeeDee into Dani's lobby at eight o'clock sharp, Crissy waved to them. "Good morning, ladies. You can go on back. Dani's waiting."

"Both of us?"

"Yes, that's what she said." Crissy patted Livy's shoulder, then DeeDee's. Crissy's husband, Drew, and their four-year-old, Amanda, sat cross-legged beside the desk looking at a picture book. Drew waved as they walked by, then returned to his reading. At DeeDee's curious look, Crissy explained, "They're hanging out here for a few. Then I'm taking him to work and her to daycare. I don't normally come in until nine, but today was an exception."

"Not due to us, I hope?" Livy searched Crissy's face for any sign of squelched resentment.

Crissy shook her head. "It's okay. For you two, I don't mind. It's just that we only have one car between the two of us."

Little Amanda glanced up from her book. "Daddy said we getting a new car today." She flashed a gap-toothed grin. "It's a blue one. Blue's my favorite color."

"How exciting." Livy pivoted toward the little girl.

Drew patted her on the head. "It's not only blue, Mandy. It's fast, too."

"Really, really fast?"

"Super-duper fast!"

Livy eyed Drew and Crissy, now focused on their daughter. If they struggled financially, they hid it well, especially Drew, with his starched off-white shirt and neatly trimmed hair. She could visualize him behind the wheel of a fast blue sports car.

"Ladies!" Dani's voice from behind reminded Livy why they were here. "Come on in." Dani beckoned them to the Green Room, where a plush massage table rested against a celery-tinted wall, spiky plants hung in the corners, and Eastern music enveloped them with an almost physical caress. "Have a seat." She gestured to the floral sofa.

Instead of seating herself on the matching ottoman, as DeeDee expected, Dani paced, her cheekbones protruding from her scrunched face. "I have to admit, this issue has me stymied. I'm going to refer both of you to an OBGYN at Swedish Hospital."

"But, Dani." DeeDee leaned forward, gripping her knees. "We want you to deliver our babies. That's why we're here."

"I understand. I want that too. But this is a complication that's a bit above my pay grade, if I'm honest with you."

Livy shook her head. "But you said nothing was wrong."

"Well, of course, I can't be sure. And you don't want to take chances if the baby starts showing signs of distress. You'll need an OBGYN in that case. She'll want to monitor them closely."

Livy widened her eyes. "What kind of distress do you mean?"

"Worst-case scenario? If the placenta isn't getting enough oxygen to the baby, the brain could start to shrink. Or it could begin to accumulate fluid."

A horrified hiss emerged from DeeDee's mouth. She raked frantic fingers across her shorn locks. "How would they know?"

"The ultrasound would show it. You will probably have one every week from now until delivery."

"What would happen if they find" — Livy gulped the words — "brain distress?" Her legs went numb, and she would have toppled if she were standing.

Dani stopped and studied them. "If the babies show signs of potential brain damage" — she inhaled — "they'd need to be taken as soon as possible."

Livy clutched her twin's cold hand. "At thirty-two weeks? Dear God, no."

"On the bright side, babies born between thirty-two and thirty-three weeks have a ninety-eight percent chance of survival. Swedish Hospital has one of the best NICU units in the state. You and your babies will be in very good hands there."

A whoosh clouding her ears, Livy barely heard Dani's optimism. Her eyes stung with unshed tears as her dreams of happy, healthy babies crumbled, a dream as insubstantial as a foggy day. Scott's heart would break at the news.

And Dad's, too.

~~~

A baby's cry pierced the night.

Livy's elbow rammed into something or someone, but she couldn't make it out in the dark. Where was the baby? Had she given birth already? She groped around whatever vast expanse she lay on, striving to open her eyes. If she could just open her eyes, she could find her crying baby. *Don't cry, Baby. Mommy's coming.*

Her mouth went dry when the cries went on and on,

and she still couldn't see anything. She tried to stand but tottered off-balance. Short, frantic breaths burst from her. The baby must be scared. Hungry. What had she named him? Or her?

Her heart raced—she didn't remember giving birth! She explored her still-swollen belly, rubbing her palm over its hilly contour. Her blood chilled. The crying baby was still inside.

Baby was dying, and she could do nothing to save it.

"Sweetheart?"

Scott? Livy opened her eyes. Faint light filtered into the bedroom, and the blessed quiet stilled her racing heart and cleared her mind. She looked into Scott's angst-ridden face. No crying baby. In fact, the baby was using the inside of her belly as its own personal racetrack.

"Did you have a nightmare?"

"Mmm." She surged upward, propping on her elbow. "I thought I heard our baby crying." She pressed a hand against her heart, letting her head fall back on the pillow. "I thought I had given birth already. But it was dying." She let out a long, slow breath. Her baby was still alive.

Scott folded her in his brawny arms and cradled her belly in his hands. "I'm thankful it was only a dream."

"Me too, honey. But deep down, I'm scared. What if this was a premonition?"

Chapter Thirteen

Howard's heart stopped when he read Margo's text. *I suggest we drop the price a couple $grand. Lots of interest, no offers.*

He sat in his driveway, too stunned to move despite the withering summer sunshine pouring through the windows of his white Prius. *Is it because I took out the pool?* His late best friend, Nils, had warned him he'd regret filling it in to make room for a new recording studio. "Have you ever heard of a house in SoCal without a swimming pool?" Nils had said.

Nils had a point. But this Northwest-bred boy had never taken to swimming. What did he need with a pool except to entertain Hollywood VIPs? A recording studio brought in dough. And his sons, Gus and Dom, had plenty of friends with pools.

Yes, the absence of a pool is conspicuous, Margo replied. *At least half the prospects comment on it.*

He dug his heel into the floorboard and punched out the letters. *There must be some other old has-been musician out there who'd rather have a recording studio than a pool.*

Howard stared unseeingly at his small rented bungalow on a quiet street in West Seattle, with a to-die-for view of the Puget Sound and its distant islands. The home's fresh coat of off-white paint glowed cheery as a spring day. Its green trim seemed to smile at him. A home with street cred, a home he'd be proud to own if it had a thousand additional square feet.

In his rear-view mirror, he saw the woman from next door pass by on the sidewalk, walking her two-toned doxie and eying his house in that sidelong way people do when they don't want you to know they're checking you out. Wouldn't it be fun to surprise her? He opened the door, leaned out, and waved. "Hello, there!"

The woman cocked her head and bestowed what she probably considered a friendly smile, but it couldn't hide her embarrassment at getting caught. "Hello," she replied. The dog yipped and strained against the leash. She pulled him back, and they moved on.

Howard guessed her to be in her fifties, despite the youthful blonde streaks in her shoulder-length hair. Too many blonde women over fifty in this town. How would he ever narrow down his choices to find his nemesis?

His phone dinged with Margo's reply. *Maybe so, but none of them have made offers on your house.*

Who'd believe he'd ever be in such a position?

He propped the door open with his knee and breathed deep, but the cool breeze couldn't touch his desperation. If he could sell his stuff — all his memorabilia: classic guitars, rock band paraphernalia — maybe he could get 250 grand for it all. But maybe not.

Now if he were to sell the Saffire School of Dance building... He had at least three years of equity built up. On the other hand, a new owner could possibly double, even triple, Livy and DeeDee's rent. As long as he owned the building, his kiddos paid discounted rent.

No, he couldn't sell the Ravenna building. At least not yet.

His frenetic thoughts bounced like wild things inside his head and beckoned down a mental path he thought he'd never travel.

He could hire a hit man to eliminate Bro for less than this ordeal had cost him. Howard longed for a world with no more baggage from his past. But would he really get away with it? Could he risk a prison sentence just to rid the world of a despicable leech?

No way. Not another stint in jail.

Been there, done that.

~~~

1983

A trip to jail, all due to a twenty-dollar collector's item.

Howard spent his first night behind bars on a cold, hard metal slab jutting from the wall. He shifted every which way in a vain effort to get warm and comfortable. His three other cellmates snored or wheezed, chasing sleep further away.

When he'd arrived Saturday evening, they booked him and allowed him one phone call. Since his mom and her fourth husband were out of town for Memorial Day weekend, he'd called Nils.

"I told you we needed to get out of there." Nils cursed. "But you had to—"

"Shut up." He matched Nils's curse with one of his own. "Can you call my boss at Safeway tomorrow morning and tell him I was in an accident? And now I'm in the hospital?"

"No way, dude. I'm not doing your dirty work."

"C'mon, be a pal. You want me to get fired?" He raised his voice over the shouting in the cellblock.

"Not my problem."

"It will be when I run out of money for band equipment. I was gonna help you buy a new snare, remember? But if I get fired, I won't have the dough."

Nils cleared his throat and mumbled another curse.

"If you call my boss, we'll go find you a new drum as soon as I get my next paycheck. Okay?"

Nils exhaled. "You son of a—"

"Thanks, dude. I owe you." Howard slammed the phone down before Nils could change his mind. He growled to the deputy, "I want a lawyer."

The deputy didn't look up from his *Field & Stream*. "Next Tuesday, kid."

He seethed as he plopped on the metal slab. Did his friends know where was? Had Nils told everyone? He pictured his bandmates, laughing, chortling at his downfall. Mocking the would-be rock star at his lowest moment. How did long-term inmates handle this high-octane level of frustration chewing away at their spirits, day after dreary day? No wonder they came out worse off than when they went in.

Dinner consisted of a chicken drumstick, which was more skin than meat, a bag of potato chips, and a carton of chocolate milk. He wolfed down the food, but a gnawing hunger remained.

He was still sleepy the next morning when the breakfast cart came around. Shivering, he took the offered plate with feigned nonchalance, then dug his fist into his empty stomach to make it stop its incessant growling—a growling so intense it hurt. Wincing, he sat cross-legged on the slab and gobbled up his breakfast—greasy sausage, a single slice of toasted white bread, and a can of Tang-like orange drink.

His jail-issued gray coverall smelled as foul as it looked. Over its left pocket, a white embroidered decal read "King County Corrections"—as if he'd forget where he was. He shifted, nearly choked. The reek wasn't just the coverall. He'd opted out of showers rather than risk the torments rumored to occur in community showers.

He snorted, folded his arms tight. Of all the misfortunes, he had to get thrown in jail during a three-day weekend. Tuesday the court reopened. Two more days.

To pass the time, he twiddled his thumbs and listened to his cellmates grouse. A young man with cornrows looked to be the friendliest of the bunch. "What you in for?" he asked Howard, all smiles.

"Stole a Jimi Hendrix shirt. You?"

"Crack. Armed robbery," he boasted as if he'd won Student of the Year.

The kid seemed too nice to be guilty of such antics. In comparison, Howard felt like a choirboy.

The other two cellmates appeared worn and beaten, oozing foul attitudes from every pore. He cringed at their shouted curses. Probably career criminals. He sure didn't wanna end up like them.

Two drunks arrived on Sunday evening. They smelled like a distillery. Now he fought nausea, as well as cold, all night.

They were released the next morning. If wishes were superpowers, Howard would be a body snatcher and walk out of this cell a free man.

At his arraignment Tuesday morning, he listened in numb shock to the charges against him. One count of petty larceny. One count of resisting arrest. He stifled a curse. What the—He hadn't resisted arrest.

He pleaded not guilty and requested an attorney.

Due to his previous record of juvenile larceny, the judge set bail at five grand. But Howard didn't have the 10 percent required to make bail. Two sheriffs' deputies escorted him back to his cell.

He called his mother, who answered on the fourth ring. When he explained his predicament, she gasped out an oath.

"Howie. What on earth did you do to land yourself in jail?"

"All I did was take this measly little twenty-dollar tee shirt, Mom. It's not like I killed someone."

He tuned out her lecture. Was it sunny outside this institutional eyesore? It better be pouring rain, so the folks walking free got to experience a little gloom themselves.

"Don't tell my boss." His throat tightened. "Nils told him I was in a car accident, and I'll be in the hospital for a few days."

"Do you know how soon you're getting out? Do you need bail money?"

"I don't know nothin'. I haven't even gotten to see a lawyer yet. Had my arraignment this morning. Bail is five grand."

Her intake of breath rattled the line. "Let me make some phone calls." She exhaled. "Glen might have some ideas."

"Can you get me out of here today?"

"It won't be today." She tsked. "I can't do anything until I talk to Glen. He'll be home late tonight."

Howard cursed. "If you hadn't taken off for the weekend, you could've helped me out *today*."

"If you want my help, Howie, you're going to have to show some respect. Call me tomorrow." With that, his mother said goodbye and hung up.

He dropped the phone, scowled at the deputy. "I want a lawyer, man."

The man might have been a robot for all the compassion he showed. "We're short on public defenders right now. This is a peak vacation season. Memorial Day weekend, you know. You'll get your turn."

One more day in this hellhole. Howard stomped back to the cell, kicked the metal slab, and winced over the pain shooting through his big toe. When he lay down again, his back protested. He shifted and twisted his body in multiple ways, but the aches and pains kept their grip.

Nobody told him jail was so boring. He missed his guitar. And his comfortable bed.

He clasped his hands behind his head and squeezed his eyes shut. No time like the present to compose some new song lyrics. But he needed inspiration. He needed fodder.

Stuck in jail, need some bail – Lame.

Bring me some booze for my jailhouse blues – Naw.

Got prisoner boredom, gonna shoot me a warden – Now that would get him twenty-years-to-life in the slammer.

"Jailhouse Rock" – Elvis had the right idea. Put a positive spin on it.

Howard started to hum. The cellmates quieted as he hummed louder then broke into song.

He sprang to his feet, forgetting his aches, regretting it the next instant. Despite his sore back, he posed like Elvis, air guitar in hand. Chin thrust forward, lip curl intact, he sang his heart out. Judging by the sudden appearance of an audience, his performance traveled to the cell across the way.

His cornrowed cellmate clapped and gyrated. The other two men smirked, but both pairs of feet went a tapping. The applause and whistles when he finished let him pretend he'd just performed for a Kingdome full of rabid fans.

~~~

Dreary day after dreary day threatened to stretch

ahead like an endless tunnel. Howard began to fear the boredom would drive him insane.

Someone yelled from the other side of the cellblock. "Sing for us, Elvis."

Their catcalls pummeled him. But he didn't feel like entertaining. He felt like kicking and yelling as he lay on his slab and contemplated this hellhole.

Singin' the hellhole blues — drowning my soul in booze —

He hummed a random melody in a minor key and opened his mouth, making sure everybody heard. "I'm singin' the hellhole blues — drownin' my soul in booze!"

The cellblock quieted. Howard eased his aching body off the slab. "C'mon, everybody. Sing it!" He strummed his air guitar, putting his whole body into it. "Drownin' my soul in booze —"

"Ya ain't gonna find no booze here," called a voice from the adjacent cell.

Howard tried again. "I'm singin' the hellhole blues! Wish I could drown in booze!"

Soon a chorus of voices chanted along. *Clap. Clap.* The cellblock rocked.

"You a rock star or somethin'?" The mean-looking cellmate's mouth twisted.

"I wish." Howard shouted over the chants. "I'm in a band. Hoping to get a record deal."

The man harrumphed.

"Hey, Elvis." Another request launched from across the way. "Do 'Hound Dog'."

"Hound Dog! Hound Dog!" the chant rocked through the cellblock.

He caved in and entertained them until lunchtime.

~~~

"Mom? Did you and Glen come up with my bail?"

"He'll have it by Friday."

"Friday?" he shouted. "That's two days away. How come you have to wait so long?"

"Don't yell at me."

"Sorry." He softened his voice. "But I don't see why I have to wait two more days."

"Money doesn't grow on trees, you know."

He bit back a retort.

"We're not rich folks. Glen can't just go to the bank and pull out money he doesn't have. And our credit line is maxed out."

"I get it." He gave an exasperated grunt and dropped the receiver into its cradle. He shook his head at the deputy. "Parents."

"Kids." The guy didn't bat an eye.

Howard made sure the man heard his angry stomps.

If something went wrong and he wasn't out of here by Friday, he wouldn't be seeing Luna Rickles again.

If not for Luna Rickles, he would've gotten out of that marketplace long before closing time. If not for Luna, he wouldn't be here.

Still, he had to see her again. He visualized her glossy hair, her iridescent eyes. Those red lips he'd like to kiss.

How had she managed to capture his essence in her five-line rhyme, anyway? Somehow, she'd known he considered life without music not worth living.

He sighed and lay on the slab, then closed his eyes and let his mind wander to his childhood. To happier times.

He wished he still believed in God. The God he'd learned about in Sunday school would get him out of here, without a doubt. He'd prayed a lot when he was a kid, while his grandma was still around to encourage it.

"Howie, you don't have to be afraid to tell God anything.

He loves you like a daddy."

Howard's daddy pulled a vanishing act when Howard was four. He wasn't sure he knew what daddy-love was all about. If God's love was anything like daddy-love, he might as well be as bad as he could possibly be.

His three subsequent stepdads couldn't compare to the real thing. The first one had been decent to him, and Howard, being little, could pretend he was Daddy, the same way he could pretend Santa Claus was real. The second stepfather mostly ignored him, leaving him to raise himself through middle school and high school. If not for Grandma, he'd be a lot worse off today.

He balled his fists. The God of his childhood stopped existing when Grandma died. But it wouldn't hurt if he talked to some God he could pretend existed.

The dinner tray came. He wolfed down a tasteless meal and tried to pray without the other guys detecting.

"Hey, God. You there?" He tipped his face to the wall and kept his voice barely audible. With the other guys hollering so loud, no chance they'd overhear.

"Get me out of here, God. I'll do anything. If you get me out of here before this weekend, I'll fly straight. I'll clean up my act. I'll never steal again.

"And, God, I'll do whatever you ask if you'll let me be with Luna. I'll be a missionary." He flinched. "Well, maybe not a missionary. But I'll never lie again. I promise." He brought his hands together in a *V.* "Scout's honor." Would God count that, since he'd never been a scout?

He opened his eyes and stared at the panel above. An odd sensation filled him—the feeling from Sunday school. An innocent trust that God would fix everything wrong in the world. In his world.

Hope and skepticism warred in his heart the rest of

the evening and well into the next day.

"C'mon, God. Show me what you're made of. Prove you're a God of love, like Grandma said. Oh, and if you see her, tell her hi for me, will ya?"

~~~

"Howard McCreary?"

Howard bounded off his slab as the thickset deputy yelled his name Thursday morning. "Yeah?"

The man unlocked the cell. "An attorney's here to see you."

There was a God.

He entered a square private room, where a kind-faced, middle-aged woman named Christine introduced herself. She played twenty questions and shoved forms in front of him to which he paid little attention. But he perked up when she said something about releasing him to her custody.

"Awesome, man."

Christine met his eyes. "Most shoplifting is considered a misdemeanor. You've been here four days already. I doubt any judge will force you to serve more time." She licked her finger and shuffled forms, pointing at one. "You had a shoplifting conviction five years ago, I see. Because of that, the judge may sentence you to community service as well as probation."

Howard exhaled, his tense muscles loosening. Community service would be paradise compared to jail.

"Here's your trial date."

Three weeks to wait.

"I'll request the judge dismiss all charges. If he doesn't go for it, I think I can talk him into time served and probation."

Howard pumped her hand. "Thanks, man."

"Just don't get yourself into any more trouble. Show up early at the courthouse. Eight o'clock sharp, okay? Dress nice." She shook a finger at him. "You want to look respectable for the judge."

"Most definitely, ma'am."

"Now, let's get your stuff and get you out of here. Do you have anybody to pick you up? Or will you be taking the bus?"

"I'll call my mom."

~~~

As he stepped into freedom, Howard relished the feel of his regular clothes.

Yes, there was a God. Emerging into the soft morning air, he mouthed a thank you to the heavens.

But now, the moment of reckoning had arrived. So far, God had kept His end. In return, Howard had promised God he'd straighten up and fly right.

But how?

Chapter Fourteen

Livy, flat on her back, stared at the serene meadow painted on the ceiling as Dr. Zahir measured her abdomen. The peaceful scene did nothing to ease the disquiet in her gut. The OB lifted the stethoscope from Livy's belly, then studied anew the sonogram Dani had sent over. "Any bleeding?" she asked in her faint Middle Eastern accent.

"No."

"That's good. If you start to bleed, you need to call my office right away." Computer keys clacked. Then Dr. Zahir got up and came to Livy's side. "You may sit up now."

Shivering despite the warm morning, Livy grasped the doctor's proffered hand and heaved herself up, then wrapped the thin paper gown around herself.

Concern creased the doctor's brow. "Let's talk about your supplements. Did you bring them?"

"Yes." Livy hopped off the table, then shuffled to her tote bag and handed over the box of tea and the vitamin bottle. Dr. Zahir scrutinized the labels for endless seconds, then typed into her computer. "How long have you been on them?"

"I started taking prenatals as soon as I found out I was pregnant."

"And the tea?"

"Just a couple of months."

"Hmm," the doctor said. "Normally, I don't discourage my patients from drinking pregnancy tea or taking supplements, in fact, I encourage it. But some of the herbs in this tea I've never heard of. Rooibos?"

"My sister and I researched all those ingredients, and they all sounded beneficial for pregnancy. My grandma is knowledgeable about herbs, and she researched them too. She told us they're good stuff."

"Well, they may or may not be. But let's just try something and see what happens. Stop consuming the supplements and tea for a week, and we'll examine you again in seven days. If your baby has started growing again, we'll have a pretty good idea what the culprit is."

Livy dug her fingernails into her palms. Grandma, natural medicine advocate, had said the opposite. *Those minerals and herbs are very helpful, and you should continue,* her text had said. *If you'd never used them, you and your babies could be worse off.* Should she take Grandma's word over an OB's? What if her baby grew worse without the herbs and minerals? Or even died?

True, she could certainly have another baby or two in the future. Yet how tragic to have nothing to show for all the stress and changes she'd put her body through in the last seven and a half months except a stillborn baby.

No, not tragic. Devastating.

Dr. Zahir interrupted her spinning thoughts. "Let's do another ultrasound Monday. Then I want to see you a week from today, next Tuesday."

"Okay." Livy's voice broke, and she cleared her throat to cover it up.

"Also, don't take any long trips before your due date. We need to keep you close to home, you know."

After Dr. Zahir left the room, Livy fumbled to put her legs one by one into her maternity jeans. Was it her imagination, or did the elastic waistband feel a tad looser? She placed two fingers inside. Oh no. Tears broke free. Spying a tissue box by the sink, she grabbed one and blew her nose hard. With tears blurring her vision, she wasn't sure how to make it to the lobby where Scott, Nick, and DeeDee waited. Yet she needed them. She needed Scott's rock-solid chest to lean against, and DeeDee's hand to cling to.

Someone knocked on the door. "Come in."

A nurse poked her face in. "Oh. I didn't know anyone was in here."

Livy sniffed. "I'm done, just trying to pull myself together."

"You poor girl." The nurse crossed to her and touched Livy's arm. "Did you bring anyone with you?"

"Yes, my husband and sister."

"How about I go get your husband for you?"

"Oh, that would be perfect." A smile broke free. "Thank you."

Before she even plopped into the chair, Scott was there, lending his chest for her head, his arms soothing her. "Bad news?"

She sobbed harder, unable to speak. He ushered her to the waiting room where she passed DeeDee on her way to the exam room.

"Deeds."

"Livs?"

"I think my baby has shrunk," she gasped out.

DeeDee's mouth elongated. Then she shook her head as though the words made no sense. Scott's head swiveled to her, but further explanation eluded her when the nurse stepped between her and DeeDee. "Why do you think your baby has shrunk?"

Livy sniffed. "My jeans waistband feels looser."

The nurse eyed her abdomen. "Baby's probably just shifted a little. They do that as they get closer to their due date." She graced a sunny smile on Livy, then placed her hand on DeeDee's shoulder blades. "This way," she directed.

DeeDee disappeared through the exam room door. Livy and Scott stayed in the waiting room.

Swinging between relief and despair, Livy held back tears until DeeDee emerged. Then Livy cried all the way home.

Chapter Fifteen

"This is Big Al from your classic rock station. We have local boy, Declan Decker, up next."

Big Al had the Wolfman Jack growl down. Howard rolled his eyes when he heard the opening riffs of his first hit song, "White Cobra," vibrating from the car stereo. "Welcome home, Declan Decker!" Al shouted over the intro.

Howard rolled into the Second Avenue parking garage and glanced at the time. He'd arrived five minutes early for his appointment at Hoyt Bank, time enough to sit and listen to the song he could sing in his sleep.

And time to talk himself out of what he was about to do. But Luna's image on the VHS floated on the edge of his vision. He could almost hear Bro's mocking laughter.

He had to do this. He'd find a way to explain it to his daughters. If they ever found out.

Tapping his phone, he reread the two emails from local stations requesting interviews. The gigs would net him a decent payoff, but they were three and four weeks away. He could replace the trust fund money by then, no problem. If only Bro were willing to wait that long.

He hummed along to his former number one hit song. He should be tired of it by now, but the memories of the day he'd composed it in his head had sustained him all these years without his muse.

If he'd never met Luna, this song would never have

been written.

~~~

1983

A sky as blue as Luna's eyes greeted Howard Saturday morning. He bounced out of bed at nine, grateful his boss had told him to take as much time off as he needed to recover from his accident. He'd planned his morning to the minute: He'd catch the ten-after-ten bus at the corner of Fremont, arrive at Seattle Center before noon, then hang out, and try to sneak in to the dance competition already underway.

His mother and Glen waved goodbye as he raced out the front door and leaped, pain-free, down the steps into the fair morning. Not a hint of rain in sight. A light breeze jostled his freshly washed hair as he walked the two blocks to the bus stop.

He shoved the last of his coins into the fare box, and then shrugged. Showing up late for paid events usually meant getting in free. He didn't give Luna's boyfriend any more thought than he did the stranger beside him.

"Next stop, Seattle Center!" hollered the bus driver.

The Space Needle loomed high above, as if it were beckoning to him. Jumping off the bus, he cased the layout of the place. Big concrete box, one main entrance. Easy to slip in unnoticed among the bodies flowing in and out of the convention center. He attached himself to a group of girls and slid inside.

A stocky female attendant eyed them suspiciously. "Hand stamps?" Howard held his breath and half-hid his bare hand within the bevy of hands. The attendant glanced at them and nodded, gesturing them inside.

He released the breath he'd been holding, then

grabbed a program and looked for Luna's name. The aged-ten-and-under competitors had already finished. He passed over the 11–15 group, the 16–19 category, and stopped at the 20–25 section. There she was. Luna Raquelle. He chuckled. So she used a stage name, too. And she'd be on stage for Round One in fifteen minutes.

A few empty seats remained in the dim auditorium, so he strode casually to the back of the room, shifting from one foot to the other as he waited. The girl onstage twirled and contorted her body in ways he didn't know could be done. When she crashed to the floor, the audience gasped. She burst into tears and fled the stage.

He scanned the audience for Luna's boyfriend among the anonymous faces—a face he'd recognize from the glimpse he'd caught on his way to jail. Big dude, eyes only for Luna.

"Ladies and gentlemen," the announcer's voice blared, "please welcome Luna Raquelle, twenty-one years old, from Seattle, Washington! Dancing to Michael Jackson's 'Thrrrriller'!"

Applause roared through the room.

At first, he saw only her luminescent yellow ponytail bouncing to the pulsating beat. Then the rest of her came into focus, and he sat, mesmerized, as she flowed across the stage in an all-black getup. She darted, then twirled, and darted again, all in precise, exact fashion, like a show he'd seen on the education channel. Foxes running and playing.

So he'd be a foxhound.

After she bowed and pranced offstage, he peered at the program. The top six finishers in each age group advanced to Round Two tomorrow, their names revealed at the end of the day. He'd have to wait through countless dancers before announcement time. While he waited, he entertained himself with memories of Luna Raquelle leaping and spinning like a dancing queen. Truly a thriller.

"Ladies and gentlemen!" the announcer's voice blared, and Howard jerked to attention. "Here are the top six finishers in each category. Please join me in congratulating the following young ladies, who will continue on in the competition." The applause thundered so loudly after each name, Howard sprang to his feet, afraid he wouldn't hear.

Five minutes later the announcer shouted the name he'd been hoping for. Although his stomach rumbled, he barely noticed. Making his way toward the outer hallways, he spied an exit door, which might lead backstage, and flung it open. As he meandered through a maze of hallways, crowded with contestants, he peeked in rooms and down long adjoining halls, finally jerking to a stop. There she was, not twenty feet away, slinky in red and black, hair loose and glowing as though lit from within. She didn't see him. She was too busy enjoying kisses from the dude he'd seen her with.

Howard backed against the wall and waited. He looked at his watch, waited some more. At least five minutes elapsed before the couple pulled apart.

Soon they started walking in his direction, gazing at each other. Howard turned sideways against the wall, his back to them, pretending to thumb through his wallet.

He snapped his head up then followed with studied nonchalance, keeping the couple in sight. They strode, arms around each other, toward an outside exit. A swarm of bodies came out of nowhere, voices echoing, filling the hallway between him and his prey.

But this must have been his lucky day, because, after a quick kiss and embrace, the guy left through an exit door, and Luna retraced her steps. She still hadn't seen him. He froze, waiting.

"Hey," he said when she stood two feet in front of him.

She jumped like a startled fox. Then recognition narrowed her eyes. "Oh wow, I can't believe you're here." Her tone suggested it wasn't a pleasant surprise. "What do you want?"

He wanted to soak in her magic. He wanted to serenade her with Lionel Richie songs. He wanted to—but no, he couldn't tell her so. "I came to watch the dancing. I think I'm lost, though. I'm trying to find a bathroom. Do you know where it is?"

A flash of relief loosened her face, and she pointed. "I think there's a men's room down that way."

"Thanks." He held her gaze. "But I also wanted to ask if you wouldn't mind hanging out with me for one day." He held up an index finger. "One day. That's all I ask."

She stood, hands on hips, head atilt. "I have a boyfriend."

"You can leave him at home."

A chunky dancer bumped him so hard he would've landed on Dancing Queen—if not for his split-second reflexes. He thrust out a protective arm and dug in his heels.

A faint smile curved the corners of her mouth. "Why would I hang out with you when I already have Brian?"

"Because." His tone held firm. "You should consider it so someday you can tell your children and grandchildren you once hung out with the famous Declan Decker. And it would be true."

Her mouth twitched. "You're not famous, and your name isn't Declan Decker."

"What makes you think it isn't my name?"

"You thought you could fool me, didn't you?"

"Even if it isn't my name, you can still claim you knew me back when."

She chuckled, her eyes sparkling. Roughly twelve inches separated them. He watched her face, oblivious to everything except smiling red lips framing whiter-than-white teeth.

"I might consider it." Her smile spread wider. "*If* you tell me your real name."

"Not fair. Luna Raquelle isn't *your* real name."

"It's my stage name. But you already know my real name. I don't go around hiding it."

"If you had *my* name, you would." The words leapt out of his mouth before he could stop them.

"Aha. Tell me your name, Declan Decker."

"Will you hang out with me?"

An exasperated sigh. "Only if you tell me your name."

He was so close, he could see her pupils contracting and expanding.

"Now tell me."

He gulped a deep breath. "It's Howard." He exhaled. "Howard McCreary."

"Really?" She stepped back and studied him. "You don't look like a Howard."

"Tell me something I don't know."

"It's a distinguished name."

"So's yours. It's an awesome name."

"You're too kind. My mother named me after the moon."

"Cool. Should I call you Moonbeam?"

She rolled her eyes. "Hey, Mr. Songwriter, I know you can come up with something more original."

He thrust his thumb in the air. "You're on. Oh, by the

way, congratulations on making the finals. I'll be back tomorrow."

"Will you now? Better pay admission." She smirked.

"What makes you think I didn't pay?"

She clasped his right hand. The caress of her thumb, soft as a spider web, tickled the back of his hand. "You don't have a hand stamp."

"Hey, you're good."

"In more ways than one."

"Good enough to win this whole thing?"

"Absolutely." She glanced at her watch, then turned and darted, as she'd done on stage, to a nearby doorway. "I need to go find my friend, Audria. She's my ride." Luna waved, and then disappeared.

He stared after her. A cloud settled in his soul and chased away the moonbeam he'd been basking in.

Chapter Sixteen

Howard pulled his fleece vest tighter around his middle as he hurried along a cobblestoned path. The streetlamp cast eerie shadows onto the geometric concrete pillars—great slabs of granite stacked like enormous Tetris cubes. Like a sci-fi movie set, the blocks formed deep shadows the homeless folks could hide in, where they could see without being seen. Definitely a gnarly place. Freeway Park straddled Interstate 5, thus the name. The landscaped expanse with its waterfalls and grassy plazas hid the ribbon of vehicles speeding along beneath it. Even without his hearing aid, the ever-present hum vibrated under Howard's feet and into his partially deaf ears. During the day, the towering pillars and steep staircases with their blind corners lured visitors to explore. Tonight, the sign behind him warned that the park closed at ten p.m. and trespassers would be prosecuted.

He checked the time—sixteen minutes to closing. Time to head up the stairs to the meeting spot. Bro wanted to meet after dark before the park closed. But Howard had to wonder, why this park? And why this specific spot?

From the park's upper sidewalk, he peered over a rail into black nothingness. As he recalled, the city had built a shallow pond at the bottom of this slab. He'd wrinkled his nose against the acidic smell of urine, an even stronger odor than in Waterfront Park when he scoped out the meeting site earlier today. Homeless men and women had lain on the grass, cocooned in sleeping bags, comforted by their meager piles of stuff. The concrete was littered with needles, food cartons, and wine bottles as broken as those who consumed them. Someone had thrown a battered old mattress into the pond, which elicited raised eyebrows from him. Who would throw their bed into the water? Perhaps a misguided attempt to clean it? Or, more likely, a drugged stupor.

Movement registered from the corner of his vision. There, over by the trees, someone furtive came his way. Dressed all in black.

Howard, his heartbeat galloping, didn't dare breathe. The man stopped and looked around, finally spotting Howard.

As before, his nemesis spoke not a word as the items changed hands. Howard checked the video's label, then tucked it under his jacket, expecting Bro to turn and disappear into the dark night. Instead, he leaned in, inches from Howard's face.

"Bayback dime." Bro's beery whisper punched Howard with unexpected force. Smelling danger for the first time, he didn't realize he'd backed away until he felt the hard railing dig into the seat of his jeans.

"What?"

"Pay. Back. Time." Bro spit the words. "Four bribe roadie."

"Huh?" Howard grabbed the rail behind him as he tipped precariously backward. *Four bribe roadie?*

"Don't blay dumb."

That voice. Even disguised behind all that rasp, it triggered a vague memory. "What're you talking about?"

Bro thrust his face closer. "Mife…" A truck roaring by on Seneca drowned out the rest. Despite his desperate grip on the rail, Howard's shoulders inched closer to the precipice.

"'S for him." With a mighty shove, Bro sent Howard tumbling over the rail, into the abyss beyond. As if in a dream, he felt himself plummet… down…down.

Drab concrete rushed by. The drop seemed to take an eternity.

As he flailed wildly for anything to grab onto, a dawning awareness pummeled his brain like a blaring alarm clock.

He was going to die.

~~~

A loud groaning woke Howard. The groans of a dying animal. Then he realized—the groans were his own.

"Sir? Can you hear me?"

He opened his eyes. Something vibrated around him, and a dark-haired man in a bright yellow vest watched him. He moved his lips to ask what was going on, but no words came out. Only more groans.

"Do you know your name?"

He tried to nod, but couldn't manage it. He lay in a tiny enclosure of some sort, chilled from head to toe, but he wasn't sure where the moving sensation came from— his head or his surroundings. If the former, this was the worst head rush he'd ever had in his life.

"Stay calm," the man soothed. "You've been in an accident, but we're transporting you to the hospital."

Slowly, with each excruciating ache, he grew aware of pain flaring in every bone and muscle, made worse by heavy-duty shivering. He couldn't remember ever feeling so cold.

He racked his mind to recall how he'd gotten here.

"Try to stay awake if you can. You're at risk of

hypothermia."

Bit by bit, it came back. Bro had tried to kill him. He rewound the memory of the frightening fall. The floating sensation. The heavy thud and splash. Yet here he was, alive and —

Wait a minute. Was he really alive? Alarmed, he lifted his head, but only managed an inch of movement, it hurt so bad. He looked around. It more resembled a gigantic coffin. Not how he visualized heaven.

If this were hell, then hell was a mighty cold place.

Medical supplies lined the walls of his tiny prison. He was alive, riding in an ambulance. How on earth had he survived such a long fall?

An ancient memory flitted around the edges of his battered head. Suddenly a scene from his past rushed him, overtook his mind, and his head flopped to the side as he relived that awful day.

Chapter Seventeen

1983

Howard lounged in the hallway after Day Two of the competition. Luna, in waiting mode until the winners' announcement, stretched her arms high, hands clasped over her head, and smiled at him. "I owe you a new limerick."

He tried not to stare at the front of her yellow tee with glittery letters shouting In It To Win It. "How come you owe me a new limerick?"

"Your name isn't Declan. I want to give you one with your real name." She reached down to her toes and grasped her ankles, then bent side-to-side several times. She peeked up at him like a coy deer. "I made it for you last night."

Straightening, she grabbed his arm and led him along the hallway. "If you don't like it, I can toss it."

"But if I do, I don't have another twenty for you."

"No problem, this one's on me." She stopped at a room crammed with hyper multicolored and multisized bodies. "Wait here, okay?"

She returned in moments, sporting a hopeful smile, carrying a framed cardboard, and held it out. He took it and read the red-inked words.

> "My new friend, Howard McCreary,
> Will strum his guitar till he's bleary.

If I tag along,
He'll sing me a song.
For life without music is dreary."

She regarded him. "Does it work?"

He lodged the cardboard under his arm and thrust two thumbs skyward. "It works, Luna Tunes."

She flashed perfect teeth at him. "Luna Tunes? You nailed me."

"I *will* sing you a song. After two limericks, you deserve one."

"Yes, I do." She bobbed her head.

"I'm going to call it 'She's An Oxymoron'." He squeezed his knuckles, making a satisfying crack.

"I'll take that as a compliment."

He'd seen no trace of Brian. Had the other man even seen his girlfriend dance her energetic heart out to "Dancing Queen"? The irony of the song choice didn't escape his notice. "Where's Brian?"

"He left when I told him I'd made other plans. But he'll be back for the announcements."

"You did that for me?"

She shrugged, glanced away, her face growing rosy. "What can I say? You're a cute barrel of laughs."

He wanted to cheer. "You're pretty amazing yourself."

They looked at each other. Seconds passed.

His growling stomach broke the spell. A long, angry growl. Followed by her laughter. Doubled-over, knee-slapping laughter.

He couldn't help joining in. "Guess I should've eaten lunch, yeah?" Food had been the furthest thing from his mind all day. "Want to go get some dinner?"

Still chuckling, she leaned her head to the side. "I

have to be back in an hour."

"There's a place across the street." He pulled her out the door into the evening's gentle warmth. The dinner rush hadn't yet inundated the restaurant, and they snagged a booth and ordered within five minutes.

"You know a lot about me by now." He eyed her and fingered the saltshaker, breathed in the greasy-burger smell of the place. "But what about you?"

She picked up a napkin and began folding it like an accordion. "What do you want to know?"

"Everything. Tell me your dreams."

"Dreams as in aspirations, or the kind you have while sleeping?"

He raised his brows. "Either. Both."

She set the napkin down, played with her hair. "I dream of being a famous dancer." A faraway look glazed her eyes. "And I keep having this one particular dream. I'm suspended in the air, spinning. Like a ceiling fan." She made a circular motion with her finger. "Afterward, I wake up feeling a natural high, but then it's a big letdown when I realize, hey, in real life, I can't do pirouettes in the air."

"You dream about air dancing." He caught a hint of wonder in his tone.

"You make it sound like air guitar."

"It doesn't sound anything like air guitar."

"Do you do air guitar?"

"Yep. Ever since I was a little guy." And a whole lot of it in jail this week.

They shared a smile. Howard made believe he saw promise and a future written in hers.

A waitress brought their food. He picked up his burger and dug in, basking in the emotions which had been knocking him upside the heart since last Saturday.

~~~

When the announcer revealed the scores an hour later, Howard grinned at the stranger next to him, as if Luna were already his. Luna Raquelle won second place in her category, losing by two points to a twenty-five-year-old from Portland. He remained sitting in the audience, reliving the moment Luna had left his side to meet up with Brian, trying to squelch the jealousy eating at his insides like battery acid.

"Trust me," she'd warned. "You don't want him to see you with me."

And now, he was left to writhe through visions of Brian hugging Luna, Brian kissing Luna, Brian—

He had to stop this.

He unbent himself, exited the auditorium, and made his way backstage.

Luna was wrapped in Brian's embrace, and Howard hovered near the opposite wall, suffering in silence.

Unable to help himself, he sidled closer.

Luna caught sight of him over Brian's shoulder, and her eyes widened. She shooed him away.

Detecting something going on behind him, Brian released her. When he spotted Howard, an ugly scowl twisted his face—the scowl of a high school bully in the presence of a ninety-pound weakling.

Brian outweighed him by a good thirty pounds and stood at least four inches taller. And, judging by his bulging shirt sleeves, he also boasted muscle-wrapped biceps.

"You tryin' to steal my girl?" Brian's closed fist made a slow, menacing arc toward Howard's face.

"Not tryin' to steal anybody's girl." Howard backed away, attempting to sound convincing.

"Brian, don't!" Luna screamed.

The fist crashed into Howard's nose. Pain reverberated through his skull and coursed out to his feet. His head bounced on the wall, intensifying the agony.

Rough hands grabbed under his arms and dragged him down a long, isolated hall. All the while, Brian kept up a litany of curses. "You're dead meat, man. You moved in on the wrong dude's girl."

Howard hurled his own string of obscenities as he flailed, trying to free himself.

Luna was nowhere to be seen. They reached an exit door. Loading Dock, said the sign. A desperate shout exploded out his mouth, but Brian only laughed, clearly enjoying Howard's powerlessness.

The cool night air cleared his head. He struggled to grip the concrete with his feet, but Brian dropped him facedown and landed a series of bone-crunching kicks on his ribcage. Each kick sent Howard closer to the edge of the deserted loading dock.

The dock's rim loomed inches away, and the first jolt of real fear quaked through him. The rim rose at least six feet off the ground. A drop that high wouldn't kill a man, but could certainly do major damage, especially if he landed on his head.

His palms scraped along the smooth cement while he grappled for something to hang on to. He gave a mighty yell, but it merely sailed into the empty night.

With a final, rib-busting kick, Brian sent Howard flying over the edge.

He landed on his side with a powerful thud. Stars danced in front of him, then faded into the blackness.

Chapter Eighteen

Howard could hardly wrap his brain around the incredible reality—he had survived a massive fall. No wonder he shivered so hard. The paramedic took his pulse as the ambulance careened around a corner, siren screaming. Tight straps held him in place.

"B–b–Bro p–p…" He had to tell this man Bro tried to kill him. But the words mangled in his raw throat.

"You took a bad fall." The man looked about his daughters' age. He fastened something around Howard's arm. "You have several broken ribs, and I suspect a punctured lung."

The worst headache he'd ever had in his life nearly overpowered the intense pain in his ribs. The band squeezed his arm. A blood pressure gadget.

"I'm going to keep talking so you won't go back to sleep. You're very lucky to be alive." The man's resonant baritone transmitted every word clearly.

"Bro…t–try…"

"I take that back. I don't believe in luck," said the paramedic.

Howard squinted at the black letters embroidered on the young man's smock. London.

"I believe God is in control. He must want you here on earth a little longer," said London.

Howard groaned again, not just from the pain this time. *So, God. Why didn't You stop Bro from pushing me?*

Thanks for the raw deal, God, letting Bro find those tapes.

"Good thing that mattress cushioned your fall."

He tried to shake his head to tell London that some homeless person had put it there, not God, but gasped against the pain. This was worse than any hangover.

London must have read his mind. "God arranged for it to be there to save your life."

"Mmm…"

"You got pretty soaked, so we have a warming blanket over you to keep you from hypothermia. You should stop shivering soon."

"Thank…"

"Do you remember what happened?"

Howard nodded, latching onto the man's eyes with the futile hope that London could see the scene unfolding in his mind.

"Good. When you're feeling better, you'll need to let the doctors know how you happened to fall into that pool. Fortunately, there was a witness who saw you fall."

A witness! Had he seen Bro push him?

"We were unable to check your phone for an emergency contact name. Unfortunately, it got submerged, and now, it's toast. You'll be asked to provide your contact information when we get to the hospital."

He opened his mouth to grind out Dom's name, but London shushed him. "Don't worry about that now. We'll get it later. We've arrived at the ER now."

The ambulance slowed, its screams intermittent, and Howard kept his eyes closed while they carried him inside, as though eyes shut tight could ward off the pain. An IV dripped into his veins, and then the drugs took over and mercifully obliterated everything.

~~~

No sooner had Livy found a comfortable position in her and Scott's queen-sized bed than her phone quivered on the nightstand with an incoming text.

Scott's arms released her as she reached for it. It was Dom with a message to her and DeeDee.

Dad fell. He's in the hospital having surgery.

Scott leaned over. "Who's texting you so late? DeeDee?"

She shifted to him and gripped his hand. "No, my brother. Dad's in the hospital."

"What happened?"

"I don't know." She called Dom's number. Background beeps filtered through when he picked up.

"What's going on?" She put the call on speaker so Scott could hear.

"Dad fell over a ledge at Freeway Park a couple hours ago. He landed in the pond."

"Oh no." A chill quivered through her, and she bolted upright. "How badly hurt is he?"

"Real bad. Hold on, DeeDee's calling." Dom made it a three-way call. "He's at Harborview in serious condition. He has a punctured lung and a bunch of broken bones."

"How did he fall?" DeeDee's sharp question spooked a shiver from Livy.

"Don't know. He's still in surgery, so I can't ask him."

Livy lifted the phone. "Dom, don't go anywhere. We're on our way."

She forgot her weariness and her pregnancy woes as she and Scott rushed to Harborview. They hurried to the second floor, where they found Dom in a waiting room pacing, his face buried in his smartphone. DeeDee and Nick rushed in moments later. Livy hugged Dom's neck. "Have you called Gus yet?"

"Yeah. He'll try to fly up here tomorrow."

"Good." They were drawing curious looks from the others in the room. She dropped her voice, mouthing the words. "Do you know if Dad was drunk?"

Dom merely shrugged. "I dunno."

"I hope they did a blood test." Livy nestled her hand in Scott's. "What would make him fall over a ledge unless he was wasted?"

Sidling closer, DeeDee nodded. "This is totally out of character for him. He's never been accident-prone."

Livy's other hand closed around DeeDee's. "He's been clean for three years."

"He claims he doesn't abuse alcohol anymore."

Dom rubbed his apricot-colored goatee. "You know that one sidewalk in Freeway Park above the pond?" At Livy's nod, he continued. "Some dude saw him fall. He landed right in the water."

Gasping, Livy squeezed Scott's hand as DeeDee tightened hers. "That's so high! How in the world did he survive?"

"We need to find someone who can answer our questions." DeeDee tugged her along to the nurse's station. "Guys, stay here. We'll be right back."

After they made several inquiries, a young nurse named Helena stepped up. "You're Mr. McCreary's daughters?"

At their nod, she suggested they follow her to a private room. Once seated, DeeDee asked about a blood test.

"Yes, that was the first thing we did." A trace of defensiveness tightened the nurse's tone, hiding an unspoken *Of course!* "There were no drugs in his system and just a trace of alcohol. Point-oh-two, which suggests he might've had one or two drinks several hours earlier."

"So, not incapacitated," Livy observed.

"No. Whatever — or *whoever* — caused him to fall over that railing, it wasn't from substance abuse."

Livy gasped. "Whoever? What do you mean?"

Compassion darkened the nurse's eyes. "When they brought him in, he was mumbling that someone pushed him."

"Did he say who it was?"

The nurse shook her head. "It was difficult to make out what he was saying. He could barely talk."

DeeDee's somber gaze reflected Livy's own thoughts. Everyone knew that place was dangerous in daylight, much less at night. People had been murdered there. Men had broken bones sliding down the waterfall. With its reputation, Livy couldn't fathom why on earth Dad had been at Freeway Park after dark in the first place. And how had he survived such a great drop?

Helena said something about a police investigation, but Livy barely heard. Her mind whirled as she and DeeDee returned to the waiting room. She beckoned DeeDee to a secluded spot, away from Gus and Dom, and they sat. Livy squeezed her knees. "Remember on Sunday when Dad got that call in the middle of lunch and he seemed upset?"

DeeDee nodded, her eyes widening.

"I-I wonder..."

DeeDee clutched Livy's hand. "If he has an enemy."

Chapter Nineteen

"Bye, sweetheart." Scott, accompanied by the fresh scent of steaming coffee, gave Livy his customary goodbye kiss, then set the coffee cup beside her ballet-dancer lamp. "Here's your decaf. Take care of yourself. We'll go visit your dad tonight."

She stretched and reached for the cup, vaguely remembering last night—she'd crashed in her own bed rather than opting to stay the night at the hospital. With urging from their husbands, she and DeeDee had agreed to ride home with them to get some sleep. The guys were right, she admitted now as she relished her first hot sip of the day. She and DeeDee couldn't do any more for Dad, and they needed to think of their babies' welfare.

Her stepdaughters tailed Scott into the room, Kinzie in a black tank and camo leggings, Lacie rocking a unicorn top with ripped jeans. Livy'd long ago given up offering them fashion tips once she learned they'd rather fit in with their grade-school peers than look presentable, at least according to her and Scott's standards.

This parenting business was the hardest job she'd ever attempted. She couldn't help wondering if parenting her own biological child would be less, or more, challenging than raising stepdaughters. On the upside, this was good preparation. On the downside—far too many to name.

She set the cup down. Kinzie and Lacie offered shy-preteen versions of a hug, and she breathed in the freshly shampooed scent of them. "Bye, girls. Enjoy your last week of school." She sat up and kissed both girls' soft cheeks, their hair brushing moisture across her neck, then smiled at her husband. "Have a good day at work, honey, and don't worry about me." She bunched a pillow behind her sore back. "Thanks for getting the girls ready and driving them to school every day." She pinned them with a look. "Do you two know what an awesome dad you got?"

They nodded in unison, and Scott planted another long kiss on her lips, his whiskers tickling her skin. She felt, more than saw, Kinzie and Lacie watching, bashful yet fascinated, trying unsuccessfully to avert their gazes.

After he and his daughters left the room, she stretched her arms high and listened to the telltale sounds of Scott's departure repeating their daily cadence. The dogs' goodbye barks. The hum of the garage door buzzing through the walls. The manly sound of his Chevy Avalanche backing out before it paused at the end of the driveway.

The familiar noises faded, and her attention shifted to her phone flashing on the nightstand. She rolled over to check it — 7:14 a.m. Two text messages awaited her. *Good morning,* Melodie greeted. Then, *Going to make it to practice tonight?*

Probably not, Livy replied, her finger hesitating over the keyboard. If she told her friend about Dad, she was opening herself up to questions she didn't feel like answering.

Is your dad okay?

Whoa. Where did that come from?

Livy shook her head in amazement. *Why do you ask?*

Crissy said something about an accident. Is it true?

How had word gotten out already? It happened less than ten hours ago. Maybe someone at the hospital had talked to the press. Or posted something on social media.

It's true. He had a bad fall and is in the hospital. He needs prayer. Keep this to yourself, please.

Will do. Crissy seemed surprised he survived.

All traces of sleepiness had vanished. *Yeah, we were shocked too. Twas a God thing!!*

She swung her legs to the floor and pushed her feet into warm fuzzy slippers. She needed to search online for news of Dad and find out just how much the public knew.

Perched on the edge of the bed, she propped slippered feet on the floral ottoman and opened her laptop. First, the local news. Searching under both of Dad's names yielded nothing recent. *Freeway Park*, she typed next. Up popped an article from last week on the city's recent sweep of the homeless camps there, but nothing about a man found injured last night.

A post on his Twitter account from two weeks ago made her grin. *I'm back, Northwest peeps! You can take the boy out of Seattle, but you can't take Seattle out of the boy. #EmeraldCity#HomewardBound.* 723 likes, about half as many comments. Too many to wade through. Dad hadn't posted anything since. He'd never been much of a social media person, seeing as he was as old school as Yale.

A new email notification pulsed at the bottom of her screen. She clicked it open. *Hoyt Bank*, it said. *Your updated statement is ready to view.*

She did a quick check of the balance to see if her fund had earned anything this month.

12,797.86?

There must be some mistake. What happened to their 260,000-dollar balance? She scanned the details, her heart lodged in her throat. A 250,000-dollar withdrawal posted yesterday. She clutched at her throat, her breaths shallow and gasping. Someone had taken out nearly all of her and DeeDee's funds!

In seconds, she had DeeDee on the phone, and they studied their account together. Between DeeDee's ragged breaths and her own dismayed cries, she read from the statement. "Client funds withdrawal? What the…?"

"I'm going to call Hoyt Bank right now," DeeDee promised.

"They're not open yet."

"Oh, crap, you're right. They don't open till nine. What am I supposed to do for the next hour and a half? Go crazy?"

They fell silent, but Livy couldn't bring herself to end the call. At a time like this, when she couldn't bear to be alone with her distress, even a silent connection was better than none.

"Wait a minute." DeeDee's breathy words held resolve. "Dad is the trustee on this account. He can withdraw from it, right?"

"You think Dad did this? Why ever would he?"

"I don't know. But who else could it be? Neither of our husbands can touch this fund."

"Do you think he could be having financial trouble? Maybe that's why he's been acting so strange lately."

"Let's go to the hospital and find out."

~~~

When they arrived, Dom had left, and they found Dad in a private room, fast asleep, oxygen tubes in his nose. "Full of morphine," the nurse, Helena, told them. His uneaten breakfast waited on a tray beside the bed.

Livy's tummy growled at the sight of richly buttered toast and a sunny glass of OJ. She winced at the bruises and wounds marring his face. Her belly impeded her attempt to lean in for a better look. She shifted and bent her knees. A bandage covered his left cheekbone, but the bruises extended to the right one as well. The odors of antiseptic and chemicals wrinkled her nose, and while the beeping monitors beside him carried on a steady percussion, she shivered as though a sudden draft swept through the room.

"He looks like he got hit by a truck."

The nurse adjusted the blanket more firmly around him. "I've seen worse, believe me." Studying a clipboard, she turned and left the room.

Livy strove to resist the fresh breakfast sitting in front of her, but she finally gave in and grabbed a piece of toast. DeeDee grabbed the other piece, then lifted the juice to her mouth. Only an unappetizing bowl of grayish yellow applesauce remained. Livy's tummy still protested, but she turned to the bed, determined to ignore the pangs. She and DeeDee needed to stop by the café on the way out.

"Dad." Livy placed the printed bank statement atop his gown. "Dad?" She hated the urgent squeak in her voice, but they needed to know what happened to their funds. At least if Dad was the culprit, they'd have a measure of peace knowing it wasn't in the hands of some random overseas cybercriminal.

But he didn't stir. Livy shook her head. "How long should we wait?"

"As long as we need to. In fact, I'll wait all day if I have to. How dare he pull a stunt like that without telling us?"

"Let's sit down. I need to get off my feet."

Livy's soles tingled whenever she stood for more than fifteen minutes, and sure enough, here came the telltale numbness. "There's only one chair." She pushed the nurse's button, and Helena returned, wheeling a wide vinyl chair into the room. Livy and DeeDee sat, fingers fidgeting, feet tapping, as they waited for Dad to awaken.

Out of habit, Livy checked her phone, which reminded her of Melodie's text. "I got an interesting text from Mel this morning." She showed DeeDee the text exchange. "But my search for news on Dad was interrupted by the email from Hoyt Bank."

DeeDee pulled out her phone. "Well, let's keep looking. I'm dying of curiosity over how Crissy found out." After some swiping and keying, she held out her phone. "Look. Here's something. 'A man was found seriously injured in a pond at Freeway Park last night around ten p.m. A witness claimed he saw the man fall into the pond. The injured man's identity has not been released.' " DeeDee's eyes bugged. "If his identity hasn't been released, how would anyone know it was Dad?"

"Think about it. Crissy is in the medical field—"

"She's a receptionist!"

"No, hear me out. Haven't you noticed how medical professionals all know each other? She might know someone who works here, and that person posted about it on social media. Or maybe Dani found out and told Crissy."

DeeDee crinkled her face. "Well, instead of speculating, why don't you just ask her?"

Livy swiped at her phone. "I'd rather ask Mel."

How did Crissy find out about Dad?

When Mel didn't reply immediately, Livy opened Facebook but closed the app after thirty seconds of scrolling without really seeing. Images of Dad falling to a near-death consumed her thoughts.

She glanced over at him. No change. The monitors beeped and hummed. The blood pressure cuff squeezed and released like clockwork.

Her phone buzzed. Melodie. *She says she saw something on Facebook.*

Livy showed DeeDee the text, then replied.

Ask if she can send us the link.

Melodie replied with a thumbs-up emoji at the same time Helena walked in. "He might be asleep for a while," the nurse told them. "The morphine really knocked him out. He's about as pain-free as possible right now. Totally oblivious." She surveyed his motionless form. "Are you two sure you want to wait?"

Livy picked up the bank statement resting on Dad's chest. "Deeds, let's go get breakfast, then talk to Dom. We'll get this figured out."

Chapter Twenty

Livy rubbed her belly as she and DeeDee pulled up to their dad's house. "I shouldn't have had that second cup of decaf at the hospital."

"Heartburn?"

"Bladder." Livy grimaced. "And the rain only makes it worse."

"I know, right?"

They found Dom lounging on the living room sofa. A bass riff boomed through his earbuds, and the house smelled like chicken wings and old pizza. He jumped and ripped out one of the earpieces when he saw them.

"Sheesh. Way to sneak up on me. Couldn't you knock or something?"

"Sorry." Livy winced. They were all new at this business of living in the same city after years of separation. "The door was unlocked, so we figured you were home."

"What are you doing here?" His stockinged feet slid as they hit the hardwood floor. "Is Dad okay?"

DeeDee made a what-do-you-think face. "He's alive, at least. But he may not be home for a while. Have you heard from Gus?"

"Yeah, he texted me that he can't make it until next week. It's finals week."

"Do you need us to bring you anything?"

Dom shook his head. "There's plenty of food here. I

can drive to CaliBurger if I need to."

"Don't hesitate to let us know if you need anything." Livy plopped to the other sofa and looked him in the eye. "You're welcome to come stay with one of us, if you'd like. We hate to see you all alone here."

"I'll be fine."

"Do you have friends nearby? If you're not going to take us up on our offer, at least try to hang out with decent people."

"My friend, Jeremy, lives on the other side of that hill." He pointed toward the backyard. "His dad is a friend of Dad's. Owns a music store."

Settling in, DeeDee crossed her still-slim ankles. "I hope he's good people."

"So, Dom…" Livy relaxed against the sofa arm. "We didn't just come here to check on you. The other reason is, we want to know if Dad is in any kind of trouble, financial or otherwise."

Dom's eyebrows shot up, the first crack in his cool teenaged facade. He gave a forced shrug. "No clue. Why?"

"Just curious." DeeDee betrayed no emotion, apparently agreeing with Livy's own reluctance to say too much until they knew more. "Livs, let's do some investigating."

"Wait a sec…" Dom's voice trailed their retreating forms, but Livy gestured they'd be right back.

Livy's heavy gait matched her twin's as they made their way to the back wing. "What did you have in mind?"

"Snooping through his files and personal papers."

"That sounds kind of underhanded."

"Well, if Dad's in trouble, don't you think we should help if we can?"

Livy preferred they wait until his condition

improved. Yet DeeDee had a point, too. Who knew how long he'd be unable to communicate. In the meantime, if they learned he did withdraw their funds, they could put that question to rest. "I suppose so."

"Let's check out his workroom." DeeDee stopped at the last door in the darkened hallway.

"What do you expect to find?"

"Hopefully a withdrawal receipt for two hundred fifty grand."

"Can you wait until I use the bathroom?"

When she rejoined DeeDee in the hall, a question that had been niggling at her brain all morning sprouted into a full-blown fear. She twisted her wedding ring back and forth, then halted when they reached the threshold. "Deeds?"

DeeDee spun to her. "Hmm?"

"What if he wasn't pushed?"

"But the nurse said…"

"I know. But think about it. Has it occurred to you…I mean, do you think maybe Dad…um…"

"What?" Even in the shadows, DeeDee's brow arched with impatient curiosity.

Please, Deeds, read my mind. I don't want to say it aloud.

"You mean, could he have jumped into the pond on purpose?"

Livy's gut churned at her twin's directness. She nodded, relieved DeeDee had guessed.

"I don't know." DeeDee rubbed her arms. "He didn't come across as suicidal. Yet he wasn't under the influence, either. Isn't that path fairly well lit at night?"

"I don't know." Livy lifted her palms in a helpless gesture, visualizing her dad strolling through the park, always in a hurry, and maybe rushing a little too much, lost in thought, not seeing the edge. Again, an odd place for him to be. Normal people avoided places like that at night.

With a scoff, DeeDee spun and stalked into the room. "No way would Dad have intentionally thrown himself over. Why would he?"

"He's in some kind of trouble. I just know it." Maybe this room would hold a clue or two as to the nature of his trouble.

While Livy glanced around the room, unsure what to look for, DeeDee went to the bare desk housing Dad's computer and opened the top drawer. Livy helped her search, but the desk drawers were nearly empty — pencils and pens, a pack of gum, and some ancient CDs. A pile of unopened mail in another. Livy shuffled through the envelopes. Citibank Mastercard. The Bon. Seattle City Light.

"Nothing here."

A cry of surprise pulled Livy's gaze to where DeeDee stood, brandishing an old VHS tape. "Look what I found."

The boxy, antiquated tape looked like an anomaly in her twin's grasp. "It says 'Me and Luna' on it. I bet it's old home movies Mom and Dad took before we came along."

"How sweet that he kept it all these years."

DeeDee tucked the tape into her oversized knit purse. "We should take this home and watch it."

"I think we should ask Dad's permission before we watch it," said Livy.

"Okay, okay." Reluctance dragging her movements, DeeDee returned it to the drawer. "But now, let's go back to the hospital and find out if Dad had any bank documents on him since, apparently, there's nothing here. The hospital should have all his stuff."

They bid their brother goodbye after he assured them again he'd be fine. Then they headed out into the damp morning, eager to get to the bottom of the missing money and Dad's baffling behavior.

~~~

"We were wondering if we could look through our dad's belongings." DeeDee, stepping to the nurse's station, wanted to take charge, and Livy let her. By lifelong habit and unspoken agreement, Livy would act as their spokeswoman next time.

"We put it all in the big cupboard by the door," replied the gray-haired nurse. "We dried his wet clothes as good as new. Help yourself."

In the room, Dad looked exactly as he had two hours before. A nurse informed them he'd been awake for an hour, but he'd gotten another dose of morphine and was out again. Filtered light bled through the oyster-colored vertical blinds behind his hospital bed. The monitor showed his steady rhythm, and the IV fluids ran unhindered. Someone had removed his breakfast tray. DeeDee opened the cupboard where a pile of clothes were folded neatly on the middle shelf, then handed Livy Dad's navy hoodie. "You check these pockets. I'll check his jeans." She kept her voice at a near whisper, perhaps fearing to wake Dad.

Livy dug her fingers inside both pockets. "Nothing here," she whispered.

"Wallet. Keys." DeeDee tossed them to a chair.

"Sssh." Livy glanced at the bed. They couldn't wake Dad yet. "Anything in the wallet?" She snagged it and peeked inside—a wet mess of soggy bills and receipts. "If the document we need is here, it's completely ruined."

"Darn." DeeDee reached up for the black vest. As she pulled it off the shelf, something beneath the clothing slid out and clattered to the floor.

Livy jumped back. Surely, the noise would awaken Dad. Nevertheless, he slept on. Balancing herself with the closet doorknob, she slowly knelt and picked up the object. "Oh hey." She held it out. "It's another old VHS tape, cracked beyond repair."

"Weird."

"This one is labeled 'Me and Luna' also. It feels quite damp."

"He had a VHS tape on him at the park?"

"Apparently so. Don't ask me why."

DeeDee wrested the tape from Livy's hands and peered at it. "Is that Dad's writing?"

"I can't tell." Livy studied the block letters. "It's printed. But who else's would it be?"

Scrunching her forehead, DeeDee drummed her fingers on the tape. "All these strange things he's up to. First, he goes to a city park at night with an old tape of himself and Mom. Then he falls into the pond for no apparent reason. After he presumably takes a load of dough out of our trust fund. It just makes no sense." She slipped the tape into her bag.

"He needs to wake up soon." Livy's voice rose to a squeak, and she took a deep, calming breath as annoyance at Dad and worry for him battled inside her. She and DeeDee went to his side and listened to his steady breathing. At least he was oblivious to all the turmoil he'd created.

DeeDee gave Dad's shoulder a gentle tap. "Dad, wake up, would you? You've been up to something very strange. Don't try to sleep your way out of this, either. We're going to keep bugging you until we get some answers."

Chapter Twenty-One

DeeDee soaked in the panoramic view of the bay from the glass elevator as she and Livy ascended to the thirteenth floor of Millennium Tower. When they arrived at the marble and glass office of Hoyt Bank, she straightened her shoulders and ran her fingers through her hair. Not much intimidated her, but she couldn't help a shiver of awe at the high-class surroundings flowing in luxury.

This time she let her sister take charge. Livy stepped to the gleaming marble counter and gave the receptionist a friendly casual smile. "Is Mr. Wyatt available?"

"Do you have an appointment?"

"No, we just need a quick consultation about our account."

The woman looked back and forth between the two of them. "Names?"

Livy made introductions, the woman checked their IDs, then directed them to have a seat. They sunk into rich eggshell leather sofas, joining a well-groomed woman in a gray plaid pantsuit—wife of a CEO, DeeDee would bet, possibly a divorcee from the cold-eyed stare—and a polo-shirted man—Microsoft engineer, high school Valedictorian—who didn't look up from his *Money* magazine.

Soft voices rose and fell in the background until Mr. Wyatt, who looked about their age, approached them with an outstretched hand.

"Olivia and Diana McCreary? What can I do for you?" After the obligatory handshakes, he beckoned them to a glass door. "Come in and have a seat." They perched in his wood-paneled office adorned with abstract art. "I don't think we've met, although I've met your father. Howard McCreary, right?"

"Yes." DeeDee eyed his shiny brass nameplate. John B. Wyatt. "In fact, that's why we're here."

Purple dress shirt, short-cropped hair. University of Washington Business school graduate. Investment banker by day, party animal by night.

"We noticed a big withdrawal the other day." Livy perched on the edge of a chair and folded her hands in her lap — only DeeDee could've heard the effort her sister took to keep her tone casual. "We think our dad must have done it, but we just want to make sure."

Still standing, Mr. Wyatt moved behind his desk. "He did. I take it he didn't tell you?"

DeeDee gripped the chair arm, her heart shuddering in relief. "He did not."

The answer could've been so much worse.

She flinched at a cold hand on her wrist. Livy gaped at Mr. Wyatt, her fingers squeezing DeeDee's arm like a blood pressure cuff. "Did he say why he needed the money?"

"No," said Mr. Wyatt. "But even if I knew, I'm not at liberty to reveal my clients' confidential information."

Gripping her own chair arms, Livy shifted on the hard wooden surface and crossed her ankles. "You know, we didn't get a notification from the bank until the next day. Doesn't the bank have a policy to alert account holders about large withdrawals?"

"Well, he came in person. He did seem in a rush, and he kept looking at his phone. But since he opened the fund, he's the primary signer on the account. The two of you are equal beneficiaries. Which means technically it's his fund, but you two are allowed to access up to fifty thousand dollars per withdrawal."

Pressing her lips tight, DeeDee watched Livy twisting her fingers over and over. "I see." She stood in an effort not to reach out and still her twin's nervous hands. "That's really all we needed to know, Mr. Wyatt. We thank you for your time."

She and Livy shook his hand. Then he escorted them to the exit. "Thank you for coming in." He handed them each a business card. "Don't hesitate to call if I can be of any further help."

They descended the elevator and stepped onto Second Avenue where a cargo truck and city bus spiked the noise level and DeeDee's blood pressure. A homeless man cuddled his backpack like a lover. "How does he sleep through all this?" she muttered to Livy.

"I will assume that's a rhetorical question that you already know the answer to."

"Mmm-hmm. But here's one that's not rhetorical. What did Dad do with all that money?"

~~~

Livy and Scott had the dining room to themselves while the girls visited their maternal grandmother. Livy took advantage of their absence to discuss a sensitive topic. "Scott, listen." She slid the paper to the side and peeked at Scott, who was twirling spaghetti noodles on his fork. He nodded to indicate he followed, and she read aloud from the daily *Times*. " 'LOCAL ROCKER DECLAN DECKER IN SERIOUS ACCIDENT. On Wednesday evening around ten p.m., Declan Decker apparently fell into a pool in Freeway Park. A man who witnessed the impact alerted a nearby couple who called 911. The witness, who identified himself only as Bruce, told the paramedics he heard a yell and saw a man falling. When he went to investigate, he found the man facedown in the foot-deep water. Decker, whose driver's license confirmed his identity, was rushed to a local hospital with serious injuries. It is unclear how or why he fell and whether drugs or alcohol were factors. Hospital personnel refused requests for interviews on the basis of patient confidentiality.

" 'Decker, real name Howard McCreary, was born in Seattle and raised in the Ballard neighborhood. In 1991, he signed his first record deal with his band, the FireAnts. That album, LunaTunes, went platinum, and he continued to record throughout the nineties. In recent years, his record sales have declined, and in January, he settled a case for several million dollars against his former manager, who sued Decker for breach of contract. Last month, the former rocker relocated back to Seattle from his longtime home in LA in order to spend more time with his family.' "

Her phone pulsed with an incoming text. Melodie. *How's Howard?*

Ha. Not "your dad," but his first name. The one only his closest friends used. She grinned as she typed. *When we left him this afternoon, he was still out, high on opiates.*

Wow emoji from Melodie. *Do they know how it happened?*

Livy bit into an authentic Italian meatball, courtesy of her husband. *I don't think anyone knows because he was alone.*

OK, keep me posted!! Pretty please!

She chuckled. "Sorry, honey." She related the electronic conversation, then moved swiftly to the issue that had her pacing and clenching her fists under her chin all day. "DeeDee and I found out some very strange things today." She told him of the missing money and everything they'd learned about the accident, watching his expression change from mild curiosity to head-scratching alarm.

"Deeds and I can't figure out if he fell accidentally — or on purpose — or if he did, in fact, get pushed. Which would mean someone intentionally tried to kill him." Her heart stuttered, but she forced herself to go on. "He could've made an enemy at some point. Maybe it has to do with Morton's lawsuit. Or maybe he's..."

She stopped, unable to voice her fear, and tipped her head at Scott, whose features went taut as a dawning awareness settled on his face. "Honey, tell me what's going on in that handsome head of yours."

He wiped his mouth with the napkin, then set it down a little too hard. "I can think of a few reasons why he might need two hundred fifty thousand dollars quickly. A new investment, possibly. Or maybe he's having legal problems. Did that issue with his agent get fully resolved?"

"As far as I know, yes. But he's always been open with us about his life. If he needed funds for a new investment or a legal settlement, he wouldn't have any reason to keep it from us. That's why DeeDee and I were so blindsided. Why didn't he just tell us?"

Scott stroked his chin, and she paused her eating, mesmerized by the complex man she'd fallen in love with two years ago. A brilliant man who had no idea how good-looking he was. That endearing chin-stroke thing he did — she could always tell the wheels of his mind had engaged. Sure enough, here came his analysis.

"I can name one reason why he wouldn't tell you."

"What?"

"Blackmail."

Livy nearly choked. Had he read her mind? "Wow." She dabbed her mouth with a napkin, buying time. "Do you really think so? But why would someone want to blackmail him?"

He cracked a tiny smile. "Because he's Declan Decker."

"You know, I remember something he told DeeDee and me when we were kids. Something like, 'When you're famous, everyone wants a piece of you.' "

Scott held her gaze. "It seems a pretty likely reason to me that someone would need big bucks right away."

"If he's being blackmailed, then there are things in his life he's kept us completely in the dark about. And Dom too." She raised her water glass to her lips, and the liquid soothed her suddenly dry tongue. She set it down with a shaky hand. "I just remembered. The video!"

"What video?"

"We found an old VHS video of himself and Mom in his belongings. At least, we assumed it was him and Mom by the label, but the tape was shattered. Apparently, he had it on him when he fell." She took another quick gulp from her water glass.

"Where's the video now?"

"DeeDee has it. But…oh!" She held her palms to her head. "There was another one just like it at his house." She hoisted herself up, then stopped when she saw the look on Scott's face.

"Sweetheart, relax. It's not like you have to go watch it right now."

She eased back in her seat. "We need to see what's on it. Maybe it's unrelated to his recent activities. But maybe it's not."

"Could he have confided in anyone?"

She lifted her palms as her heart rate slowed to near normal. "I have no clue. I'll reach out to some of Dad's contacts in the music business and see if anyone's heard from him recently."

"What about your other brother in California? Wouldn't hurt to ask him."

"He's supposed to fly up here this weekend. In fact, honey, maybe you'll pass him in the air when you fly down there Friday for your conference."

"Speaking of that…" Scott stared out the window at the dusky evening. "I'm a little worried about leaving you here alone for four days. If I could get out of it, I would. But the company's paid for it, and it's nonrefundable."

"No need to worry." She gave his muscular forearm a reassuring pat. "DeeDee and Nick are just a few blocks away."

"True." He ran his finger back and forth across his creased forehead as if he were trying to iron it out. But the furrows remained.

Bad sign.

"Honey?" Livy leaned in until her belly hit the edge of the table. "What's on your mind?"

He eyed her, his fork suspended. "I'm wondering if God is planning a Job-type trial for us. I mean, we were already dealing with pregnancy complications. Now your dad is in the hospital after suffering a fall that should have killed him." He shook his head. "I hope and pray this is as bad as it's going to get."

She stared at her plate, unable to reply.

When she looked up, he was staring at her middle. "How is Baby today? Still active and kicking?"

She caressed her belly. Time to switch to a more positive topic. "You have a very energetic child, honey. It's funny, I've been so preoccupied with my dad that I haven't been as obsessed with my pregnancy. It's too bad a different tragedy had to happen to get my mind off my troubles."

Chapter Twenty-Two

While Scott loaded the dishwasher, Livy sat at the table and chewed her fingertips as if the action could spur her mental creativity. "Honey, when you're done, would you mind helping me with this message?"

"Sure. Who are you sending it to?"

"Deeds, our brothers, and ten music contacts who know Dad."

He came and sat beside her. Between the two of them, they composed a message that got immediate attention.

> Dear friends:
>
> You have probably heard the news that our father had a serious accident yesterday. We are concerned about him and want to know if you have talked to him or seen him in recent days. If so, please private message me.

I was sorry to hear of his accident, came the response from the manager of Jubilee Music. *Unfortunately, I have not seen or communicated with Declan in several months.*

The remaining five who bothered to reply said roughly the same thing. By seven o'clock, when she grew convinced no one else would reply, she drove to DeeDee's, interrupting her and Nick watching an episode of *Dancing with the Stars*.

Livy chuckled when she let herself in. "You look like you're growing out of the couch." Black-clad DeeDee had sunk so far into the equally black sofa's plush depths that the two appeared melded.

DeeDee groaned and pointed to the TV. "I'm jealous of those women who can move so freely."

Nick draped his arm over her shoulder. "Sweetheart, you'll be dancing again soon."

"I know. It's hard being patient." DeeDee made a pained face at her husband, then turned to Livy. "Come to the sunroom with me, Livs, and let's call Dom." She squeezed Nick's leg. "Babe, you get to stay here and tell me who won." He rose and helped her to her feet, and she and Livy flip-flopped into the next room, where Livy related Scott's blackmail theory.

DeeDee's mouth twisted. "I wish we knew what was on that video he had."

"It could be perfectly innocent."

"It could be perfectly incriminating. Nothing else makes any sense."

DeeDee picked up her phone and put it on speaker. Dom's teenage-boy hello mumbled through the speaker. They'd probably interrupted a video game. "Dom, we're hoping you can help us understand what Dad's been up to." Livy could picture Dom sit up straight at DeeDee's no-nonsense tone. "Do you have any idea what he was doing in Freeway Park at night? Or why he would need a big chunk of money?"

A moment of silence, then, "You already asked me that. I told you I didn't know."

"Sorry to ask again, but this is really important." Livy's apology softened DeeDee's abruptness. "I know you don't have any solid information, but can you think of anything he might have said or done in the last few days that seemed odd? Did he ever act vague or secretive?"

"Um, he spent a lot of time at his computer."

"Was that unusual?"

"Sort of."

"Did he seem upset? Preoccupied?"

"Yeah, he did. I just figured he was ticked off at his Realtor 'cause his house isn't selling."

Finally, a clue. Livy checked DeeDee's expression to see if she noticed, too.

DeeDee replied with a nod and a thumbs-up. "I hope you have their contact info for us. What's their name?"

"Margo somebody."

"Dom," DeeDee said in her I-mean-business voice, "we need you to search Dad's stuff and find her name and phone number. There's got to be something...a business card, documents, what have you. Please go look and call us back."

"'Kay."

After DeeDee ended the call, Livy slapped the futon cushion. "We should check Dad's Facebook accounts, his personal and professional pages, for someone named Margo."

They leaned over DeeDee's phone, scouring all the pages on Dad's public Facebook account to see if he'd liked anyone named Margo or any real estate business. "There must be a hundred music agents here, but no Realtors so far," DeeDee murmured.

"And of course, every rock band that ever existed is represented here." Livy scrolled further down. "Even some Christian bands. Look. NeedToBreathe. MercyMe. He certainly has good taste."

"They all know each other." DeeDee grinned. "Aha, look. Waverly Real Estate, Los Feliz Blvd, Los Angeles,

CA." She clicked on the website. "Here we go. 'Our agents.' " A few clicks later. "Margo S. Pilar, Senior Broker." She raised her hand for a high five. "We found her." An attractive brunette in her fifties gave them an open-mouthed smile as though she couldn't contain her bushels of happiness. As though selling real estate in California were the most exciting career ever.

"Let's call her."

Livy shifted to face her. "We haven't really planned what we're going to ask her. We can't just call and say, 'Hey, our dad is acting weird. Do you know why?' "

"Good point. Why don't we ask her if she's talked to Dad in the last twenty-four hours? At least we can start there." Before Livy could protest, DeeDee clicked the number. "It went to voice mail," she mouthed at Livy. "Hello. This is DeeDee McCreary calling, Howard McCreary's daughter. I understand you're my dad's real estate agent. So sorry to call you this late. My sister Livy and I were wondering if you'd talked to our dad in the last couple of days. We'd appreciate if you could call us back tomorrow."

Two minutes later, DeeDee's phone rang. She pressed the speaker.

"This is Margo Pilar." Her voice held a faint accent. Hispanic, perhaps. "Don't worry about the late hour. I'm up till almost midnight most nights." A carefree chuckle, exactly like Livy would've expected her to sound. "I talked to your dad yesterday. What would you like to know?"

DeeDee recapped her on the accident, and Margo clucked.

"Oh, I'm so sorry to hear it. How is he?"

"The doctors believe he's in for a long recovery. Anyway, we wanted to know if you'd observed anything unusual with his state of mind."

A sigh whispered from the other end. "You mean besides his extreme frustration? His house isn't selling, and I'm afraid he's blaming me for it. You know, with all the bad luck he had before he left LA, and now nobody wants his house. I hoped for his sake he'd get away from all the bad stuff by moving up there. But apparently not. I advised him to stay until his house sold, but he wouldn't hear of it. He couldn't wait to get out of LA."

"Did he give any hints that he was in some sort of trouble?"

"As a matter of fact…"

DeeDee clenched her teeth, and the same veiled impatience surged through Livy.

"Something he said made me think he was in dire straits for money. Now, what was it…? Oh yes. He said, 'You're my last hope, Margo.' "

"Last hope for what?"

"For funds, I assumed. He didn't elaborate."

Finally, DeeDee turned a knowing look on Livy. "Thank you for your input. We appreciate your time." They said their goodbyes, and DeeDee clicked off.

Triumphant, Livy tapped the phone. "See? He's in financial trouble. The kind of trouble that could result from blackmail."

Her phone rang in her pocket. "Oh, it's Dom. Hello?"

"Hey."

"We found the Realtor's name, and we've already talked to her. So you can go back to your video game."

"I wasn't playing a video game. I was looking for the Realtor name like you asked. And I found something in Dad's nightstand."

"What?"

"I found this photo, and I think it's what upset him."

"What photo?" Livy and DeeDee spoke in unison.

"A photo of your mom."

"Okay," DeeDee said. "But why would it upset him?"

"She's with some guy. I can't see his face, but he's bigger than Dad."

Livy met DeeDee's shocked gaze.

"Wowness," DeeDee breathed. "Is there a name or anything on it? Can you tell when it was taken?"

"It's really old. You know those old cameras that used to print out photos?"

"Polaroids?"

"Yeah. It's one of those."

"That is old." DeeDee rubbed her scalp. "Look on the back. Any name or date?"

A long pause. "Your wife was cheating on you."

"*What*?!" Livy nearly dropped the phone.

"That's what it says on the back. 'Your wife was cheating on you.' "

Livy doubled over, her hand on her chest. "Thank you, Dom. We're coming by for that photo. See you soon."

DeeDee ended the call, her shoulders relaxing.

"Wowness," Livy echoed. "That would explain his state of mind."

"But it doesn't answer the other question: Who sent him that photo?"

Chapter Twenty-Three

1983

Howard opened his eyes. An angel's face floated above him, and he blinked, wanting to hold onto this dream. Or maybe he'd died and gone to heaven.

The angel spoke in Luna's voice. "Howard?" His vision cleared. Luna's eyes bored into him, brows drawn together. He scanned the sterile room, a tiny, colorless room filled with medical equipment.

He cursed and tried to sit up. "Yow!" He gasped, pain stealing any other words.

She placed a firm hand on his chest. "No. You can't get up yet."

"What the h—"

"Shhh. You'll be okay."

He peered at her. A deep red bruise marred the skin beneath her right eye. An angry red cut split her lower lip.

"What happened to your face?"

A nurse rushed over. "Howard?" Her face was kind yet firm. "How are you feeling?"

He hurt all over, as if jail hadn't inflicted enough pain. He shifted, trying to get comfortable.

"Ow!" If he were the crying type, he'd be bawling by now.

"You need something for the pain?"

He nodded, grimacing and sucking in agonized

breaths. The nurse left, and he surveyed Luna's face again.

"You gonna tell me what happened?"

"You don't remember?"

"I remember what happened to *me*. Your lowlife boyfriend beat the living crap out of me. But what happened to *you*?"

Luna's eyes gleamed with unshed tears. Her voice dropped to a whisper. "He tried to beat the living daylights out of me, too. After he dragged you away, I ran to find a phone booth and called 911. Brian found me and punched me. I screamed for help. Then some guys jumped on him and subdued him. The cops came and hauled him away. Eventually, an ambulance arrived too, but it took them awhile to find you." She sniffed. "He broke your nose and several of your ribs."

"He broke my nose?"

"Yeah." She tilted her head. "But, you know, it gives you a tough look. You look like a real rocker now." The sheen of tears dimmed, and she grinned. "It's kind of sexy."

He didn't care about sexy right now. Instead, he held out his hand. "They're gonna put your ex on probation." He closed his fingers over hers. "He's gonna make it his mission to find you. Then, when he gets out of jail, he'll hunt you down."

She winced. "I'll be in a place where he'll never find me."

"Where?"

"At Audria's aunt and uncle's. Brian doesn't know them. He'll never find me there."

Worry seeped away, and he relaxed. "Let's stay together, okay? I'll make sure you're safe."

She smiled and wrapped a shiny tress around her finger. "You're my hero." The smile faded, and she lifted her chin. "As long as you promise you'll never do to me what Brian did."

"I promise. He punched you before?"

Grimacing, she nodded. "Just one other time. I told him if he ever pulled it again, he'd be history." She leaned over and planted a gentle kiss on Howard's lips. Her hair tickled his cheek. "And now he's history."

Howard reached up and embraced the back of her silky hair. Pain stabbed him, but he ignored it. He took his time as his eyes and hands roved over her face, caressing the cut on her lip with the lightest of touches. When they finally kissed, long and deep, he went spinning over the edge again. But this time he relished it.

Chapter Twenty-Four

The first thing Howard saw when he opened his eyes was Luna's face superimposed on the ceiling. He squinted, and the vision disappeared. He blinked, not sure what he'd seen. The specter had Luna's face, but wore a black beanie and sported a much heavier body.

Luna, 110 pounds soaking wet, never wore black. "It washes me out," she'd claimed. But apparently, his late wife was experimenting with gothic fashion and eating well on the other side. He chuckled to himself, happy she was having a good time up there. Voices undulated around him, one agitated, the other firm, but his ears refused to cooperate.

The second thing he saw was a fair-haired nurse leaning over him, poking him with something.

He squeezed his eyes shut against the overpowering pain coursing from his head to his toes, then opened them again, remembering how he got here.

His mouth felt as dry as an LA summer. "Hey." He cleared his throat. "Wha–what hospital... is this?"

"Harborview." The nurse cocked her head at him. "Glad to see you're alert. You've been out for a few days. How do you feel?"

"Like hell." His groan reached the off-white ceiling. "Hurts... so bad."

"We've got you on heavy-duty pain meds. You got pretty banged up, to put it mildly. The police came by yesterday, wondering how it happened."

As if he needed more problems. He couldn't tell the cops what really happened. He couldn't tell anyone. The publicity would ruin him.

"I–I got mugged...."

She raised her brows. "Yeah, no surprise since you were walking through Freeway Park after dark. Why were you there?"

"Meeting…a fr–friend."

"In the park?" Doubt dragged out her tone.

He closed his eyes in hopes she'd stop asking questions.

"When you feel better, the cops will be back to interview you."

Which would give him time to prepare a plausible story. When he got out of here, he was going to track down Bro and make him pay in the most excruciating way.

When he opened his eyes, compassion softened her face, seeped into her brown eyes. He must look like a wreck.

"H–how long have I–I been…?"

"Two days. You came in Wednesday night. It's now Friday afternoon." She checked the Fitbit on her wrist. "Three thirty-five p.m."

Bro would be long gone by now. Once that despicable, boneheaded lowlife found out he'd survived, would he try again? Howard would go the rest of his life with a target on his back if his nemesis were never caught.

He simply couldn't understand why Bro would want to hurt him. He'd gotten the 250-grand video, and Bro got the dough.

The video! He couldn't let that fall into the wrong hands. "By the way, did anyone find a" —he stopped for breath — "a video in my jacket?"

"A video?"

"An old… VHS of my… wife."

"I don't recall a video," the nurse said. "But your stuff is right here in this closet. I can look for you."

"Thanks," he rasped. "It means a…lot to me."

She rummaged through clothes he recognized, knelt to eye level of the lower shelves, then felt along the upper shelf. When she turned, regret filled her eyes. "Sorry. I'm not finding it."

If he'd had the strength to bury himself under the bedclothes, he would. After all the trouble he'd gone to for that recording — the funds he'd "borrowed" from his daughters, the heavy risks he'd taken — he had nothing to show for it?

What kind of a God ran this universe, anyway? He closed his eyes, willing the nurse to go away and leave him in his misery.

~~~

Risky stifled a groan when Bro leaned in too close.

"Did you get it done?" His rough voice scraped her nerves.

She glanced down the hall to the closed door. "Shh, keep your voice down. The kids are asleep." An almost-sneeze tickled her nose against the strong aroma of weed. These days, he always smelled of it. How was he able to keep his job?

He grasped her upper arm, and she twisted away. "Tell me what happened."

She looked at the ground. What a coward she was. "I–I couldn't do it."

"You couldn't do it."

She recoiled at his sarcasm. "Someone came in, so I

left."

"You know you're making things more difficult for both of us, don't you?"

She stepped back. "I'm not a murderer, Bro. I don't want to do your dirty work for you anymore." A fierce almost-whisper. "And why do you think I would get the job done if you couldn't even do it?"

His mouth contorted into a snarl, and she fled to her car, slamming the door behind her.

~~~

A day like any other day at Harborview Hospital dawned. Machines hummed. Nurses padded along the corridor. Soothing voices undulated over the intercom.

"When do I get to go home?" Howard asked the nurse as the blood pressure cuff squeezed his wrist. Thank God, the pain had subsided, and his mind felt almost clear for the first time since the day of the fall.

"When the doctor gives you the all-clear."

He cocked his ear. "I need my hearing aids."

"Your hearing aids are here. Your son brought them by."

She reached behind her, and he could see the box in her hand, her fingers moving around inside.

"Much better," he said after she inserted the devices. "You're awesome." The machine beside him pulsed with a clear steady beat. The hum from the hallway clarified into actual snippets of conversation.

But the nurse didn't reply. At a male voice from the hall, she spun around, and Howard forgot his pain and distress when a uniformed policeman materialized in the doorway.

Now his pain was no longer merely physical.

"Howard McCreary?" queried the heavyset

thirtysomething man. He didn't wait for a reply but approached the bed. "Detective Flynn. Are you up to answering a few questions about the incident in Freeway Park on Wednesday?"

The nurse cast a nervous look at the cop and left. Howard silently rehearsed his script, scratching his raw cheek where the bandages had been.

"Can you tell me what happened?"

He forced a quick nod, grateful it didn't hurt too much. "Yeah, I was taking a shortcut through the park...."

"Why?"

"It was a pleasant night, and I felt like some fresh air." He glanced at the doorway, at people walking by. Nurses, interns, visitors with somber faces. A young woman slowed outside his room and peered inside, alarm twisting her face at the sight of a policeman before she hurried on.

"What were you doing in that part of town?"

He took in a mind-clearing breath. "Had a date."

"At?"

"The Hilton." Partially true, at least. A "date" with the parking garage. In fact, the hotel probably towed his car away by now.

"What was your date's name?" At Howard's look, the officer explained, "We may need to get a statement from her."

"Don't recall her name. She wouldn't know anything anyway." Howard had to look away from the cop's probing gaze again. "Afterward, I thought I'd head over to the twenty-four-hour Subway for a bite to eat—"

"Why didn't you just eat at the hotel? You were already there."

Oops. Unprepared for this plot twist, he stammered, "Well...um... I was..." His mind scrambled for a plausible excuse. "I wasn't there to eat, if you know what I mean." He forced a smirk. The cop could take that however he wished. "And I was craving a foot-long chicken bacon ranch. In hindsight, I regret it."

The cop gave him a long appraising look. Could he tell Howard was lying? "Once you got to the park" — a deliberate clearing of the throat — "what transpired to make you end up in the pond?"

"Uh, a couple guys jumped me, and I fought back."

"Did they steal anything?"

Howard eased in a deep breath. The worst thing he could do was appear nervous. "Hard to say. It's pretty much a blur in my mind now."

"There was a witness who had a slightly different take."

"There was?" He'd completely forgotten the paramedic telling him the same.

"He didn't say anything about any muggers."

He thought fast. "Maybe he was one of them."

The cop chuckled. "I doubt it. He was a frail old homeless man, living in a tent." He propped the notepad against his substantial belly. "You were found facedown in the pond with broken bones. Clearly, this was no ordinary mugging. Now, are you going to tell me the truth?"

Howard's heart lurched. "Guess I should've clarified that I was walking along the upper promenade. The muggers went for my wallet, but when I fought back, I must have gotten too close to the railing." He scrunched his face, the angst genuine. "I went right over the edge."

Silence followed, broken by the cop's labored breathing as he scribbled notes.

"Did you get a look at them?"

"No, they were both dressed in dark clothing. I

couldn't make out their faces."

"By the way, I asked the hospital's chief of staff if you had your wallet on you when you arrived. He said you did."

Howard clutched his chest, feigning relief. "So they didn't get it!"

Another suspicious look. "You're lucky to be alive, you know."

"You're not the first to say so. Apparently, I landed on a mattress, which broke my fall."

"We interviewed a few other folks who hang out there, but nobody was able to shed any light on the incident. We were hoping you could tell us something helpful."

"I wish I could. Thank you for looking into this, and I hope you catch the guys."

"We have an officer who patrols the park. If the crooks strike again, I'm confident he'll catch them."

Howard exhaled his tension. "That would be sweet." Even sweeter if he could bring Bro to justice.

On his own terms.

Chapter Twenty-Five

Howard's mind chewed on Bro's final words for what felt like hours before the rotund Detective Flynn returned, this time with a female partner, Detective Satterthwaite.

Bro had snarled "four bribe roadie" just before he pushed Howard over the railing. But Howard hadn't a clue what it meant. His mind traveled years into the past, to all the tours, the various road assistants his band had hired. To the best of his knowledge, he'd always treated his roadies fairly and paid them generously. Had he inadvertently wronged one of them, and was now paying for it?

It made no sense.

The officers entered while Howard clung to the arm of a nurse who was leading him to the bathroom. What time was it?

He craned his head at the window behind him and to his right. Bright daylight beamed in, but couldn't penetrate the cloud hovering around the cops, with their hard questions and equally hard gazes.

"I'll wait," Flynn said, his girth drooping from the sides of the whitish vinyl chair. His partner leaned against the sink.

"Do you mind closing the door?" Howard shot back over his shoulder. When he finished, he half hoped the officers would be gone, but no. There they waited, carrying on a quiet conversation. At least they'd honored his request to close the door.

The nurse departed after helping him back into bed but left the door ajar about an inch. "Can you close the door?" he repeated to Flynn, who eyed him, his expression unreadable.

"This will just take a few minutes. Quick update. We tracked down your car make and model, then went over to the Hilton to interview the parking garage manager. He confirmed a car of that description had been left there unclaimed for forty-eight hours before they had it towed. We then reviewed camera footage from the evening of your assault."

Howard lay still, trying for casual, but each time he moved, massive pain in his ribs forced a grimace.

"Some of the elements of your story still aren't clear," Flynn went on, his manner disarmingly calm. "You see, the security cameras showed you arriving at the parking garage at about nine forty that evening, then heading straight for the street. You didn't go into the hotel at all."

"You must have had the wrong car."

"No, we got a close-up of the driver. It was you, all right."

Howard forced a cough, then groaned with all the intensity he could muster. Maybe they'd go away if he moaned loud enough.

"Yet you told us you were there for a date. It must have been the world's shortest date, yeah?"

Satterthwaite cracked a smile, then wiped it away.

Howard closed his eyes against Flynn's cocky smirk mocking him.

"We're also confused about the route you allegedly took to Subway." The cop tapped his pen against a metal clipboard in an annoying series of rat-a-tats. "You said you took a shortcut through Freeway Park, where you were mugged. But once you left the parking garage, all you had to do was walk one block south on Sixth, and one more block west on Seneca. Instead, you crossed the street in the opposite direction and ventured into the park. Obviously, you weren't heading to Subway."

Flynn stopped tapping, and Howard opened his eyes. He met the cop's penetrating stare.

"The 911 call was placed at six minutes after ten p.m., less than half an hour after you parked."

Long pause.

Don't answer.

"This is sounding suspiciously like a drug deal gone bad. I think you're protecting someone."

Howard narrowed his eyes at Flynn, matching his stare. "I've been clean for three years, Detective. I don't see why it matters what time I was there or for what reason. The fact is—I *was* assaulted." He tapped his chest. "Obviously. The more time you spend questioning me, the longer it will take to catch 'em."

Flynn stood. "We'll be in touch." He took a card out of his pocket and left it on the counter. "If you decide to cooperate, give me a call."

He waddled out, Satterthwaite tailing him. At the opened door, two identical faces peeked in, both chins dropped about two inches.

His kiddos! They'd heard everything!

The tension in his chest released. He'd never been so glad to see his daughters. They might be angry, even furious, over what he'd done. But he could count on them to seek justice.

On the other hand...maybe not. Their gazes followed the cops out the door. Then they approached his bed. DeeDee crossed her arms, her eyes as hard as blue flint. "Drug deal gone bad, huh, Dad? That would explain a lot." She whipped her hands forward, the two Luna photos clutched in her fingers. "Be honest." She flipped one over to expose the scrawled words.

Your wife was cheating on you. The accusation stabbed him anew.

DeeDee's words needled him through a fog. "Did this drive you to drugs?"

Livy thrust the bank printout onto the bed like she was playing Rock Paper Scissors. Paper won. "Be straight with us, Dad. Are you being blackmailed?"

"Shut the door," he said.

DeeDee shoved it closed. The loud click punctuated the tense atmosphere.

From his vantage point, their cross-armed stance formed a no-nonsense wall. His little girls had grown up to be assertive, anti-BS young women. "The cop was wrong. There was no drug deal." He met DeeDee's hard stare. "Someone sent me that photo. Maybe someone connected with your mother's ex-boyfriend." He locked eyes with Livy. "And you're right—I was being blackmailed."

They just stared at him until DeeDee lowered her arms. "By whom?"

"Some dude who called himself Bro emailed me out of the blue one day—"

"He sent the photo?"

"No, according to the delivery guy, it was a woman. But I got the email the same day as the photo."

"A woman?" Livy tugged her hair. "Did you get her name?"

"No. There was no name. The courier said she was an older blonde woman."

Two sets of identical blue eyes flashed at him. "Audria?" Practically in unison, the name of their mother's best friend burst from them.

Audria. Of course. Yet…

"Nah." DeeDee was first to reject the idea. "Aunt Bestie wouldn't do that."

His sentiments exactly.

Livy nodded. "Plus, if it were Audria, why would she say 'your wife' instead of Luna?"

"And why would she use that method if she had something so important to tell Dad? She'd just call him."

"Although…" Livy tipped her head to the ceiling. "It's been ages since we've talked to Audria. Since Deeds and I started going to church, she doesn't reach out anymore."

Howard scratched a spot on his arm not covered by a cast. "She is one of the few people who would have an old photo of your mother. She also might know if your mother really did cheat. Why don't you ask her, see what she says?"

DeeDee put a finger to her chin. "But according to her Facebook posts, she and Jake are in Vegas. It'll have to wait till next week when they get back."

"Oh?" he said. "When did they leave?"

As though seeking confirmation, DeeDee glanced at Livy. "Yesterday, I think? Or the day before?"

"The photo was delivered to me last week. Before she left. You ought to go to the delivery office and show them a photo of Audria, see if they remember whether she came in."

Livy grimaced and pointed to the bathroom. "Excuse me a minute, you guys. Be right back!"

Luna had needed to stay near facilities at all times while she was pregnant. "Not a problem." He met DeeDee's skeptical gaze. "If you get a chance, drop by Emerald City Couriers before five and ask for Julius. The address is online. It's close to your childhood home. Might be fun for the two of you to drive by your old house."

"You mean today?"

He glanced at the clock. "It's almost four. You probably won't make it. But don't wait too long. It's already been over a week."

"If it was Audria, I will be amazed."

"If it was Audria, I just hope the delivery guy recognizes her after all this time."

Livy waddled from the bathroom and came to lean against his bed. "Okay, Dad." Her silky hair swung as her stare intensified. "This is getting really confusing. An older blonde woman who might be Audria and some dude named Bro. Why don't you tell us everything."

~~~

By the time Dad finished his story, Livy shook her head back and forth like an out-of-control pendulum. DeeDee stood frozen, fist under chin, eyes wide as saucers. Through the cracked-open window, the sounds of business as usual seemed to invalidate the drama playing out in his room. "Kiddos, you need to understand I did this for you."

Beside her, DeeDee's jaw clenched. "For us? Dad, you must be joking."

"I couldn't let that tape go public. For your sakes, for your mother's sake, God rest her beautiful soul. For Gus and Dom. I never intended to upset you. Can't you get that?"

In Dad's world, protecting his family from the leeches and the unscrupulous had always been his highest aim. She leaned against DeeDee, shoulder to shoulder.

"I was planning to raise the two hundred fifty and pay it back in a few weeks."

"What do we do now?" A despairing whisper seeped from Livy's lips.

"You need to hire a bodyguard to keep everyone out of this room," said Dad. "Bro must know by now I survived his murder attempt. Seems likely to me he'll try again."

With the level of danger amped up, Livy sagged inside. As if pregnancy woes hadn't drained her already…

"Then, find out who the man in the photo is." Dad turned pleading eyes on them. "I want to know who sent it, and I want to know who Bro is."

"How do you expect us to do all that?" DeeDee's jazz hands chopped the air. "We have absolutely nothing to go on."

"I know someone who might be able to help you. Your grandma Gaia."

"You want us to tell her what happened to you?" Livy twisted her wedding ring 'round and 'round.

"And about the stolen money?" DeeDee added.

"No need." Dad motioned them closer. "I have an idea."

Chapter Twenty-Six

Livy turned into Grandma Gaia's cobblestoned driveway in Portland as the afternoon sun sent dazzling light into Grandma's flower garden, intensifying the rainbow effect. Livy loved Grandma's roses, which sported a wide mix of hues. Some as orange as a sunset sky. Others with blooms of palest lilac.

"If I were an artist"—DeeDee stopped to caress a yellow rose petal as they made their way along the paving stones—"this garden would be the first thing I'd paint."

"I know, right?" With their overnight bags in tow, they stepped up two concrete stairs to Grandma's black beveled front door. Livy rang a doorbell embedded in the stone facade, then opened the door as Grandma had asked. "I hope she submitted an entry to the Rose Show."

A multicolored tapestry, hanging next to the door, greeted them. It sported the New Age Tree of Life, which Grandma swore by as a harbinger of good fortune. The irony of adapting a Biblical symbol for non-Biblical purposes was not lost on Livy. Across the room, a shelf of goddess sculptures adorned the mantle above the granite fireplace. Livy'd considered them cool and sacred in her pre-Christian days. Now they just made her shudder.

She and DeeDee followed a sweet-smelling aroma to the kitchen, where Grandma stood at the counter in an apron of psychedelic fabric, her hands busy in a mixing bowl.

"Lambkins!" She still used the warm term of endearment from when they were children, even though they were almost thirty. "I'd hug you, but I'd get dough on you."

"That's okay, Grandma." DeeDee wrapped her arms around Grandma's narrow waist. Then Livy followed suit.

"Did you have a nice drive down?"

Livy grinned. "Besides having to stop three times for bathroom breaks? Pretty uneventful."

Grandma didn't need to know that they were disobeying doctor's orders by making this 170-mile trip. Let her believe they were here for one purpose only: to return their mom's photos to Dad. "What are you making?"

"Orange vegan cake."

"Smells good. Can we help?"

"No, you two didn't come here to bake. Why don't you go on up to the attic and get your mom's things?" She stopped and wiped her hands. "Follow me. I'll show you where they are."

Memories rushed Livy as they climbed the steep, dark stairs to the attic bedroom, the room where they used to stay as children whenever Mom went to rehab. Weak light filtered through the tiny window until Grandma flipped the light switch. Musty odors tickled Livy's nose.

Grandma tugged on the old wooden window sash. "This room needs some air." She opened a door and reached up to the closet shelf. "Here's a shoebox where she stored a lot of old photos. There are some scrapbooks and photo albums, too. Why don't you grab those?"

She eased the shoebox carefully off the shelf and set it on the double bed where Livy and DeeDee used to sleep. The room had seemed massive then, with its high sloped ceiling and ancient chest of drawers. The chest remained, as did the bed, but now Livy saw the small, shabby room with new eyes. No longer a haven from a troubled homelife, simply a child-sized attic room where it would be far too easy to hit one's head.

Drawn to the fresh spring air wafting in, she crossed to the window overlooking downtown. The wooded West Hills, towering a thousand feet high and dotted with radio towers and luxury homes, dwarfed the skyscrapers just as they had twenty-five years ago.

"Thanks, Grandma," DeeDee said behind her. "These will keep us busy for a while."

Livy eyed her mother's shoeboxes and photo albums stacked haphazardly. "Grandma, did you bring all this stuff with you when you moved down here?"

"No, it was after your mom passed. I brought all her belongings back here, at your dad's insistence. All her clothes, books, jewelry...I took it all. That woman he hooked up with, your nanny, didn't want any of Luna's things around."

"Really?" DeeDee sat and picked up a photo album first. "That doesn't sound like the Joy I knew."

"I suspect she was suffering from a guilty conscience."

Livy joined DeeDee on the bed and opened a shoebox. "You could be right."

Grandma caressed their shoulders. "Just give me a quick rundown on your babies before I turn you loose. When is your next ultrasound?"

DeeDee sighed out her pleasure. "Monday afternoon."

Grandma paused her massage. "I'm a little concerned you quit taking all those wonderful herbs and minerals."

"We've only been off them a few days," said Livy.

"Dr. Zahir just wants to see if it affects the babies' development."

"Well, let's hope for a positive outcome tomorrow, then, shall we?" Grandma gave their shoulders one final squeeze. "Definitely let me know what they find."

"Of course, we will."

"Have fun reminiscing. Goodies will be ready in about twenty minutes."

They nodded as she left the room, silent, taking in all the scattered reminders of their mother's history.

Once Grandma was out of sight, DeeDee removed the two photos from her bag. "Okay. Here's the guy we're looking for." She set them on the bed and grabbed a stack of photos from the shoebox. "Look." DeeDee held up a photo of a smiling baby. "This goes all the way back to her baby years. Wasn't she cute?"

More photo flipping kept them busy. Spicy aromas from the kitchen, mixed with sweet images from the past, brought back old times. "She had the most darling tap dance costumes."

"In this one, she could pass for one of us. Good one of her and Grandma when Grandma still dressed like a sixties' flower child."

The photos Livy dug through in the shoebox followed no particular order. "Here's one of Mom with Audria. Look how young Aunt Bestie looks!"

DeeDee gave the photo a cursory glance. "What were they, about sixteen?"

Livy glanced at the back. "Yep, 1976. Sixteen years old." She grasped another stack of loose photos. "There are a ton here of her and Audria with other people I don't recognize."

Which reminded her of Dad's claim that an "older blonde woman" had sent him that photo. A woman who fit Audria's general description. She and DeeDee needed to decide how to pursue that angle.

But at DeeDee's next words, all other thoughts fled.

"Wedding photos!" DeeDee squealed.

Livy leaned over. "Oh, it's been years since I've seen these."

"Haha, look at Nils! What a nerd."

Livy doubled over at the best man's goofy expression. "They were all just babies then."

"How adorable, barefoot on the beach. Remember when Dad used to tell us their wedding story? He was so proud."

~~~

May 1984

Howard's bare toes wiggled in the sand like fingers kneading PlayDoh. Luna, ethereal in white, squeezed his hand. Beyond them, the sea churned. Overhead, gulls squawked their congratulations. He tried to focus on the woman minister's words about the sacredness and meaning of marriage, but his heart and mind refused to cooperate.

A ring for my lady, My lady in white.

At Luna's left stood Audria, teary-eyed and sniffling. On his right, Nils shifted from foot to foot. Despite today's landmark occasion, Nils was antsy to get to their gig.

A dream come true, e-ver-y night.

He and Luna would make lots of yellow-haired, blue-eyed babies, starting tonight. He'd take them to Sunday school, be the best dad, the best husband, God had ever seen.

Reverend Gladys's next words drew him back into the moment. "Do you, Howard, take Luna to be your wife?"

"I do." He peeked at Luna, whose dreamy smile still trembled on her face.

"Do you, Luna, take Howard—"

"I do."

"You may kiss your bride." He grabbed his wife, then dipped her backward and planted a wet kiss on her lips while the crowd whistled and catcalled.

Don't need no shoes or ten guitars—

He finally pulled back, his hands cupping her face, his eyes holding hers. As they shared a smile filled with promise and a future, he forgot the crowd, the wet sand, the breaking waves.

I got the sun, the moon, and the stars.

Chapter Twenty-Seven

Smiling over the long-ago images, DeeDee set the wedding photos aside and thumbed through an old-fashioned red album. She fingered a page of faded photos encased in cellophane pockets. "These are all just Mom with friends. I don't see one of her with that guy."

"Keep going."

The old cellophane crackled as DeeDee flipped to the last page. "Here he is!" She grabbed Livy's wrist. "Mom with that guy."

"How can you tell it's him?"

"The clothes. See? I bet it was taken the same day." She slid the photo out, then flipped it over. "Ha. She wrote, 'Me and Brian. Summer of eighty-two.' "

"Let me see." Livy drew the photo close, and they studied it together. A very young version of Mom sat on a vintage seventies plaid sofa, nestled under the arm of an athletically built, early-twenties man. Both smiles showed sparkling sets of white teeth. "Eighty-two? Then whoever wrote the caption was either confused or lying. She hadn't even met Dad then."

"I wonder what his full name was." DeeDee pressed the heel of her hand against her forehead. "Sheesh. I just realized Grandma might know who he is. Let's show it to her."

"We need a good excuse for asking, in case she wonders why."

When they got to the kitchen, Grandma was pulling the cake from the oven. She collected three matte black stoneware plates from the cupboard, and they gathered around the heavy wooden kitchen table. "Find anything interesting?"

"We did. This." DeeDee brandished the photo.

Grandma swallowed. "What's that?"

"We're wondering who this guy is."

A crease crinkled Grandma's forehead as she bent closer. "Oh yes. I remember him."

"Do you remember his last name?" DeeDee showed her the name and date on the back.

Pursing her mouth, Grandma shook her head. "I've completely forgotten. Why are you interested in him?"

Folding her hand over the photo, DeeDee met Livy's eyes. Here came the question they were expecting. "Dad was reminiscing about the time he and Mom met. We think this must be the guy he stole her away from."

"How long did they date?" Livy asked.

"Oh, a few years, I think. He was a bit older than her and even had a little son."

"Hmm." DeeDee took a bite of cake, savoring the zest of orange. "But the child wasn't Mom's?"

"Oh no. You would know it if he were."

"And Mom broke up with him after she met Dad?"

"I believe so. But it wasn't because your dad swept her off her feet. It was because Brian punched her one too many times. Which is why I didn't like him, to be honest."

DeeDee speared another bite of cake, trying to imagine her peace-loving mother dating someone hot-tempered. It didn't quite compute. Maybe that was what attracted her to Dad. He was one of the kindest, most even-keeled people she'd ever known. Not that he didn't have his faults, but a bad temper wasn't one of them.

"He beat your father up, too," added Grandma.

DeeDee scowled. "Really? Dad never mentioned that."

"You ought to ask him about it."

"You bet we will."

~~~

When they finished eating, Livy and DeeDee returned to the attic. "Let's try the scrapbook." The extra weight Livy carried left her nearly panting from a mere flight of stairs. "Maybe we'll find Brian's last name there."

The scrapbook held tattered remnants of Mom's youth—old dance recital programs, party invitations, wedding announcements. One page contained dried flowers held on with yellowed tape, each meticulously labeled with a memory—"wildflowers from camping trip, summer of '75," "poppies from Disneyland trip, '72," "daisies from Katie's yard." Livy flipped each page, checked each ancient memento, looking for one particular name.

A sudden rainstorm pounded against the window, and she shivered in the unexpected chill. As DeeDee stood to turn on the overhead light, Livy flipped the page, and her pulse quickened. "Oh!" She pointed with a shaky finger. "I think I found it."

DeeDee leaned over to peer at the *Seattle Times* cutout from 1981. It was a letter to the editor titled "Kingdome Ticket Prices Unfair."

Livy skipped over the five-line paragraph to see the writer's name circled in proud red marker.

She gasped and tapped her fingernail twice on the name: Brian Brodie.

"Brodie," breathed DeeDee. She snapped her fingers. "Aha!"

"What?"

"I think I know what Dad heard. It wasn't 'four bribe roadie.' It was 'for Brian Brodie.' "

Livy leveled a dropped jaw at DeeDee. "Of course!" She grabbed DeeDee's hands, and they danced a celebratory jig. "You're totally, absolutely brilliant."

They plopped to the bed, all grins. DeeDee palmed her jeans' back pocket. "Now what did I do with my phone?"

Livy fumbled in her sweater pocket. "We can use mine."

"Great. Do a search."

"Facebook first." Her hand trembled so bad, her finger missed the icon. She tried again, then keyed his name in. Beside her, DeeDee's breath stilled.

Livy sighed as the search concluded. "There are a ton of Brian Brodies on Facebook."

"Add Seattle to his name, see if that helps."

After another fruitless search, Livy opened Google. *Brian Brodie, Seattle.*

Topping the list—a headline from the *Seattle Times* dated two years earlier.

Livy gasped. An obituary.

"Listen to this, Deeds." She held up the phone for DeeDee and read aloud in slow disbelief. " 'Brian Robert Brodie, Jr., of Burien passed away February 27 from complications of liver disease. He was born June 30, 1955, in Renton to Brian Robert Brodie Sr. and Cecilia Brodie. He left behind a wife, Darlene, and...' "

"Go on."

Livy jabbed at the screen. "It won't load any more info unless I'm a subscriber."

"What a scam."

She thrust the phone away and eyed her twin. "Our

hottest lead turns out to be dead for over two years."

"This guy was about the right age," DeeDee pointed out. "Five years older than Mom. I bet it's him."

"I wonder if the blonde woman who sent Dad the photo was the wife." She picked up the phone, still showing the obituary. "Darlene."

"Let's find out if she's even still alive." A quick obituary search turned up nothing. The handful of Darlene Brodies on Facebook lived in other states. "She might have remarried and have another last name by now."

"Hmm. The mysterious blonde woman's identity remains unknown." Livy set her phone on the bed and propped her elbows on her knees. An unexpected shaft of sun had shoved away the spring shower. She stared at the slanted rectangle on the wood floor. "I'm even more confused now. Bro said to Dad, 'Payback time for Brian Brodie.' If Bro was exacting revenge on Dad on Brian's behalf, then Bro isn't the guy in the photo. So how are the two connected?"

DeeDee scrunched her forehead. "Hmm. Bro...Brodie. Brian's son, maybe?"

Livy thrust a triumphant hand in the air and smacked DeeDee's open palm in a victorious high five. "I bet you're right. We just need to find some way to find out if he had a son."

"Subscribe to the site, then."

"Nuh-uh. I refuse to subscribe to a site just to access one obituary."

Chapter Twenty-Eight

Livy and DeeDee gathered up their mom's things and went downstairs where Grandma urged them to finish the cake. "I've had more than enough." She placed a warmed slab of moist cake beneath each of their noses, and they dug in.

"This is awesomesauce, Grandma." As Livy popped the last bite into her mouth, visions of Bro pushing Dad to an untimely death twisted through her mind. But she forgot Dad's troubles when DeeDee groaned and clutched her middle. At the sight of her contorted face, Livy wobbled upright and gouged her belly against the table edge. DeeDee's moans drowned her cry of pain.

Steadying herself against the table, she rubbed the sore spot vigorously. "What's wrong?"

Another moan. "Cramps," DeeDee gasped.

Grandma sprang to her feet. "Are you bleeding?"

Her face gray and agonized, DeeDee white-knuckled the table edge and tried to stand. "Oh!" She doubled over. "There's another one." Her shout curdled Livy's stomach. "Oh no, something wet just landed in my panties."

Grandma got to her side in seconds. "Here, let me help you to the bathroom. We need to see if it's blood."

In the bathroom, DeeDee crouched over the toilet and wailed. "My water broke."

"We'd better pray." Lurching to her twin's side, Livy placed both DeeDee's hands in hers, sucking in deep breaths to calm her own heart rate. "Heavenly Father, please be with DeeDee and her baby." DeeDee stilled beneath Livy's touch. "Please comfort her heart and place Your hand of protection on the baby, that no harm will come to her. Amen."

She opened her eyes to Grandma's disapproving frown. Apparently praying to the heavenly Father was not politically correct.

"I can't believe this." DeeDee sobbed. "Why did this have to happen when I'm almost two hundred miles from home?"

Fists on hips, Grandma glared at them. "How could a bunch of old photos be more important than your babies' welfare?"

Because at the time, Dad's welfare had trumped everything else.

"I would have told you to stay home had I known you were under doctor's orders. In fact, I'm surprised your husbands let you out of their sight."

"Scott didn't have a choice." Livy cringed under Grandma's disapproving gaze. "He's in Orange County at an engineering conference." As for Nick, Grandma didn't need to know about his strenuous objections that morning. "What if something happens to you or the baby?" he'd groused at DeeDee. They'd argued for fifteen minutes before he finally conceded that yes, Grandma could easily handle any emergency. "But if anything goes wrong, I won't forgive myself for letting you do this." They'd even prayed together before she and DeeDee hit the road.

Suddenly exhausted, Livy leaned on the counter. "You're right, Grandma, but like we told you, we wanted to do it for Dad."

Grandma tsked. "Couldn't it have waited until after

delivery?" She drew her brows together and turned to DeeDee. "Is there any blood?"

Sniffing, DeeDee doubled over with another contraction, managing to shake her head between gasps.

"Go get in my car." Grandma's verbal whip-crack energized them to action. "Time to get you to the hospital."

~~~

A weak cry, so faint she might have imagined it, floated through the dim room. DeeDee reached through the dusk for her baby, but it was as futile as trying to get there on a treadmill. Perhaps if she amped up her pace, she'd find her infant. But the air thickened, and she dropped her arms in defeat. A faintly acidic odor tickled her nose. Voices came at her, and something warm and soft filled her grasp. "Here she is, your beautiful baby girl," said someone nearby. The voice undulated up and down, the pitch rising and falling like an auditory strobe light. "She's seven weeks early, so we're taking her to the NICU."

DeeDee clasped the bundle tighter and sniffed a delicious powdery scent. She heard Livy's steady voice through the murk. "Deeds, you made it. Your baby is fine. Just really tiny…"

"Three pounds, eleven ounces," said the disembodied voice again.

"I've called Nick," said her twin. "He's flying down here now. He should be landing soon."

DeeDee ached to take a good long look at her baby, but her frozen eyes refused to open. Was something wrong with them? Her head felt like a helium balloon about to float away. Maybe this was a dream, and her baby was still inside her.

Her baby, Xena.

Xena Olivia Rush, the warrior princess.

She and Nick had chosen the name in hopes their daughter would grow to be as strong and capable as the fictional heroine in character, morals, and spirituality.

Livy was speaking again. "Isn't it awesome? They were able to save your baby. Praise God, right?"

"Mmm," DeeDee managed, pulling the sweet-smelling bundle closer. "Mmm."

~~~

Nick covered DeeDee's hand with his solid one, and she forced a feeble smile. His flickered in response. "How do you feel?"

Night had fallen, and she blinked against the overhead light. "In love."

He chuckled. "How about physically?"

"Oh, that." She sighed. "Sore all over." She placed a hand on her abdomen.

He squeezed her hand. "We made a beautiful baby, sweetheart."

Her smile widened. "That we did."

"And she's going to be okay, I think. The doctor will be in soon to talk to us."

A blonde woman in a smock, who reminded DeeDee of Dani, strode in. She peered at her clipboard, then back at them over black half-glasses. "Mr. and Mrs. Rush?"

Nick stood. "Yes?"

She put out a hand. "I'm Dr. Reynolds. Congratulations on your new little one. Xena is a darling name, by the way." She tilted her head at DeeDee with a rueful half-smile. "Not the way you planned her birth, I'm sure. If we'd had time, we could've attempted to delay your labor with a magnesium drip, but she decided she was ready before we were. Anyway, we got all your records from Dr. Zahir emailed today, so we're all set to care for your little preemie."

DeeDee cringed, imagining Dr. Z's reaction to her rebellion.

"That's the good news."

Nick raised his brows. "What's the bad?"

"She can't go anywhere for a few weeks, at best. Are you prepared to stay here in Portland until she can go home? The hospital can help make lodging arrangements for you if need be."

"They can stay with me." A voice from the corner spoke up. DeeDee hadn't even realized Grandma was sitting over in the shadows. "I live two miles from here on Mt. Tabor."

Dr. Reynolds beamed at Grandma. "Perfect. And you are…?"

Introductions ensued as DeeDee battled with the reality that she was stuck here, hours from home, for who knew how long. Oh, if only she'd listened to Dr. Z and not made this trip.

~~~

Oh, if only she and DeeDee had heeded Dr. Zahir's warning not to leave town. Livy gripped her Jaguar's wheel as she steered around a stall on northbound I5 in Tacoma. A red SUV's rear straddled the line between the shoulder and the right lane, backing up traffic for the last mile and a half. Three hours on the freeway had soured her mood, and she hadn't even reached Seattle's snarling traffic. She and DeeDee had shrugged off Dr. Z's warning, figuring the odds were slim anything could go wrong on a mere two-day trip. Deciding that Dad's quest for justice sat pretty close to the top of their priority list.

After two overnights at Grandma's with no change of clothes, no twin sister, and numerous texts to her worried husband, she was more than ready to be home. At least replacement clothes were easy to obtain. Not so her husband. She missed him desperately, and he missed her. As promised, he'd skipped the afternoon portion of the conference so he could call her once each half hour on her way home, just to reassure himself all was still well.

She'd miss having DeeDee to do pregnancy with. She'd miss her newborn niece's first few weeks as well. But she relaxed in the knowledge that the baby's life was saved and tiny Xena would survive.

"Thank You, Lord," she breathed for the four-hundredth time since Monday. "Please watch over my baby. Help Baby grow and thrive and heal it so it will develop normally."

Ha. From that swift kick she just felt, Baby must have heard. Tomorrow was her rescheduled ultrasound. One more day to learn how her baby was faring. She'd called Dad this morning to update him on his newborn granddaughter. "Congratulations, Grandpa."

Of course, being Dad, he'd plied her with numerous questions. He wanted to know every minute detail—length, weight—and then, at last, he paused.

"Don't you think it's odd that both your babies had the same growth issues?"

"I agree, Dad. I've always heard no two pregnancies are exactly alike. Even with all our similarities, we assumed the same would also apply to us."

Would her own body give birth far too early also?

Her left hand cradled her belly, rejecting the fearful thought, while her right hand maneuvered the car through thickening traffic. A hit Christian song lifted her mood and sent her left toe tapping.

Dad had been pleased with their discovery of Mystery Man's name. "Brian Brodie...hmm," he'd said. "Good work, kiddo. You're getting us a little closer to nailing Bro." She'd asked him when he was going home, and he'd told her, "Probably tomorrow. The hospital is arranging for in-home care."

Her phone beeped. Dad. Her thoughts must have summoned him.

Two minutes later, traffic came to a standstill, and she peeked at the text.

There's a family named Brodie in Burien. Going to hire a PI to find out more.

Chapter Twenty-Nine

DeeDee eased her sore body into Grandma's cushy armchair and exhaled out all the stress of the last few days. Already she missed her precious baby girl something fierce.

Grandma sat next to the cold fireplace, crocheting. "Where is Nick?"

"He went to stock up on baby stuff. Tax-free. We need a car seat, a stroller, diapers, et cetera."

"What a considerate husband you landed. And he's going to be a great dad."

"I know, right?" A grateful smile pushed at the corners of her mouth. "I knew from day one he was my person."

"You're very lucky. Not everyone finds their soulmate."

Not lucky. Blessed. "What are you making?"

"Two baby blankets. I bet you can't guess who they're for."

"That's sweet of you, Grandma." She lifted a bottle of water to her lips and took a long drink, then set it on the table next to her. "Hey, I got a text from Livy this morning." She shifted in a vain effort to find a position that didn't hurt. "She says the waistband on her maternity jeans feels more snug today. She thinks the baby might be growing again." She didn't add the additional news in Livy's text about locating the Brodie family. She and Livy promised Dad they wouldn't tell. And it wasn't likely Declan Decker's problems would make the news here in Portland.

"So happy to hear it." Grandma wrapped multicolored strands of yarn around a crochet hook. As the yarn pooled next to her, she gently toed Freddy, her black and white cat, away. "And she stopped taking the tea and supplements?"

"She did. It's hard to believe herbs or minerals had anything to do with it, though. I trust Dani implicitly. Why would she vouch for something that would harm us or our babies? It's completely foreign to her mission as an alternative medicine practitioner."

"I know, it is odd." A question hung in Grandma's tone. "I wish I could see the stuff for myself. There's a natural supplement shop over on Northeast Broadway that might be able to give us another opinion."

"I should've brought them with me." DeeDee frowned. Then the tension in her jaw relaxed. "There's a website for the tea. If you don't mind ordering it online, you could get a box shipped to you within a couple of days."

After finishing the stitch she was working on, Grandma set the yarn on the hearth. "Let's go do it right now. You can do the driving."

Grandma carried Freddy as she and DeeDee made their way to the computer in Grandma's dining room. DeeDee sat and pulled up the website, specifying Crissy Collins as the distributor who would get credit for the sale. She selected a box of the prenatal tea and clicked the cart.

"Click PayPal," Grandma directed, "and that will take care of the payment. And request two-day shipping."

Next DeeDee found the website for the supplements

Dani had given them and ordered a thirty-day supply. "All done. They should both arrive on Friday, if all goes well. Looking forward to getting a second opinion."

"I'm sure they're fine." Grandma's confident tone sounded forced. "But it will be nice if my friends at Nature Well could put your minds at ease."

DeeDee stood. "Indeed. Now that's done, I am itching to see my tiny babyette."

"So am I. Come on, let's get over to the hospital."

"I'll text Nick and ask him to meet us there."

~~~

When Livy's phone rang ten minutes later, she assumed it was Dad. On the CarPlay screen, she hit accept. "Hello?"

A snuffling female voice filled the car. "Livy?"

"Mel?"

A noise suspiciously like a half-laugh, half-sob shoved everything else from her mind.

Mel sniffed. "Can you talk?"

"Of course."

"Good. I just tried calling DeeDee, but she didn't answer."

"DeeDee's been preoccupied. Her baby—" Another loud sniff from Mel halted her. "What's wrong?"

"Have you seen today's blog on StarSights?"

"Heavens no. I've been stranded in Portland the last two days." She braked as she neared a red pickup going approximately thirty miles per hour, then swerved around it. "What's it say?"

She could picture Melodie, managing to remain stiff-backed even while leaning forward at her dining room table, peering through reading glasses at the tiny font on her laptop.

182

"I should warn you…it's not good."

"I'm driving. Can you read it to me?"

"Okay, here goes." Another sniff. " 'For all you beautiful Declan Decker fans, we have an update just for you'—exclamation mark. 'Unless you've been living in Antarctica for the past week, you will have heard that Decker was seriously injured in Seattle's Freeway Park and remains in the hospital. But today, his sad tale took an unexpectedly sordid twist. An anonymous source claims Decker was at the Hilton for a tryst with "an unidentified woman" after which he meandered over to Freeway Park. When we asked the source how they got this information, they only said, "I have connections." ' "

Livy snorted. "Mel, don't tell me you're taking that seriously. I know for a fact it's not true."

"I-I don't know what to think. On one hand, you know what they say. Where there's smoke, there's fire. On the other, some people will say anything if it profits them."

"Whenever I read that column, I picture some wannabe fiction writer sitting all alone in a dark room, hunched in front of their computer, making stuff up. I bet it's some unemployed twentysomething guy living in his mom's basement. In an old rundown bungalow in Rainier Beach."

Mel must be more smitten with Dad than she'd thought. After just one date. Otherwise, why would she care about some silly gossip column? Livy gentled her voice. "Sounds like you have strong feelings for my dad."

"Is it that obvious?"

She chuckled. "Don't worry. I won't tell him."

"How is he doing?"

By the time Livy finished updating her friend, she neared Tukwila. She glanced at her dashboard GPS, where the town of Burien formed an insignificant dot in the northwest corner.

If she took the next exit, she could take a quick detour and head over to Burien. Once there, she might be able to find the Brodie residence. And possibly catch a glimpse of Dad's attacker.

Chewing her lip, she pondered her options.

Curiosity took over her hands, steered the wheel to the right, toward the suburb of Burien and Brian Brodie.

~~~

Howard itched to leave this colorless place—just another hospital lacking in personality or unique characteristics. He longed to see his new granddaughter. He wanted his old life—his pre-Bro life—back. A life in which the worst thing to happen was songwriter's block. Yet each time he moved, pain still made him grit his teeth. His newly arrived son, August, stood there, trying to mask his shock, his red hair flopped in his eyes, his childhood freckles faded almost to nothing. Behind him, Dom's black Keds squeaked across the tile floor, back and forth. You'd think he was the worried dad and Howard his injured son.

"Dom, relax." Howard snorted. "You're pacing like a maniac."

Dom halted as if he'd hit a wall.

"Look at you two," Howard went on. They'd last been all together at Christmas, several months ago. "I'm amazed how alike the two of you look. You could be identical twins, if you weren't two years apart."

"We know, Dad."

"You told us that last time."

Gus held out his phone to display a pale blue screen outlined in red, covered in words. Howard's own name at the top leaped out. After all these years, his stage name in lights still elicited a thrill.

Balancing the phone in his palm, Gus steadied it before Howard's face. "My friends've been asking me, 'What's your old man been up to, dude?' See, check this out."

Howard took it and brought it close to his face.

The words on the screen, tiny as caterpillar legs, gripped him around the heart and squeezed. "Decker... seriously injured in Seattle's Freeway Park... An anonymous source... tryst with an unidentified woman..."

He'd sue that police department. Their interview with him was confidential. Who had leaked this — and how? Someone at SPD? Or had one of the hospital staff overheard? He'd insisted the cops close the door to prevent this very scenario.

Even though he knew the truth, those who read this could easily assume it was factual. He slammed the phone down on to the blanket covering him. He'd worked hard to clean up his act and shed the "party animal" reputation he used to be known for.

"Look, guys, this is hogwash. There was no tryst, no woman. It was an unfortunate accident after a mugging. This writer is just making stuff up."

At least he hoped so. He hoped it was simply a coincidence that this person's fake news happened to mirror his story to the cops. Because if not...

Someone he should have been able to trust had betrayed him.

Chapter Thirty

Livy slowed at the Burien address she'd found in the online White Pages. Number 4325. The Brodie cottage had nothing to distinguish it from other nondescript, half-shabby residences on the block. Unmowed lawns and crumpled cars betrayed the neighborhood's declining status. Livy imagined blaring TVs left on all day by parents who worked long hours for low pay at the local strip mall or grocery store or friendly neighborhood diner. School-aged kids playing video games, eating whatever they could find in the cupboard while Dad and/or Mom worked.

A life much like hers and DeeDee's during Dad's prefame years. Some days, all they had to eat was Honey O's. It didn't help that Mom hadn't been able to conquer her slavery to heroin.

A teenage girl sat on the porch steps of the house next door, absorbed in her phone and drinking from a soda pop can. No car in the driveway. Did she have parents at home to watch out for her? Perhaps her mom was a struggling single mother, getting by on food stamps and sporadic child support. At number 4325, no movement or sign of life. A used-up, exhausted old Honda hunkered in the driveway.

She needed to decide whether to stop and watch the house for a few minutes or give up this crazy plan. After stopping at the curb and killing the engine, she steeled herself against the guilty twinge, knowing exactly what her husband would say if he knew what she was doing. Okay, then. She'd sit here for fifteen minutes, then be on her way.

Removing the old photo of Brian and her mom, she set it on the passenger seat and tapped her foot. Took out her phone and scrolled through Facebook. Then checked her email.

A movement to her right made her look up. A man in a tee shirt and cargo shorts flip-flopped in her direction. Staring at the sidewalk, hands in pockets. His basketball player legs ate up the pavement. No phone in his hand…a rare sight these days.

He paid no attention to the heavyset young woman strolling beside him and pushing a sleeping little boy in a stroller, a can of Diet Coke resting in the cupholder.

As they got closer, Livy saw the woman's mouth making conversation, the man finally turning to focus on her.

Livy rolled down the passenger side window. "Excuse me."

The man stopped midsentence and leaned in, rubbing a skull tattoo on his neck. Sunlight flashed from the plug stretching his ear lobe. "Hey." From the gray-streaked hair and laugh lines, she pegged him as roughly a decade older than her. The woman stood about a foot back, annoyance twisting her lips, clenching her jaw.

"Do you live around here?" Livy directed her question at the man peering in her window.

"I do." He pointed. Straight at number 4325. "Right there. Looking for someone?"

She froze at the unexpected reply, studying him. Could he be her quarry? Sneaking a peek at the photo of Brian beside her, she checked for resemblance.

None at first glance.

When she looked up, he'd followed her gaze to the seat. Had he spotted the photo?

No, she'd anchored the photo partially under her purse, which blocked his view.

Garnering her wits, she attempted a disarming smile. "Yes, I'm looking for some old friends. The Brodies. Do you know them?"

Instead of replying, he narrowed his eyes at her. "And you are?" His voice tipped up at the end, challenging, suspicious. His gaze slid down to her bulging middle.

She grappled for a name to give him, falling back on her stepdaughters' names. "Lacie," she told him. "Lacie McKinzie. But…"

"Don't remember any McKinzies. There are lots of us Brodies around. You must have the wrong address."

He stepped back as though her car had sent an electric shock through him and put up his hand in a farewell. Livy fumbled for her phone. She needed to get a photo of him. If this was Bro, Dad might recognize his build and overall look.

While he crossed the front lawn of 4325, the woman and baby close on his heels, Livy lifted her phone and snapped a photo of his back.

The man stepped to the door.

He stopped and turned to usher his family inside. As he did, he glanced back and met Livy's eyes. Heart thudding, she dropped the phone into her lap, stretched her lips into a forced smile, and waved as if he truly were a dear old friend.

Heart in her throat, she started her car. Feeling the man's eyes on her, she meandered her way through the neighborhood, purposefully slow, as though making a leisurely trip to the store. When she reached the highway, her hands trembling on the wheel, she floored it, unable to get away fast enough.

~~~

Xena sighed contentedly at DeeDee's breast, sucking as if her life depended on it. DeeDee stroked Xena's velvet-soft head as the baby rested a tiny hand on her chest. A surge of something wondrous rippled through her. A better high than the opioids she used in her teens. A warm spa, the finest whiskey, a blazing fireplace — none could compare to the natural high she got from nursing her baby.

So this is what euphoria felt like.

She couldn't bear to imagine how she'd feel if anything happened to Xena.

Her baby's tiny eyes, covered by flaps of translucent veined skin, were still the narrowest of slits. Dr. Reynolds told her they'd probably fully open by her original due date. Still weeks away.

Xena, light as a bundle of warm air in DeeDee's arms, bobbed her little head as she nursed. Such a precious sight. The good news was she'd gained five ounces. The bad news: She had to live in an incubator for several more weeks, with mother/daughter time allowed every two to four hours for feeding. At night, when DeeDee returned to Grandma's for much-needed sleep, the nurses fed Xena with milk DeeDee had expressed. During the day, she often stayed in the NICU between feedings, pacing from the parents' room to the incubator for a gazing session, checking her phone for messages, posting social media updates, looking out the window at the unremarkable view four floors below. Vehicles clogged all six lanes of freeway. A commuter train sped toward downtown.

Homeless tents dotted the hillside beyond, exactly like the camps in Seattle. Why would anyone want to live beside a busy, noisy freeway? If you could call that living.

Sensing movement behind her, she tilted her head to see Nick at the door. He stood, simply watching, a beatific smile arcing his mouth. Now her little family was complete.

Thank You, Lord.

Chapter Thirty-One

The morning was warm for early June, at least ten degrees warmer than Livy's drive home from Portland yesterday. She cracked her car window. Breeze filtered through and cooled her overheated skin. Another pregnancy woe she hadn't been prepared for.

She put on her blinker for the freeway off-ramp. "Dad," she said into the phone after she'd told him of her excursion in Burien yesterday, "you don't need a PI. I found out what you needed to know, and it didn't cost you a thing."

"I don't want you taking risks, though. That's the PI's job."

He had a point. She had no desire to follow Bro around. Any spare energy she had went toward her "nesting" instinct she'd heard other mothers talk about—helping Scott furnish the nursery, cleaning the house. Once weariness overcame her, only then would she lie down and try to rest.

"All right. I'll let the PI take it from here. Just keep DeeDee and me posted, okay? And FYI, I'm on my way to visit Audria. She posted on Facebook that she and Jake got home yesterday. I didn't tell her why I wanted to see her."

"Don't overdo it, kiddo. When is Scott getting back?"

"Tonight. He's going to Uber home so I can rest."

"Good man."

Livy reached Audria's coral ranch home in Bellevue

and parked in the driveway. She opened the wooden gate to a path lined with huge planters, a mix of pansies, zinnias, and geraniums spilling over their sides like flowery rainbows.

Audria wrapped her in a breathtaking hug, wreathed in smiles. The familiar scent of her perfume — Obsession — brought tears to Livy's eyes. "Aunt Bestie, it's been way too long."

"Yes! It has." Audria patted Livy's belly. Only Aunt Bestie, and few others, could do so without Livy recoiling. "Just look at you!"

The first thing she noticed was Audria's hair, an elegant shade of silvery gray.

The second thing she noticed: her friend had lost about twenty pounds. "You look great! So thin and fit. And you changed your hair color. It's beautiful."

"Thanks. I decided it was time to stop fighting Mother Nature."

"Was this a recent decision?" *Like, within the last week?*

"Oh no, it's been gray for months."

Of course, Audria hadn't sent that photo. Deep down, Livy had known it. But what a relief to have confirmation.

Jazz music serenaded them as they sipped decaf at Audria's stainless-steel island. Livy's gaze settled on a vase of red mums centered on the countertop — a blaze of color in the monochromatic kitchen. Audria spent the next half hour telling about her trip to Vegas while Livy fidgeted and rocked the barstool to and fro, anxious to get to the real subject. She sipped from a mug stenciled with a map of Italy and curved her feet around the chair's metal legs.

She could cross Audria off her list of possible blonde women, but her friend still might know something useful about Mom's past.

"Well, I've gone on and on, haven't I? And you haven't even had a chance to tell me how you're doing. I'm excited about DeeDee's baby and so *relieved* she's healthy! Do you have photos?"

"You know I do." Livy picked up her phone and scrolled through the photos DeeDee had sent, showing them off one by one.

"Oh, how precious," Audria cooed.

The last of the photos scrolled by, opening the door for Livy to walk through. "By the way, speaking of photos, DeeDee and I found one of Mom at Dad's house from way back when. I bet you'll remember it." She lifted the photo of Mom and Brian from her purse and set it on the table in front of Audria, scrutinizing her expression.

As Audria's eyes widened, her lips stretched into a delighted smile. "Oh, what a treat! I remember taking this picture. Wonderful memories."

"You took it?"

"I did."

"Do you remember the year?"

"I couldn't tell you exactly, only that it was taken pre-Howard." Audria's eyes darkened. "That guy was an absolute jerk."

"So you knew Brian."

Astonishment rippled Audria's face. "Wow, I'd forgotten his name. How did you know it?"

"Dad told us about him." Livy flipped it over, the words on the backside visible. "Someone wrote this and sent it to him."

Audria's shoulders stiffened as she drew herself up. A curse flew from her lips. "Whoever wrote this is lying. Your mother never cheated!"

Livy slumped in relief. "But who could have sent it?"

"I can't even begin to guess. When did he receive it?"

"Sometime in the last couple of weeks. It devastated him."

"Is that why he fell in the park?" A twitch in her eyelid marred Audria's otherwise smooth face.

Livy wondered if her friend's mind had traveled back to Livy's own life-changing accident three-odd years ago. On that long-ago day, her distressed state of mind, her frustration from her family's unwillingness to delve deeper into her mother's death, had contributed to her lack of attention to the traffic around her.

And her leg would likely never be completely normal again.

Her heart twinged as she thought of Dad. He'd likely never be his old self physically, either. She pondered how to answer Audria's question without lying. "He says he was mugged."

Audria nodded. "That's what the news said."

Livy let that one slide. "By the way, thanks for the flowers you sent him while he was in the hospital." She stayed in safe territory and updated her friend on Dad's current state. But in the back of her mind, a question wouldn't leave her alone.

What motive was behind the message on the photo if it wasn't actually true?

Chapter Thirty-Two

"**G**ood morning, Dad." Livy adjusted the volume on CarPlay. "Has it really been more than a week since your accident?"

"A week and two days. Feeling better every day."

"Good to hear. I'm on my way over to check on you. Are you up and about?"

"Yep. How did your ultrasound go this week?"

Mel's street approached, and Livy swung the wheel to the right. "Oh, Dad, praise God. The baby is growing again. It's almost caught up to where it should be at thirty-five weeks."

"That grandchild of mine is going to make it into the world, healthy and thriving. I feel it in my bones."

"If your bones are telling you so, Dad, it must be true."

He chuckled. "I read something interesting on the internet the other day."

"Tell me."

"Did you know that the offspring of identical twins are genetically the same as half-siblings? Which means your two babies will be closer biologically than the usual first cousins."

"That's really interesting." She slowed as she neared Mel's tidy off-white bungalow. She'd only been here once, a few months ago. "By the way...I'm bringing a friend who's been asking about you. And she's bringing brunch."

"Melodie?"

Livy pulled to a stop in front of Mel's house. "Do you mind?"

"If she doesn't mind my body cast, then I guess I don't mind either."

"Great. We'll be there shortly."

She strode to Mel's green door and rang the bell. When the door opened, the aroma of freshly baked cinnamon rolls wafted out. Mel's stiff smile betrayed her nervousness as she flung the door wide and eyed Livy's belly as if to cover up Dad dominating her thoughts. Livy received her friend's hug and followed the aroma into the kitchen. The delicious culprits cooled on a counter cluttered with spices, seasoning bottles, jars of tea bags.

Perched on a stool, Livy crossed her legs at the ankles. "How does it feel to have the next three months off?"

"I love summer break even more than my students do. Anyway. You have to tell me all about DeeDee's baby." Mel stopped at a cupboard. "Want something to drink? I have lemonade, iced tea, regular tea, coffee…"

"Decaf coffee if you have it. I'm off tea for a while. Doctor's orders."

"Not even prenatal tea?"

"Not even." While Mel brewed coffee, Livy gave her friend a quick update on the baby's growth issues.

"Crissy is going to feel terrible if it turns out her tea had anything to do with your baby's problems."

Livy blew on the fresh coffee Mel set in front of her, watching the steam curl away. "Well then, we won't tell her."

"My lips are sealed." Mel propped the tray of rolls on her forearm. "After your baby's born and you're done nursing, you ought to try her energy tea." She showed

Livy a small, square box similar to the prenatal tea. "This is called Pep-T. She says it got her through Amanda's toddler years. It has ginseng, cinnamon, a few other herbs."

"Thanks for the tip." Livy could afford to pay the tea's inflated prices, so why not keep helping Crissy. "I'm looking forward to the day when I can drink tea freely again. And eat normal food. You know how long it's been since I've had a cinnamon roll?"

"Why can't you eat cinnamon rolls during pregnancy?"

"Baked goods give me really bad heartburn."

"DeeDee too?"

"Yes, unfortunately."

Mel wrapped the tray of rolls with tinfoil. "Okay, I won't make you look at these." She handed some paper plates and napkins to Livy. "Can you carry these for me?"

"Sure." She took the items. "If he doesn't fall in love with you after he gets a taste of those, he needs his head examined."

Mel widened her eyes in mock fear. "Oh, the pressure."

Grinning, Livy stood. "Come on, girlfriend. He knows you're coming and is looking forward to seeing you." Okay, Dad hadn't exactly said that. But hadn't his voice acquired a lilt when she'd told him?

She toted her coffee cup to the car, Melodie on her heels, and they made it to Dad's West Seattle street in thirty minutes. Strong wind gusts from the Sound whipped the fir trees in undulating waves. Downed branches and overturned bins littered Elliott Drive. "Looks like quite a windstorm came through here today," she said as she pulled into Dad's driveway.

"Cute house," Mel said. She took her time removing

her seat belt, then opened her purse and refreshed her lipstick. Turning her face this way and that in front of the mirror, she finally let out a less-than-satisfied groan.

"You look gorgeous." Livy opened her door, banging it into a toppled recycling bin. "Don't be nervous." Too late, she remembered Mel's claim that telling a nervous person not to be nervous was as effective as telling a Southerner not to drawl. Livy's husband proved the truth of that. Only time could "cure" a Southern accent. And nervousness.

Livy eased her way out of the car next to the partially filled bin. Its lid yawned open, contents starting to spill out. When she leaned over to right it, her bump got in the way. "Mel, can you help me with this, please?"

Mel came around and set the bin upright, closed its lid, then pushed it to the sidewalk, narrowly missing a woman walking her dachshund. The dog greeted Mel with a single sharp bark.

With a little screech, Mel jumped back. "Good doggy! Nice doggy!"

"Back off, Doc," the woman commanded the dog, yanking his leash. "He's very friendly," she said to Mel with a smile.

Mel stared at the dog dubiously. "I can tell! Have a nice day." She hurried back to Livy and let out a deep sigh. "That was a timely distraction."

"How so?"

"For half a minute, I completely forgot to be nervous." Turning a grin on Livy, she said, "Bring on Declan Decker, girlfriend."

~~~

"DeeDee, you got a package."

Grandma peeked into the guest room where DeeDee

rested between hospital visits. Exhaustion so intense it clawed her bones had driven DeeDee to bed two hours ago, and she didn't think she ever wanted to get back up again. Nick lay next to her, rubbing her lower back as she lay motionless. For some reason, the aches and pains had worsened today. She just needed to stay off her feet for a while.

Grandma's announcement jerked DeeDee into an alert state. "Mmm?" she managed as Grandma approached, holding a box in her hand. "What's this?"

"Your tea shipment."

"Mmm."

"Want me to open it?"

DeeDee closed her eyes again, relishing Nick's massage. "Mmm-hmm." Opening her eyes a slit, she noted the closed blinds. She had no way to know if it was afternoon or evening. "What time is it?"

"Almost noon. After I open it, I'll take it over to the shop and get their take."

"Cool. Thanks."

"You just rest." Grandma set the box on the bed and slit it open with a nail file, dug through packing pellets, then pulled out a cellophane-wrapped box that DeeDee recognized.

"That's it."

Grandma slid her finger under the sealed cellophane and tugged it loose, then removed a pouch. She crumpled up the cellophane and left it in the shipping carton, then folded the lid of the box back into place.

Something elusive knocked at DeeDee's weary brain. Something about the process Grandma used to open the box. What was it?

"I'll head over there now." She tossed a look at Nick. "Take care of your wife, Nick."

He nodded almost as wearily as DeeDee.

"Grandma. Wait a minute."

She ground to a halt and turned.

Energized with sudden curiosity, DeeDee rose to her elbow. "Can I see the box for a sec?"

"Sure."

Grandma handed it to her, and DeeDee took it in her hands, rotating it while she scrutinized, then removed one of the bags. She brought the familiar, yet not familiar, pouch close to her face and sniffed it. *Something's not right.*

"Weird." She held it to the light. "This one doesn't look or smell the same. The stuff we bought from Crissy looks like tiny twigs and pine needles. But this looks like little red and gold potpourri. Also..." Her spine tingled with a dawning awareness. Nick's hand slowed, then stopped, his fingertips resting lightly on her skin. "Our tea never had cellophane on it. Crissy gave them to us taped shut with a little round seal."

She searched Grandma's face for a logical explanation but found only alarm.

"Are you saying...?" Grandma's words came out strangled as though she were fighting for oxygen. "You think your tea may have been tampered with?"

"I-I don't know." DeeDee tipped her head to check Nick's reaction. He only stared at her, his mouth hanging half open. "I can't think of any reason why Crissy — or anyone else — would want to tamper with it. Besides, she's our friend. She's never shown even a trace of animosity toward us."

"Hmm." Grandma dropped to the edge of the bed. "This is very strange. Maybe you should contact her, explain the situation, and see what she says."

DeeDee balled a fist. "You bet we will."

Chapter Thirty-Three

Dad only had eyes for Mel, Livy noticed when they entered his family room where he lay on the couch. His glance barely grazed her and stayed on Mel instead. His welcoming smile gave her hope that perhaps their mutual attraction might turn into something more lasting.

She waved at Gus and Dom, absorbed in a basketball playoff game on TV.

"Hey, hey," said Dad. "Something smells good."

Mel smiled and showed him the contents of the tray.

"I bet those are as delicious as they look," he said.

"Dad, they're to die for." Livy moved to the couch and started to sit. A beep from her phone startled her. A text from DeeDee. *Call me. Urgent.*

She gasped. Had something happened to Xena?

Leaving Mel and Dad in animated conversation, she waved her phone at them and went to the kitchen, where a gray-haired nurse stood at the counter preparing a sandwich. The woman looked up, smiled, and nodded a greeting.

"Hello," Livy replied. "I want to thank you for taking care of my dad."

"Absolutely." The woman lifted the tray. "Your dad has been a very cooperative patient. I'm Karen, by the way."

After Livy introduced herself and Karen left the room, Livy settled at Dad's midcentury kitchen table with a retro lamp on one end. She might as well be sitting on the set of *Mad Men*.

"Hey," said DeeDee's agitated voice.

"What's going on?"

"It's the tea!"

"What's the tea?"

"What made our babies stop growing."

Livy gasped, hearing the meaning behind the mangled sentence. "How do you know?"

"Grandma and I ordered the same prenatal tea from the company website, and we got it today. Livs, it's a different tea than what Crissy gave us." DeeDee's words tumbled and fell as she explained.

Livy's heart contracted when the truth hit. "How could Crissy have made such a major screwup?"

DeeDee's sobs brought a spasm to Livy's heart. "I'm not convinced it was a screwup. It feels deliberate, but we need to ask Crissy what was going on before we make a judgment. Although I don't even know how to ask without exploding."

"She's such a nice person. I think we should give her the benefit of the doubt until we find out what happened. Oh, by the way" — Livy dropped her voice — "I'm at Dad's, and I brought Mel. She knows Crissy better than we do. I could run it by her, see what she thinks."

"Yes, please do. Then let me know what she says." Long, shuddering pause. "By the way, how is Dad?"

"Still not a hundred percent, but doing better." It came out forced as she strove to switch to a happier subject. "He looked pretty pleased when he saw Mel." She could visualize Deeds stretching a grin on the other end. "They're talking away, didn't even notice I left the room."

"Hmm. Well. Let me know how it goes. And I want Mel's take on Crissy."

~~~

"I'm not usually this immobile." Howard stifled a groan. The nurse had assisted him to the living room so he and Mel could talk in a quiet setting. He lay back in his La-Z-Boy, cursing his helplessness, regretting that he agreed to let Mel see him like this.

"It's not like you can help it."

He accepted the cinnamon roll Mel offered. She'd even brought paper plates. A woman with both musical *and* culinary talents? Glory be. "Have a seat. You don't have to wait on me."

Today, she showed off her long, slim legs in a snug pair of jeans topped with a loose purple shirt. She perched a few feet from him on his plush navy sofa and balanced the tray atop the coffee table books—*Rolling Stones' Encyclopedia of Rock* and *History of Music: From Caveman to Pop Star*—books more for show than for reading. But the pictures were interesting enough. Especially the one page devoted to yours truly.

He broke off a gooey sliver of roll and chewed. The sweet glaze rolled over his tongue like warm ice cream. "Wow." He swallowed, scrutinizing the roll as if searching for the secrets of its goodness. "This is a work of art. I don't think I could write a song that sounds as good as this tastes."

Mel laughed. "Thanks. I doubt anyone's ever paid me such an eloquent compliment." She used a fork to cut off a slice, managing to make it look like her hands were dancing. "I–I hope you don't mind me asking..." Mel placed the bite-sized treat on her tongue and shot him a glance, then focused on chewing. She eyed the partially eaten cinnamon roll as though deciding whether to consume all those calories. "What happened exactly at the park that night? I understand you were mugged…?"

"Yes." No need to go into detail. He watched her give in to temptation and eat another bite, then lick the fork. "I don't remember much except waking up in an ambulance with the worst pain of my life. Everyone says it was a miracle I survived and that I'm lucky to be alive."

Another bite. This time she licked glaze from the roll, and he stared, fascinated. He wanted her to keep going, but she stopped and flashed a gleaming white smile at him.

Just like Luna Tunes used to do.

"God protected you." Her no-nonsense statement made it sound like fact, not mere opinion. "You must be special or something." She lifted twinkling eyes.

He had to chuckle—she looked so embarrassed. He wished he could convince her what a gem she was. It was a rare woman who could turn rosy so quickly.

"I'm glad God is a fan of mine." He raised his eyes to the ceiling. "Thank you, God," he said, immediately regretting his flippancy. He needed to redeem himself. "And I'm a fan of His. In fact, I'd get His autograph if I could."

"You already have it." Her smile had disappeared, and she concentrated on the doughy bite in her mouth.

"What do you mean?"

"The Bible could be considered His autograph."

"Hmm." He tipped his head. "Guess I hadn't thought of it that way."

"You could also call it His autobiography." She reached in her purse. "That reminds me. I have a book you might like to read."

He caught a glimpse of flowers and streams. A girly book. He didn't have the heart to refuse her gift, so he took it. *Strength For My Trials,* said the title. *Psalms for the hard times in life.*

"It helped me so much after my husband passed," she went on, lacing her fingers through the loosened strands of hair framing her face. "I hope it helps you, too."

"Thank you." He anchored it beneath his leg, stroking the spine. "It's thoughtful of you." *Even though I'm never gonna read it.*

Livy rushed in belly first, nearly panting. "Sorry to interrupt." She gestured at Melodie. "I need to talk to you."

Squelching a ripple of disappointment, he waved them away. "Go talk. I'll be fine."

Livy didn't even notice. Her open mouth and agitated movements provoked his alarm. "Is everything okay?"

She finally focused on him. "I'll explain later. Mel, can we talk in the kitchen?"

~~~

Inhaling the bacon, egg, and coffee-scented air in Dad's kitchen, Livy fisted her hair behind her head and relayed DeeDee's story.

"Are you serious?" Mel faced her, fists on hips, lips pursed. "She screwed up your tea order?"

"You think it was a screwup?"

"I can't imagine why she'd do it intentionally."

"Did your tea come wrapped? Or sealed?"

"They used to come wrapped in cellophane. On my last order, they came sealed."

Crissy could have swapped her tea with Mel's. But then, why would she?

"So odd." Livy anchored herself against the counter. "How well do you know Crissy?"

Mel tugged on her glasses and pinched the bridge of

her nose nearly tight enough to wrench the skin right off. Livy couldn't blame her. None of this made any sense. "I must not know her as well as I thought. Because that seems out of character. Look at her job…you have to be really organized and detail-oriented to do what she does." She slid her glasses up and gave a helpless shrug. "I don't know what to tell you."

"What kind of person would mess with people's orders? Especially tea for preggie ladies?" A storm was building in her heart. Crissy could've seriously messed up her baby's well-being.

Hot waves overtook her, and she tugged the ceiling fan switch on. Her mind spun in sync with the fan, steady and sure, piercing through the muggy thoughts. She looked her friend in the eye. "We need to confront her. And I think it needs to be done face to face. With both of us."

Chapter Thirty-Four

Howard shifted as Mel and Livy waved goodbye and rushed out the door. Something to do with the babies, Livy explained, but she didn't elaborate. A shopping trip for baby clothes, maybe? For a moment, he felt lost. Despite the fact that he sat here surrounded by people who watched over him. His sons. The nurse. The security guys he'd hired, roaming the grounds. So why the deflated feeling?

The rooms hadn't changed. The sun broadcast its friendly light through the picture window. Gus and Dom still hollered at the game in the TV room. The nurse's upbeat smile remained.

But the good cheer had left the room. The same moment Mel did.

~~~

Livy aimed her Jaguar toward Evergreen Birthing Clinic. "It's one thirty now. Dani only stays open until three on Fridays. We'll just walk in unannounced."

"I agree it'll be more effective to confront Crissy here than at her apartment."

Trying to loosen her tense shoulders, Livy pulled to the curb. "How about we bathe this in prayer?"

"Good idea."

When they finished petitioning the Lord for success and answers, Mel lent her arm to hoist Livy out. The clinic door jingled their arrival into the pine-scented lobby with its familiar soothing music. A young couple at the reception desk swiveled and eyed them. A sliver of Crissy's blue hair peeked between the two. With a nod, Livy signaled Mel toward the row of chairs.

Livy plopped into a vinyl seat and glanced at Crissy. Still occupied with the patient. She couldn't wait to see Crissy's face when she saw them.

"Take a seat," Livy heard Crissy say in her pronounced accent. "Dani will call you in a few minutes." The man and woman turned, and Crissy's gaze fell first on Mel, then on Livy, who masked a grin at the utter astonishment mutating the other woman's face.

"Livy. Mel?" Crissy half stood, then returned to her chair. "What are you two doing here? Is everything okay?"

Livy stood, then waddled to the desk, and cast a nonchalant smile at the expectant young couple taking seats. "Everything's fine. I just need more tea. I was hoping you have a stash of it here."

"Oh." Crissy froze a moment. "I, uh, stopped selling the tea."

Mel set her elbows on the counter. "You did? Why?"

"Too much work, not enough payoff."

"Bummer," said Livy. "I left my supply in Portland, and I need some. Which reminds me. Did you hear DeeDee had her baby already?"

Crissy shook her head, her eyes shifting between Livy and Mel. Nervous silence fell.

The phone rang. Crissy's trembling hand snatched it up as if it were a lifeline. "Greetings. Evergreen Birthing Center." Tension tightened Crissy's voice as her eyes flashed questions at them. "How may I help you?"

Behind her, Dani greeted the patient, and Livy turned

her head so Dani couldn't see her face. She didn't need any distractions. The couple's voices faded away into the depths of the clinic.

Crissy's eyes widened when she saw them still waiting. She coerced upbeat words at the person on the other end. "Cool beans! When would you like to come in?"

Livy motioned to the chairs. "Let's wait till she's off the phone." She plopped to a chair like she weighed 200 pounds and listened to Crissy move the phone conversation into personal realm, asking the caller about her husband, child, job. *Might as well ask her the price of tea in China, girl.* Livy smothered an eye-roll, certain Crissy delayed them on purpose. She needed to use the bathroom, but she didn't dare go anywhere. She tightened her gut and tried not to squirm, but the baby chose that moment to kick her bladder.

"Argh," she whispered, clutching Mel's arm. "I need to go. Don't let her leave."

Mel nodded, and Livy lurched to the ladies' room. Just in time.

~~~

Heart pounding, Livy limped out of the bathroom to the lobby, stunned at what she'd just seen. A thirtysomething woman with a toddler read a magazine in the lobby. Mel leaned on the counter chatting with Crissy. Over the throbbing pulse in her head, Livy heard Mel holding her friend captive with tales of middle-school life.

"Sorry to interrupt." Livy angled her hip against the desk edge and mustered a pleading look at Mel. "But I need to get home." *Don't object, Mel. Just trust me on this.* She turned a bright smile on Crissy. Could Crissy tell it was as fake as her own? "I'll bring my baby in after it's born."

"Sounds good." Crissy's pretend smile faltered. "Take care of yourself and give my regards to DeeDee and her little one." No mistaking the genuine relief in Crissy's tone. Clearly, she couldn't wait for them to leave.

Out on the sidewalk, Livy nearly burst with her pent-up news.

Mel scrutinized her. "Why didn't you ask her about the tea mix-up?"

"I found something while I was in the bathroom." Livy pressed one hand into her chest and pointed with the other. "Let's go over to Stumptown Coffee, and I'll tell you."

"I can't wait that long. Tell me as we're walking."

"Okay." They waited on the curb for the walk light. "So, after I used the bathroom and washed my hands, I looked around for paper towels." She practically had to shout over the traffic noise. "I opened the supply cupboard, and guess what I found?"

The light changed. "Um, tea?"

Livy stepped into the crosswalk. "Lots and lots of little boxes of Crissy's tea. All beautifully wrapped in cellophane." She held up her phone. "See? I got a photo."

Mel slowed her pace and steadied Livy's phone. "She lied to us."

"Yes, she did. And I want to know why."

"You could've said something at the time."

"I had this strong sense I needed to play it cool."

They reached the opposite curb. Two preteen girls exited Stumptown, eyed Livy's belly, and giggled. Livy stopped herself from rolling her eyes, remembering what it was like to be twelve.

Mel opened the door for Livy, and Livy shuffled to

the end of the line. "I think we ought to stay here until we see Crissy leave. I imagine she leaves through the back door, so let's watch for her car."

"She drives a red Honda," Mel said. "That she calls Ronda."

"I like it." Livy laughed. "When she's gone, let's go back over there and tell Dani what we found out. Crissy's her employee. It should be Dani's call on how to handle it."

"I'm game." Mel tossed her a thumbs-up.

Livy concentrated so hard on the comings and goings across the street, she struggled to keep up her end of the conversation. After half an hour of swapping band-tour stories, Mel leaped to her feet. "I see her."

All Livy saw was a metallic-blue Lexus RX 350 turning right out of Evergreen Clinic's driveway. "You saw Ronda?"

"No. That Lexus." Mel, her face animated, tempered her shrill tone. "I got a look at the driver's face. It's Crissy."

"A Lexus? What about the red Honda?"

"She must have traded in Ronda for Rex. I can't believe she did that."

Livy grinned, recalling Drew's recent conversation with his daughter.

Daddy said we getting a new car today. It's a blue one. Blue's my favorite color.

It's not only blue, Mandy. It's fast, too.

Really, really fast?

Super-duper fast!

The Lexus blended into traffic. "Don't those things cost about fifty grand?" Had that actually popped out of her mouth? The price of goods rarely concerned her. "Uh-oh, now I sound like my husband. He's rubbing off on me." She'd heard it often happened in marriages. It occurred to her she was rubbing off on him, too. His relaxed demeanor, the ever-serious expression softened by laughter more and more. He'd even promised to look up dance tutorials on YouTube and learn to waltz.

Thoughts of Scott fled Livy's mind when Mel stood. "Come on. We need to get over there." She punctuated the sentiment by flinging open the door.

The clinic's front door was locked. They tried the back door. Also locked. But Dani's Toyota remained in the parking lot, so Livy texted her.

At your back door. May I come in for a chat?

The door flew open. Dani stood there, a beacon in the entrance. "Livy, I'm so glad you dropped by! Is DeeDee's baby doing well?"

"Oh, you heard."

"Yes, the hospital in Portland sent me the records."

"The baby, Xena, seems to be developing normally. But I wanted to chat with you about another matter." Livy made introductions as they followed Dani into the dim halls.

"Hi, Mel. I've heard of you. You're Crissy's friend." Her quizzical glance at Livy called for an explanation.

"She's here for moral support." Livy dropped her voice as though listening ears might still linger. "I'm here about Crissy."

"Oh, really? Let's go talk in my office." Dani directed them to two chairs, then sat across the desk in a puddle of dusty afternoon sun. A traveling cloud intercepted the sunlight, and the brilliance fled. Dani tapped her tightly folded hands on the polished surface, her smile having vanished with the sun. "What's on your mind?"

A smorgasbord of emotions flitted across Dani's face as Livy told her everything. Alarm turned to disbelief, then concern. "Crissy's up to something, Dani." Livy held up her phone to show Dani the photo. "I was hoping to examine one of the teas for myself, but like I said, she claimed she didn't sell it anymore. I wondered if you'd let me purchase one." She pointed to the restroom across the hall. "So I can compare it to what she gave me."

Dani, shaking her head, half stood. "It's unbelievable that Crissy would tamper with your tea. But you're right—it could explain the growth issues." She straightened to her full height. "Let's go take a look at those boxes in the cupboard." She crossed the hall to the restroom, Livy and Mel on her heels.

Livy blinked against the sudden brightness flooding the room. As Dani tugged the cupboard door open and peered inside, Livy looked over her shoulder. Then three gasps resounded in unison.

Save for some towels and cleaning supplies, the shelves were completely empty.

Chapter Thirty-Five

Howard's gaze kept sneaking to the little flowery book atop *Encyclopedia of Rock*. He sat back for a moment, relishing the irony of the book's placement. James Brown's wild-eyed, grinning face on the encyclopedia's cover. Beside James, a booklet of Psalms featuring a sunny day and sheep relaxing by a stream as though they were sharing a picnic lunch.

He reached for the book, hesitated, then picked it up. Without effort, it fell open to the middle.

" 'When you wish revenge against an enemy,' " he read, " 'meditate on Psalm 35. "Let them be confounded and put to shame that seek after my soul: let them be turned back and brought to confusion that devise my hurt. Let them be as chaff before the wind: and let the angel of the Lord chase them. Let their way be dark and slippery: and let the angel of the Lord persecute them. For without cause have they hid for me their net in a pit, which without cause they have digged for my soul. Let destruction come upon him at unawares; and let his net that he hath hid catch himself: into that very destruction let him fall. And my soul shall be joyful in the Lord: it shall rejoice in his salvation." ' "

Let Bro be confounded and put to shame. Let Bro be turned back and brought to confusion. Let him be as chaff before the wind: and let the angel of the Lord chase him. Let his way be dark and slippery: and let the angel of the Lord persecute him.

Let destruction come upon Bro unawares; and let his net that he hath hid catch himself: into that very destruction let him fall.

He paused at the next line, unsure if he really meant it.

And my soul shall be joyful in the Lord: it shall rejoice in his salvation.

"God," he heard himself mutter, "if You're really up there, if You're listening, see to it that Bro is caught and brought to justice. If You do, my soul will most assuredly be joyful."

~~~

"I really haven't known Crissy that long," Mel admitted as Livy sped south on Highway 99 toward Crissy's apartment. "About a year. I guess I don't know her as well as I thought. I never dreamed she'd pull something like this."

"Did she ever tell you much about her upbringing?"

"I know she was born here. But her parents divorced when she was small, and her mother moved back to Brooklyn, where she raised Crissy. She came back here about ten years ago after her mother died so she could get to know her half-brother and her dad again. Her mother always refused to let her spend time with that side of the family."

Livy slowed at a flashing yellow light. "Sounds a little sketchy. Did she have a stepdad growing up?"

"She had a couple, if I recall."

"She sure had us convinced she and her husband were hurting financially. Turns out they're doing well enough to buy a brand-new Lexus."

Mel placed her fingertips on Livy's arm. "I would never have sent you to her if I'd known her true character."

Livy glanced over. "Don't blame yourself. If you hadn't recommended it, we'd never have met Dani. She's awesome."

"Crissy insisted she wanted to meet you two. 'Declan Decker's twin girls,' as she called you. So when she landed this job at Dani's, and with the two of you expecting, well, it just seemed like the perfect opportunity."

"She *insisted* on meeting us? Didn't that wave any red flags?"

"Not really. I mean, she's such a big fan of your dad's, and—Oh, I just remembered…"

Livy braked at a red light. "What?"

"I'm remembering what she said when she first messaged me. Something like, how cool that you know his daughters. Is he a jerk to them too? Although she used a different word than *jerk*. I asked her why she thought that, and she said her dad told her. Then I asked her why she was on Declan Decker's fan page if she thought he was a jerk, and she said she didn't care what he was like in person, she'd always loved his music. And she wanted to meet you two."

"How did she know you knew us?"

"You're in my friends list."

The light turned green. Livy punched the gas, and the car jerked forward.

Mel's head bounced against the headrest. "Ow!"

"Sorry, I didn't mean to peel out." Finally, a tangible clue that someone might have it in for Dad. "My dad is many things, but I've never heard anyone accuse him of jerkiness. Did you ever find out why her dad thought so?"

"I didn't think any more of it. I figured maybe her dad asked your dad for an autograph and got the cold shoulder. A lot of celebrities are like that. But now that I know your dad, I can't picture him being anything but kind to his fans."

A thought hit her like a lightning bolt. "What was Crissy's maiden name? Do you know?"

From the corner of her eye, she saw Mel's quizzical gaze. "I think it was a pretty common one. Like Williams, Miller, something like that. Why?"

Sure, the odds of Crissy having the last name of Brodie were highly unlikely. "I'm curious if her dad actually knew my dad. If so, I might remember the name."

"Turn left at the next light. Her place is two blocks down."

Slowing, Livy glanced around. "She doesn't live in the best neighborhood, does she?"

"Notice the pot shops every other block. Green crosses everywhere."

Livy wrinkled her nose. "You can even smell it in the air."

"A new Lexus would stick out here, wouldn't it?"

Mel's statement proved prophetic around the next corner. In a spot facing the two-story complex, sunlight splashed across a blue SUV's flawless paint job. "There's her thief-magnet. I hope she has a Club for it." Livy pulled to the curb behind a crinkled Kia with a missing rear bumper, and they got out. A raindrop hit her head, and she peered at the sky.

"I didn't think it was supposed to rain today."

"Me either." Mel quickened her steps, then slowed when Livy couldn't match her pace. The clouds overhead thickened and erased the sun. Drops of rain marked their territory on the cracked sidewalk, and a cool wind raised goosebumps on Livy's bare arms. "What if Crissy doesn't let us in?"

Mel lifted her shoulders and cast her a wry look.

"What are we going to say to her?"

At that, Mel merely smiled. "Leave that to me."

They neared the blue SUV, and Livy stopped. "That's not Crissy's car. It has Wyoming license plates." She glanced around the parking lot filled with aging cars, long faded from their glory days. A handful of newer, shinier cars and pickups drew her attention, but she didn't see Crissy's anywhere. "I hope she's home."

"We can at least try. She's in number two thirty-eight."

The complex, like the vehicles packing its lots, had seen better days. Its beige paint was probably attractive once upon a time. Outdoor staircases led to the second-level walk-up units, and Mel strode to one of them. Shouts and curses echoed from behind a closed, banged-up door. Whether TV voices or real life, Livy couldn't tell. She shivered. What a place to raise a child.

They reached Crissy's unit after traversing through an aroma of freshly smoked weed, and Mel knocked. "Just a sec," yelled a male voice from inside. The door flew open. Drew stood there, one earbud hanging loose, his phone in hand. "Hi."

"Hi, Drew." Mel stepped onto the welcome mat. "Is Crissy home?"

"Crissy?" His brow crinkled like he wasn't entirely sure who Crissy was. "She's not here."

"Oh. Well, will she be home soon?"

He paused, still with that baffled look on his face. "No. No, she won't. Didn't she tell you? She moved out. And took Mandy with her."

Chapter Thirty-Six

Howard squinted at the tiny words in the meadows-and-sheep booklet. "When you're drowning in adversity…"

He pressed his lips together. Beyond a doubt, this applied to him.

> …let Psalm 31 comfort your spirit. "Have mercy upon me, O Lord, for I am in trouble: mine eye is consumed with grief, yea, my soul and my belly. For my life is spent with grief, and my years with sighing: my strength faileth because of mine iniquity, and my bones are consumed. I was a reproach among all mine enemies, but especially among my neighbours, and a fear to mine acquaintance: they that did see me without fled from me. I am forgotten as a dead man out of mind: I am like a broken vessel."

A broken vessel. As forgotten as a dead man. A reproach. How did this writer know so much about him?

"Talking to yourself?" Karen the punctual walked into the room, sensing exactly what he needed—a reprieve from his brooding solitude.

"Only because I am my own most captive audience." He closed the girly book and slid it underneath his leg, but her eyes followed his movement.

"Oh, I'm sure that's not true with all the records you've sold." She leaned down and lifted his wrist. "But even rock stars need their blood pressure checked."

He grinned at the teasing glint in her eye.

"What were you reading just now?" She nodded in the direction of the book partially hidden beneath his right thigh. The cuff squeezed his arm.

"Religious verses. From the Bible."

Head cocked to one side, her face lit. "That's wonderful. Are you a Christian?"

"Depends on how you define the term."

The cuff loosened, and she ripped the Velcro apart. "One twenty-two over eighty-four. Not bad." She set the cuff on the coffee table and perched on the ottoman, leaning toward his wheelchair. "I define the term Christian the way the Bible does. Someone who's saved by grace through faith in Christ."

"Oh." He'd heard those terms as a child, but they never made sense. "I have no idea if that applies to me."

"You'd know it if it did."

"I sort of remember asking Jesus into my heart as a kid."

"Well, there's a whole lot more to it than that. Like…"

"I know." He wasn't in the mood for a sermon. "My two daughters and the lady friend you just met are Christians. Fact is, I'm not a churchgoer like them, but I believe in God." A pain throbbed through his chest, and he closed his eyes. "Though lately it's felt like He doesn't like me much."

Had that really popped out of his mouth? He barely knew the woman. But something about her inspired trust. Her kind face lacked any guile as she pressed wrinkled knuckles under her chin.

"Why do you think He doesn't like you?"

The words poured out as if they'd been waiting for the right audience. "Years ago, I promised God I'd be the best husband and father and man if He'd only make my wishes come true. He kept His end. But I didn't." He patted his shattered ribcage. "And now look at me."

"You were praying to Santa Claus."

He ought to be offended. But somehow, he didn't have the strength to summon any outrage. A feeble smile stretched his lips. "I never thought of it that way."

"A lot of people pray to God as if He's their Heavenly Sugar Daddy rather than the infinite God of the universe. I've done my share too."

"Really." Discomfort wormed into his spirit, growing keener by the second. Had he sold God short all these years, and this was payback?

He closed his eyes again, resisting further discussion, and she got the message. Patting his knee, she said, "You need to rest now. Let me help you to your room."

Visions of his God-fearing grandmother haunted his memory. Somewhere in the still-unpacked boxes, Grandma's big leather Bible hid. He blinked at the sudden urge to find it, to see all her notes in the nostalgic, comforting scrawl he remembered from childhood. He'd always sensed a bigger Presence with her. Maybe holding her Bible could recapture that feeling.

~~~

The pungent scent of fresh-cut marigolds broadcast throughout Mel's living room. The locker-room smell of the yellow and orange blooms had never appealed to Livy, but she had to admit they added an eye-popping splash to Mel's earth-toned décor.

Livy anchored her hand on the sofa arm as she sat. "I'm curious about the energy tea Crissy sold you. I have this terrible feeling that…"

"What?"

"I…" She couldn't bring herself to voice her suspicion and waved her hand helplessly. "I need to see it."

While Mel went to fetch the Pep-T box, Livy twirled her wedding ring round and round until her friend returned. "Here you go." The box was adorned with simplistic drawings of women running and lifting weights, like a greeting card.

Livy, her fingers shaking, opened it and removed a pouch, then compared it to the photo of the genuine prenatal mix DeeDee had texted her. "It's the same." She gasped, showing Mel. "Just as I suspected. Crissy switched your energy tea for our prenatal tea."

"Wow." Mel, her mouth in an *O*, shook her head over and over. "No wonder it didn't seem to work after a while."

"Because you were consuming rooibos and ginger, while DeeDee and I were drinking" — she examined the ingredients list — "ginseng and anise." She looked at Mel's stricken expression. "You had to have wondered about it, didn't you?"

"I did. It didn't look or taste the same, so I asked Crissy about it. She said they were modifying some of their ingredients and simplifying their packaging. Based on consumer surveys, she claimed. And I believed her. What a great BS-er she was."

Hand shaking, Livy fumbled for her phone. "Just going to search for those herbs and their effects on pregnancy." Even though, in her gut, she already knew what she would find.

" 'Avoid ginseng during pregnancy,' " she read. Her voice cracked. " 'It can cause birth defects and impair fetal growth.' "

Mel's face went slack-jawed. "Thanks to Crissy, your babies stopped growing."

Something prickled behind Livy's eyes, and a tear ran down her cheek. She took a screenshot, then a photo of the tea bag, and, sniffing, texted both to Deeds.

Livy's phone chimed seconds later. She showed Mel the mad-face emojis DeeDee sent. *That girl must be a megapsycho!!*

Full-on sicko! Livy replied.

"I don't get it." Mel, distress erupting from her eyes, tugged a strand of hair as though jump-starting her brain. "I don't understand why she'd do that. I never guessed she had such a cruel streak." She reached for her laptop. "I'm going to check her social media."

Livy peered over Mel's shoulder as she logged on to Facebook. "I looked for Crissy's profile once, but didn't find it."

"Here it is. She goes by Crystal on Facebook."

"Crystal Collins?"

"Crystal Luna. No last name."

She couldn't have heard right. "Did you say Luna?"

A furrow formed on Mel's brow. "What's with the funny look on your face?"

"Well, Luna was my mom's name. And it's not a super common name."

"It's sure a pretty name."

A whisper of an idea teased Livy. "Can you open her friends list?"

"Sure." Mel did so, but the list was blank. "She's got it set to private."

Livy clenched her fists in frustration. She needed to see Crissy's connections, see if the man from Burien popped up. Crissy's middle name, not to mention the tea mix-up, couldn't be a mere coincidence. If Brian had never gotten over Luna, might he have named his daughter after her?

The obituary! That day at Grandma's, she'd found Brian's death notice, but no children's names.

Should she subscribe to the site and access the whole article? The idea annoyed her, but it was the only way to get the information she needed. She'd do it first thing when she got home.

Mel returned to Crissy's timeline. "I don't recall her posting anything about leaving her husband." Her tone tightened as though fighting back tears. "The last thing she posted was two weeks ago, and it was a promo post for her tea business."

Deflating into her seat, Livy sighed. "Now what?"

Mel swallowed, cleared her throat. "I'll try texting her. She doesn't know we're on to her."

"Then why would she remove the tea from the cabinet?"

Livy's phone rang. "It's Dani. Hello?"

"Hi, Livy," the midwife said. "I thought you'd be interested to know that I received an email from Crissy a few minutes ago, tendering her resignation effective immediately. It looks like your suspicions were probably correct."

Dani sounded as professional as ever, save for the tight edge in her voice. Livy couldn't blame her for being upset with Crissy for leaving her in a lurch, not to mention causing possible harm to Dani's patients. "You won't believe what Mel and I just figured out."

Dani's dismayed gasps broadcast through the line as Livy updated her on Crissy's tea-bag swap. "I can hardly believe she'd do that, Livy. In my opinion, you and DeeDee might consider consulting an attorney to seek legal action against her."

"We will consider that. Thank you for the idea, Dani."

"Again, I'm so, so sorry this happened."

"Not your fault, Dani." Livy said goodbye and hung up, grateful Dani believed her.

Mel fingered a strand of hair while Livy recapped the conversation. "I agree. You ought to sue the pants off her."

First, she needed to know how DeeDee felt. "Maybe."

"By the way, please don't tell your dad that my friend was responsible for your pregnancy problems. I don't want him to find out I was the one who introduced you. Can you imagine what he'd think of me?"

"Don't worry. I won't say a word. But I'm sure he wouldn't hold you responsible for your friend's actions."

Mel pressed a finger on her cheek. "I wonder where Crissy went."

"Her parents?"

"Both of them are dead. But she still has family in Brooklyn. I hope that's not where she's headed."

"You should text her. Say something like, 'Hey, it was good to see you again today. Want to get together?' Did she give any hints today that she had moved out?"

"No. I'm as surprised as you are." Mel picked up her phone and typed. "Okay, I'll try your idea."

A minute later, her phone rang. "It's her!" She put it on speakerphone. "Hello?"

"Why did you and Livy come to my apartment?" No hello, only Crissy's voice, loud and challenging.

Why did you screw up our tea, you sicko? Livy wanted to yell back.

Mel sought Livy's eyes. "Did Drew tell you?"

"Yeah, he texted me. But why did you come over?"

After launching a question at Livy in her glance, Mel recovered her cool and let out a breath. "I was worried about you, girlfriend."

"Why?"

"I just sensed something off at the office today, but I didn't have a chance to ask if all was well."

"No, all is not well," Crissy spat out. "I had to leave Drew."

Mel's whole face reacted. "Oh, Crissy. Talk to me, girlfriend."

"Drew and I had a big fight last weekend. All I said was, I needed to go help my brother move. He went ballistic and tried to keep me from leaving."

"Why?"

"He hates my brother. Doesn't like me and Mandy being around him. Then he tried to keep me from taking Mandy."

"How is Mandy doing?"

"It's been hell on her."

"So where are you now?"

"I'm staying with my brother and his girlfriend. Drew can go suck eggs."

A loud chirp resounded from across the room. "What *is* that?"

Mel cast an annoyed look at the offending object. "Just the bird clock on my mantel."

Five more cheeps sent Livy scrambling for her own phone. She'd told Scott she'd be home for dinner. With the girls at their mom's for the weekend, they planned on a quiet evening at home.

She tuned out the rest of the conversation and sent her husband a text.

Hi, honey. I'm leaving Mel's right now. See you in a few.

She scrawled Mel a note—*Find out where she's living if you can*—waved goodbye, and headed for home, anxious to tell Scott everything. Even though he'd be furious with

Crissy, he'd let Livy cry in his arms and would have words of comfort and wisdom.

~~~

DeeDee paced before the NICU window, watching, but not really seeing, the rushing headlights on the freeway far below, her phone fastened to her ear.

On the other side of the line, her twin's voice wrapped comforting strands around her heart. "Deeds, Audria was not the woman who sent the photo."

"I never believed it was her."

"Maybe Crissy sent the photo."

At Crissy's name, DeeDee nearly hurled a curse. "I never want to hear that name or see that face again. I wouldn't be surprised if she sent it. She's proved what she's made of. "

Something about the photo still nagged at her. A fuzzy memory dangled at the edge of her mind, then, like a Seattle rainstorm, burst into her awareness. "I just remembered something. Dad suggested we go back to the courier place and talk to the driver who delivered the photo. Remember?"

"No, when was this?"

"In his hospital room. Oh wait, you were in the bathroom. He gave me the guy's name—started with a J. Julian, I think. Something like that."

"What are we supposed to ask him?"

"Dad thought we should show him a picture of Audria to see if he recognized her."

"But it's a moot point now, since we know it wasn't her."

DeeDee moved to Xena's incubator and peered at her baby girl's tiny sleeping face. "True." She lowered her voice a couple of notches so as not to awaken Baby. "We could show him you-know-who's photo. Psycho Woman's. It's possible, with so many customers per day, he could've gotten some details mixed up. Maybe it wasn't an older blonde woman at all. Maybe it was a blue-haired twentysomething. And maybe he'd recognize her."

"And, since you're there and I'm here, that means I get to be the designated driver for this assignment."

"Lucky you."

Livy snorted. "Also, I need to find that obituary again and get the Brodie children's names. All I have to do is subscribe to their website. It's worth a few more unwanted emails to get that info."

"If it lists a son's name, what do you plan to do with it?"

"I'll let Dad know, and he can decide whether to go after the guy."

With her free hand, DeeDee clutched the side of the Plexiglas and held her breath, listening to Livy mutter while she surfed. "Just a sec. Got to put you on speakerphone." Another pause. "Here's the obituary site."

Quick intake of breath. "What's it say?"

"The website wants my life story and my darkest secrets in order to subscribe." Despite the sarcasm, DeeDee heard no laughter in Livy's words.

More pacing, from window to crib and back again before she heard her twin and the hint of something odd in her voice. "It says, 'He' — Mr. Brodie — 'is survived by his daughter, Crystal Luna (Williams) Collins of Seattle, and his son…' "

Livy paused so long, DeeDee checked the display. "Hello?"

"I'm here. I'm just having a hard time processing this."

"That Crissy is Brian's daughter?"

"Yes, but… What did you say was the name of the delivery guy Dad wanted us to talk to?"

"Julian. Or Julius. Why?"

"How odd." Long breath. "The obit says, 'He is survived by his daughter, Crystal Luna (Williams) Collins of Seattle, and his son, Julius Robert Brodie of Burien.'"

Chapter Thirty-Seven

"Risky."

Crissy sighed. Days like today, when the weight of her misdeeds pressed down hard on her, she wished Julius would stop calling her by her cutesy childhood nickname. In light of the risks she'd taken for him, it hit too close to home.

Her mom always told her that her name, Crystal Luna, meant Luminous Moon. A name to suggest a dreamer, a granter of wishes. Not a villain, despite what she'd done. Bro didn't need to know how relieved she was that DeeDee's baby had survived. She'd come to like the twins and would've considered them friends if not for her half-brother. If he hadn't been so bent on revenge against Declan Decker. If he hadn't dangled 250 grand in her face…

If he hadn't threatened to tell Drew her dirty secret if she didn't aid and abet.

Her brother stood at the bedroom doorway, eyes narrowed at her. "This better be over."

She turned from the bed where she lay Amanda down for the night. "I promised you, Decker's twins have no idea what I did to their tea." Crissy cast one more glance at her sleeping daughter. Disney princesses danced and posed across the fleece coverlet. Innocence protected her daughter from bogeymen.

Yet the real bogeyman waited just outside Amanda's

door.

But Julius would never harm his niece. Or her.

Would he?

She eased toward the door and switched off the light. She joined her brother in the hall and wrinkled her nose at the strong smell of weed hovering around him, her head tipped back in order to meet his eyes. "I carried my end of the bargain. So don't you dare tell Drew that Mandy isn't his."

He drew back at her fierce whisper. "If Drew had any brains, he'd see that Mandy looks exactly like his best friend."

"If you say anything after I did what you forced me to do, you'll regret it. I'll tell the cops about your attempted murder against Declan Decker. Which, by the way, Bro, you never told me you were planning. You gave the impression you were only after his money."

His eyes, the color and shape of almonds, sharpened with irritation. "You would've tried to stop me."

"I totally would've. Why did you want him dead?"

"If not for him, our dad would be alive. He'd'a lived to see his grandchildren, like Decker gets to. I've told you this a thousand times. We would'a been rich. I wouldn't've come home from school hungry every day 'cause Dad spent all his money on booze. I wouldn't'a been the school bully magnet. Do you know how embarrassing it was to wear clothes from Goodwill all the time?"

"And I've already told you Dad's life was of his own making."

He planted his feet and crossed his arms, blocking out her rebuttal. "No, he drank 'cause Decker got the girl and the life he wanted." His volume rose with each word. "With hardly any effort. Your friends...the twins...got the best of everything. I bet they weren't bullied at their fancy private school. It was awesome seeing them suffer for once. But Dad…" He thrust a finger close to her face, making her flinch. "He didn't even have enough money for a demo tape after Decker turned him down."

Crissy stifled an exasperated sigh. He'd spewed the same rant too many times already. She tugged on the waistband of her size 16 jeans. All this stress was melting the weight off her. She'd soon be back to her size 10 self if this appetite loss continued.

Julius leaned against the hallway wall, beneath the framed photo of himself as a ten-year-old posing with Dad. "We need to get out of this house ASAP. People are already nosing around asking for us."

Her heart lurched. "Like who?"

"Some pregnant lady stopped by the other day saying she was looking for the Brodies. Said she was an old friend. She looked kinda familiar."

"Did she give a name? What'd she look like?"

"Good-looking, long hair. Gave her name as Lacie McSomething."

"What'd you tell her?"

"Said she must have the wrong Brodies."

Was someone actually spying on them? Or was it his paranoia talking?

She needed to talk herself down off the edge of this cliff. "She probably just went to all the addresses under that last name that she found online." The reasonable explanation arrested the dread building inside her. His suspicion was rubbing off on her.

When she looked up, his expression blared an alarm all over again.

"What?"

He shook his head. "Nothing."

"Don't lie. I can tell by your face something's up. If you know something I need to know, you better tell me."

He gestured her to the living room where his girlfriend cradled their sleeping son on the shabby sofa, her earbuds fastened tightly. He motioned Crissy to the square of linoleum that served as a "lobby."

"I wasn't going to tell you this." He glanced over at Jennifer holding Hunter and sipping from her ever-present can of Diet Coke, then dropped his voice until Crissy stood on tiptoe to hear him. "Right before I pushed Decker, I told him it was payback for Brian Brodie. I figured it couldn't hurt since he was a dead man anyway."

Cringing, she felt her face twist. "Why did you say that?"

His eyes darkened with a rage that scared her. "I wanted him to think about what he'd done to Dad while he burned in hell forever. But he acted like he had no clue what I was talking about."

Her heart rate slowed. "He probably didn't. Why would he remember Dad?"

"Yeah, good question." Bro propped his elbow on the wall and his stubbled jaw in his hands. "Why would a big shot rock star remember the guy whose woman he stole?"

Crissy clucked. "Has it ever occurred to you that, if Dad had married Luna, he wouldn't have met my mom and I wouldn't be here? It bugs me that you keep bringing it up."

Julius had enough humanity left in his heart to drop his head. Then he lifted it and eyed her. "But there's still the little matter of Decker's refusal to promote Dad's music career...."

"Maybe it's because Dad sucked."

Julius's nostrils flared. "He could've given Dad a chance."

She strained toward him, hands on hips. "I'm sure Decker learned his lesson after Dad tried to blow up his concert." She forced an extra measure of sarcasm. "I'm sure he never ever refused anyone ever again."

"Dad died a drunk, and Declan Decker went on to earn millions. We're simply correcting the imbalance." He pushed away from the wall and paced to the fireplace and back, scratching his head as he stared at the patchy beige carpet. "Plus, it was fun messing with his head. You should've seen the look on his face when he saw that photo of Dad and Luna." He gave a short chuckle.

She folded her arms and gripped her elbows, rocking from one foot to the other. His mood was infecting her. "I can tell you're worried about something."

"Yeah, what if Decker remembers what I said to him? What if he sent the pregnant lady to spy on me?"

Her heart lurched a second time. "You're scaring me, Bro." Too much weed was turning him into someone she didn't know anymore. But she didn't dare say it. She crossed to the front window. Peeking out the blinds, she said, "I don't see anyone out there, okay?"

"Doesn't mean someone won't track us down eventually."

"I know." She let the slats fall and turned to him. "How soon can we get out of here?"

"The new house is supposed to be vacated by this weekend."

"That's a whole week from now. Too long. Why don't we just leave the state? No one would find us on the Oregon Coast."

"Are you joking? The sellers aren't going to give us a refund."

"I know that." Yet she'd do anything to keep Amanda safe. Including reneging on her agreement with Bro. "But with Decker surviving…"

"He'll get his someday, even if I have to follow him into hell to make sure."

~~~

A beep awoke Howard, and he fumbled around in an attempt to find the source. When the second beep summoned, he reached to his nightstand and clasped his phone.

An email from the private investigator awaited him. Wide awake now, he swiped to open it.

> Hello, Howard. In the matter of locating family members of the late Brian Brodie of Burien, Washington, I am submitting the final report of my findings. Attached is your invoice of $1,250, which is the balance remaining after deducting your $4,000 retainer for ten hours of investigation.

Howard grimaced. This better be worth it.

> The owner of the house at 4325 South Florida Lane, Burien, is listed as Julius Brodie.

What?

The familiar name clicked into focus and chilled his blood. Could this be the same Julius?

> I snapped several photos of him, per your request, which I have attached. They were taken at various angles and in a variety of daylight, plus a video of him walking, also at your request.

> Thank you for allowing me to be of service

to you, and please do not hesitate to call me
if I can do anything more for you.

Very truly yours,

Paul Prince, PI,

Seattle, WA.

Howard clicked on the photos and scrolled. The first
photo captured the subject from the back—long and
lanky, face hidden. The physique hinted at a similarity to
Bro. The next one had been snapped from across a street,
undoubtedly from the front seat of the PI's car. He could
make out the face, but couldn't tell if it was the Julius who
delivered the photo. As Howard recalled, Julius had a
bushy beard. This man didn't. Of course, that didn't mean
anything. He needed a close-up.

Five photos later, he got his close-up and zoomed in.
He sucked in a breath. Without a doubt, this clean-shaven
face belonged to Julius of Emerald City Couriers.

But was he also Bro?

He opened the video to check the man's gait and
movements. Paul had filmed him in his driveway,
between the car and front door. Howard replayed it
several times, scrutinizing the speed of the man's gait, the
length of his steps. His mind searched for the memory of
their first exchange. Had Bro walked toward him that
night with the same quick, businesslike stride? The slight
dip of the head, suggesting a man accustomed to looking
down at folks?

If he could just get proof that Julius was Bro, he'd take
it to the police.

And this time, he'd come clean.

Chapter Thirty-Eight

Livy pounded on Dad's door. *Dad, please don't be asleep.* She rolled her eyes at the irony. Five years ago, his evening would just be starting at nine p.m. on a Friday night. Life, even at its best, could unravel as quickly as a snagged nylon stocking.

In her eagerness, she tried the doorknob, and it opened with no resistance. Maybe he'd become complacent about unlocked doors because of the two ex-football players guarding his domain. Or, more likely, Gus or Dom was the culprit.

She found Dad sitting up in bed staring at his phone, ignoring the *CSI* episode on the wall-mounted Sony TV. "Sorry I didn't call first, Dad, but I have some really urgent news."

He lifted his head. His face, as still as cold wax, chilled her. Then the wax transformed into a glad smile. "You do? I have some for you too. You go first."

"I know who Bro is!"

His brows leaped. "How did you find out?"

"His father's obituary. His name is Julius Brodie."

"Yes, I know." He gestured at the phone with a small chuckle. "The PI just sent me a report and some photos. It's him, all right. Bro is the same guy who delivered the photo. Works for Emerald City Couriers."

Thank You, Lord Jesus.

She cast him her best stern-daughter look. "Now you

need to go to the police so they can go after him. And tell them the truth this time."

"But this isn't proof. At least, not proof that'll stand up in front of a grand jury. It would be my word against his."

Livy glanced around as if the décor could give her some insight, and her gaze fastened on the TV, where David Caruso's scowling face filled the screen.

What would Lt. Horatio Caine do?

She snapped her fingers. "Fingerprints."

"Hmm?"

"We need his fingerprints." Hands clasped to her head, she turned in tight little circles, thinking, stopping only when a surge of dizziness hit her. "That video! Dad, you still have it, right?"

"Yep." He pointed. "Check the nightstand over there."

She opened the drawer, but the room's fading light swallowed up the contents. A dark object brushed her fingertips, and she pulled it out.

The tape. "Dad, do you remember if he wore gloves that night in the park?"

Dad scrunched his face. "Sheesh. I don't remember."

She shrugged and set the video down. "It must have his fingerprints on it. Oh, and I still have the photo."

She found the photo and placed it side by side with the tape. "Here you go. I hope the cops find his fingerprints on them."

"But his prints might not be in their database. There'd be nothing to connect Bro, my assailant, with Julius, delivery dude."

Please, Lord, help us find that connection.

She snapped her fingers for the second time. "Where's that envelope?"

"What envelope?"

"The one that contained the photo. It'll have Julius's prints all over it." She held up the video. "Get Bro's prints off this." She raised an imaginary envelope. "And Julius's prints from this." Her gaze moved between her two uplifted hands. "And see if they're the same!"

"I don't think it's that simple, kiddo."

"But it's a starting place. Sure, the cops would have to get Julius's prints in order to prove our thesis. That's what they do."

"I believe they'd have to have probable cause to question him."

"Dad." Livy shook the tape at him. "Just give them the envelope and tape, tell them everything, and let them worry about the details."

"Honestly, I don't remember what I did with that envelope."

Her fists clenched. The most important piece of evidence against Bro—lost. Dad's shoulders drooped in tandem with his head. "It probably ended up in the recycling. I asked the boys to gather it up and take it to the bin."

Livy darted for the door. She refused to give in to despair. "I can go check the bin right now."

"Hold on. It got picked up the other day."

Hands clutching her head, Livy halted. "Oh, that's right. When Mel and I were here that day, we noticed the bin got knocked over in that windstorm." She threw out her hands. "The envelope is gone." She clenched her fists, her hope fleeing as if swept away by the windstorm.

He shook his head. "Speaking of Mel, can I trust you to keep this business with Bro confidential? I don't want to make the details known, especially not to her. I'd prefer to tell her myself, in my own way and time."

Funny, Mel had asked her the same thing. Perhaps it meant…

"You haven't told her anything yet, I hope?"

"No, Dad, I haven't. I'll keep it zipped."

"Anyway, we need to think of other options to get the evidence we need. Do you want to try to get Julius's fingerprints some other way?"

Livy widened her eyes. "Like what?"

"Like go to his workplace and send an empty envelope to, say, DeeDee's address. And make sure Julius is the one who delivers it."

"I can't do that, Dad. He'll recognize me, remember? So he'd recognize Deeds, too." She paced from the door to his bedside and around in circles, her palms clutching her head as if she could squeeze the perfect idea from her brain cells.

He shifted, apparently seeking a comfortable position, then opened the app on his phone and fiddled with the setting, sighing as the mattress adjusted. "I think better when I'm comfortable."

"Dad, I think we should pray."

He didn't look so sure, but how could he refuse her? "All right, then. But I'll let you do the honors. That's your department."

"Fine." She came and knelt awkwardly beside his bed and clasped his hand.

"Dear Lord God, we thank You that You are a God who loves justice and truth. We ask that You would guide Dad and me while we seek justice for this terrible deed committed against him. We pray You would guide us to the truth. We plead with You for clear evidence of Bro's identity, Lord. You see everything, even that envelope that could possibly resolve this case. We leave this matter in Your mighty hands, Father God, and trust You to work it out for our good. Amen."

"Amen."

She couldn't be a 100 percent positive, but she might have caught a glimpse of hope in his eyes.

"Now I have a job for you."

"Anything."

"I need you to find something for me. My grandmother Lorraine's old Bible."

Chapter Thirty-Nine

The vision of Livy's overjoyed expression after she brought him the long-lost Bible lingered in Howard's mind long after she'd said goodbye. He propped the ancient book on his outstretched legs and thumbed the fragile pages, suddenly realizing he didn't know where to start. Should he open it at random and just begin reading?

The book fell open on its own to a page in which Grandma had inserted a decorative bookmark. Romans 10, said the page heading. A red outline caught his attention, and he squinted at the tiny type inside. *That if thou shalt confess with thy mouth the Lord Jesus, and shalt believe in thine heart that God hath raised him from the dead, thou shalt be saved. For with the heart man believeth unto righteousness; and with the mouth confession is made unto salvation.* A double-underlined note in blue pen filled the margin:

HEART BELIEVES ➔ MOUTH CONFESSES.

He eased his back against the headboard at the stirring in his heart and gazed into space. Grandma's note implied belief leads to confession, not the other way around as the first part of the passage seemed to suggest.

Confused, he read it again. In the first part, the writer put confession before belief. In the second part, the other way around. Grandma obviously considered part two correct.

Which came first, the chicken or the egg? Belief or

confession?

And why did it suddenly matter to him?

He needed to talk this over with the nurse.

He pressed his bedside alarm to summon Karen, and moments later, Dom entered. "Whatcha need?"

"Is Karen still here?"

"No, she left at ten. The night nurse just got here. Want me to get her?"

"No, that's okay." But wait. Someone else he knew could help him interpret the passage. A pretty someone with waist-length hair, cowboy boots, and a mean guitar.

He'd text her in the morning. In the meantime, he silently prayed the familiar childhood prayer: *Now I lay me down to sleep. I pray the Lord my soul to keep.*

Because God better not take his soul before he found out what the Romans verse meant.

~~~

Howard watched Mel's long graceful fingers as she lifted a USC Trojans cup to her lips. "By the way, I read my Grandma's Bible last night."

"No, seriously? What did you read?"

He recapped the reading, and his resulting confusion. "In fact, let me go get the Bible, and I'll show you." Using the directional buttons on the wheelchair's arm, he wheeled to his room, pulled the Bible to his lap, and returned to the living room. The excitement of Mel's presence left his heart pumping like he'd run a marathon. He'd lost a lot of his edge since the fall. The physical therapy he'd scheduled should get him back to his old youthful self.

Hey, if Mick Jagger could still strut across the stage at seventy-plus, so should Declan Decker at fifty-plus.

Mel's grin lit up her eyes and heartened his spirits as

she scooted closer. He thumbed to Romans 10 and Grandma's note, explaining his dilemma.

"Hmm," was all Mel could say at first. "I've never thought about it quite that way before." She closed her eyes, evidently chewing on this. Opening her eyes, she broke the waiting silence. "The way I see it," she said, "confessing the Lord Jesus is just a reflection of what is already in the heart. Like marriage vows confirm publicly the couple's decision to commit to each other." She sipped the espresso Gus brewed that morning—"frat-style," he'd claimed—wrinkling her nose at the hard-core taste. She leaned in, sending a cloud of flowery scent his way.

"Gotcha." Howard lifted his own cup to his mouth, relishing the hot jolt. "It seals the deal."

A relieved chuckle. "Yes, exactly."

"So if I believe and confess, I will be saved?"

Her eyes sparkled. "You sure will."

"Saved from what, exactly?"

The sparkle morphed into dubious regard as though she thought he might be challenging her. The doorbell rang like an unwelcome alarm interrupting a pleasant dream. Mel looked at the door. "Would that be the nurse?"

Howard gave a half-shrug, the most he could manage without pain. "She's supposed to be here at ten, and she lets herself in." He glanced toward the back of the house where the bedrooms hid. "I better get that. I don't know what the boys are doing." The chair lurched forward as he navigated toward the front door.

"Let me get it for you." Mel crossed the room and disappeared into the entryway. He heard the click of the wooden front door. "Good morning." The cadence of her simple greeting turned it into a question, as though Mel doubted her own words.

An unfamiliar female voice replied, followed by a familiar yip. He'd heard that dog before. He wheeled toward the sound. When he reached the door, his blonde next-door neighbor stood there holding something in one hand, her doxie's leash in the other. "Hush, Doc." She smiled at Howard. "Sorry to disturb you, but my husband found something of yours in our yard. I think it must have blown over there during that windstorm last week."

"Something of mine? What is it?"

"Just an empty envelope." Smiling, she glanced between him and Mel. "By the way, I'm Sharon."

"Good to meet you. I'm Howard. And this is my friend Melodie."

She peered at the envelope. "Yes, Howard McCreary." A blush crept up her neck and flooded her cheeks. "Are you...?"

"Am I what?"

"Are you—Oh, never mind." Her face cleared, and she thrust the envelope forward. "Anyway, I wasn't sure if you needed this, but I thought just in case..."

Just in case she needed an excuse to formally meet Declan Decker, Howard suspected. Why would someone bother to return an empty envelope? Why not toss it in the recycling—

He stifled a gasp as reality dawned on him. "Holy moly, I wonder if that's the envelope I've been looking all over for." He grasped the vital manila envelope with unsteady fingers, almost fearing to look at it. What if...

The missing link between Julius and Bro. He clutched it to his chest like precious treasure.

The woman beamed. "I'm so glad I didn't toss it then. You two have a nice day." Before Howard had a chance to thank her, she turned to go.

As soon as the door clicked shut, Mel spun to him.

"That must be a pretty special envelope." Her eyes sparked at him, begging him to tell her more so she wouldn't have to ask.

Howard returned to the living room, and Mel plopped to the sofa, leaned back, and crossed one long, narrow leg over the other. "I've picked up bits and pieces from Livy about what happened to you. But she didn't say anything about a missing envelope."

He might as well tell her what she wanted to know. Judging from her expression, if he didn't tell her, she'd ask Livy. "In a nutshell, I know who pushed me that night. And this envelope is the clue that will nail him."

"You mean, you weren't really mugged?"

"Technically, no. But it was easier to let people think that since, at the time, I had no evidence as to the guy's identity." He held out the envelope. "Well, now I do."

Her eyes wandered to the evidence in his hand. "You know the guy?"

"Not personally, but now I know his name. Not clear yet on the motive. Anyway, I'm hoping his fingerprints are on this envelope."

"That's why you were looking for it."

"Yes. One of my sons must have put it in the recycling, but the windstorm…"

Come to think of it, Livy had prayed for exactly this. What had she said?

We ask that You would guide Dad and me while we seek justice for this terrible deed committed against him…. We plead with You for clear evidence of Bro's identity, Lord. You see everything, even that envelope that could possibly resolve this case. We leave this matter in Your mighty hands, Father God….

Had God sent the windstorm even before Livy prayed? Chills ran up his spine. If God was truly all-powerful, He could proactively answer a prayer, right?

"The windstorm?" Mel was saying.

"Yeah." He couldn't meet her eyes. "Livy prayed we'd find a clue to the perp's identity, and voila. The evidence shows up at my doorstep. Coincidence? I think not."

"No, not a coincidence. It's God's way of showing His personal care for you."

A shiver ran through him, and he hoped Mel didn't notice.

"Livy prayed for justice," he said. "And truth."

"God hears the prayers of His children."

He longed to spill the whole story, but something held him back. Maybe he ought to tell the cops before he shared it with others, even this lady beside him. He sensed her trustworthiness, couldn't imagine she had a traitorous bone in her body. But still. He needed to zip it.

"Now that you have the evidence you need, what's next?"

"I plan to turn it over to the cops."

"Perfect." She pressed her fingers together, then relaxed her hands in her lap. "Do you mind if we revisit our earlier conversation? You asked me a super important question right before your neighbor came over." She tilted her head. "I didn't get a chance to answer it."

"Sure, go ahead."

"You asked me what God saves us from. Remember?"

He nodded, remembering childhood Sunday school lessons. "I know the answer. He saves us from our sins." A shudder went through him at the awful word. *Sin*... despicable deeds other people did, not him. A word used to generate fear and guilt and manipulate children into good behavior. His grandma used to tell him, "Being mad at your friend is the same as murder in God's eyes,

Howie."

Sure, he was angry at Bro. And justifiably so. He'd bet God was, too. But it wasn't Howard who had murder in his heart.

He might not be as bad a sinner as that hell-bound son of a…Yet he'd shoplifted as a youth, lied, lusted, made empty promises to God. In that case, he supposed that made him as much a sinner as any normal American guy.

Sinner…A word to shatter self-esteem. But then his daughters got "saved." In truth, they hadn't suffered any loss of self-esteem. They didn't appear to be under any coercion to "behave." In fact, both girls seemed at peace, despite difficult pregnancies and other trials life threw their way. Both of them married strong Christian men with good hearts.

If his daughters and sons-in-law had been saved from their not-so-heinous sins, he had to admit he didn't see a downside. "What's the upside? In other words, what's in it for me?"

"Fellowship in heaven with God. A forever family. Eternal peace."

His breathing quickened. "Okay, I'm sold. Sign me up. What do I need to do?"

Her smile stretched so wide, so Luna-like, it knocked the breath from him. "Believe on the Lord Jesus Christ, confess His name, and you will be saved."

Chapter Forty

Something kicked Livy in the middle of the night. She shuddered awake to a sweat-soaked pillow and her husband's solid back pressed against her baby bulge.

A cramp seized her like a too-tight hug, and she cried out. Scott stirred and emitted a loud snore. "Scott, honey." She shook his shoulder, calling his name over and over. "I think I'm going into labor."

Adrenaline pumping through her veins left her weak, but couldn't touch the pain. "Honey! Please, wake up. The baby's coming." Mentally, she counted the weeks until full-term. This baby wanted to be born five weeks early. Late preterm. But another cramp made her double over, gasping.

Scott rolled over and jerked upright. "Sweetheart?" He rubbed his eyes. "Did you say the baby's coming?"

"Yes! I need to get to the hospital."

She managed to slide out of bed and grab the prepacked overnight bag she kept near at all times. Scott got to her side and took it from her. "Let me help you get dressed."

"Thanks." She slid on the tee shirt he handed her and a pair of sweats. "What are we going to do with the girls?"

"Oh. Right. Guess I'll call Shari's mom to see if she can come stay with them." Already he had his phone out, calling. "Since she's only a mile away."

If only his mother were nearby instead of in Dallas.

Or that her own mother were still alive. They wouldn't need to make themselves targets of Amy's perpetual bad mood.

Scott spoke for a few minutes, then ended the call, easing out a longsuffering sigh. "She has things to do tomorrow and suggested I call Shari."

Livy grimaced and not from the pummeling in her abdomen. Scott's ex had a new life, a new husband. "She's even less likely to agree."

"Right." He texted Shari, and Livy moaned while they waited for his ex-wife to reply. What if they couldn't get a sitter? Would she have the baby right here on the bed?

No, they'd have to take the girls with them. She pictured Kinzie and Lacie whining and protesting all the way to the hospital.

No good scenario presented itself. Oh, why didn't God give mothers at least a week's notice whenever He decided to tweak the timing!

Scott's phone beeped. "She says she can come, but it'll take her roughly half an hour to get here from Kirkland."

Livy groaned. Panic lanced through her and stole her breath.

"How many minutes apart are your contractions?"

"Not–not sure. I've had two since I woke up."

"Are you bleeding?"

"No. Not yet."

"Can you make it until Shari gets here?"

"I—I'll try. Hold me." Scott's embrace would ease her fright, a sensation almost worse than contractions.

He held her for seemingly endless silent, waiting moments, and Livy gradually relaxed. She glanced at the time. A little past four a.m. No wonder Amy got cranky.

She counted the time. Her contractions were coming

almost seven minutes apart, and she realized the baby's kicks had awakened her, not the labor.

Maybe she had a little breathing room, after all.

But when Shari finally arrived, mouth in a frown, Livy felt the rush of liquid down her legs. "I think my water just broke, honey."

Scott eyed her soaked sweatpants, then the puddle on the floor.

Shari waved them off. "Don't worry about the mess. You just get going. I'll clean it up."

"You're a gem," Livy gasped out, anchoring herself against Scott's sturdy arm.

Scott cast a grateful glance at his ex-wife. "Thank you, Shari. Feel free to take the girls back to your place if you need to."

Shari nodded. From her alarmed expression, Livy was certain her face must show every frightening emotion she was feeling.

Moments later, they were in the car speeding to the hospital. The contractions were coming hard every six minutes. Scott kept throwing worried glances her way. The streetlights illuminated beads of sweat on his forehead like tiny flashing beacons. "You'll be okay, sweetheart. It'll be fine," he kept saying, over and over, apparently heedless of her cries.

"No, it won't, not if Crissy succeeded in damaging my baby." Loud sobs wrenched from her mouth.

"I've been praying since we left." Scott took one hand off the wheel long enough to squeeze her knee. And then the red sign loomed ahead of them: EMERGENCY. Tears flowed as she realized her and DeeDee's dream to be there for each other's deliveries would not materialize. DeeDee wouldn't be home for another week, at least, possibly two. Having her baby should be a joyous occasion, not this fretful, frightening experience. She needed DeeDee holding one hand, Scott the other.

She wasn't ready for this.

~~~

Minutes blurred together, stretching to hours. *Breathe. Breathe. Push. Breathe. Breathe. Push.*

At last, a wail, hesitant at first, gained steam, then filled the delivery room and invaded Livy's heart. "You have a beautiful, healthy baby boy," came a voice to her left. A nurse laid a wet bundle on Livy's chest, and she looked upon her newborn son's face for the first time.

Elation, mingled with an unfamiliar tenderness, filled her heart. "Kane," she said, as certain of his name as she'd ever be. "He looks like a Kane." She checked his fingers and toes, so miniature they nearly disappeared into the rest of him. Ten of each. *Whew.* Two minuscule ears, one stubby nose. Two sharp, dark eyes peering up at her. And a head as soft as a ripe peach.

No visible damage from the tea fiasco. Scott smiled down on them. "Kane Lorenzo. I like it. What about his middle name?"

"You go ahead and pick it, Daddy."

"Okay, then. Decker."

A strong, manly name, like Kane.

"Kane Decker Lorenzo, welcome to the world." Livy caressed his wet, tiny back and pressed kisses on his soft head. Tears ran down her cheeks, and she sniffed. "Welcome to your world."

Chapter Forty-One

After stopping to sip from a cold can of Dr Pepper resting on her car bumper, Crissy hauled two small boxes toward the moving van Julius had rented. They were finally making their escape from this town, this neighborhood. This miserable street. Sure, the wooded island property contained two rickety fixer-uppers, one for Julius, one for her, but it was good enough for her and Amanda to build a new life together. Close enough for Drew to still see his daughter. And who knows, maybe Drew, the only man she'd ever loved, would be willing to reconcile.

But today, she had a new life awaiting her. She pondered the uneasiness churning her gut all morning. Their escape felt too easy. Any moment now, their flight could be interrupted by police cars coming to carry them off to jail. Were they really getting off scot-free after all the wrongs she and Julius had committed?

Sweat ran down her brow, and she peeled off her black beanie and wiped her forehead.

Her phone rang as she carried the last of the boxes to the van.

Drew.

She set the box on the driveway. "Hey."

"Hey." A heavy pause, filled with sadness, filtered through. "When are you going to tell me what's going on?"

"I told you I promised Julius I'd help him move."

"It takes three weeks to move? It's weird he'd buy you a Lexus just for helping him. You never told me where he got the money."

A muscle twitched in her jaw. "The equity from the house sale." She swallowed hard. "Plus, it turns out our dad had some money in his estate we didn't know about."

"The Lexus is his way of keeping you under his thumb. You know that, right?"

"Drew, I'm tired of fighting about Julius. He's my brother, and I owe him for all the things he's done for me since I moved here. Plus, he's a far better provider than you ever were." She hung up on him and smiled down at her daughter, who carried a bag of toys. "Mandy, honey, are you excited?"

Amanda gave a half-hearted nod. "Mmm-hmm. Is Daddy coming too?"

Crissy sighed. Mandy hadn't stopped asking about Daddy since they'd fled. Poor thing. Her daughter's little four-year-old mind couldn't grasp why Daddy didn't go with them. "I know Daddy would like to be with us, but he knows we have to help Uncle Julius fix up our new house."

"Daddy could help too."

"No, Daddy's busy at work. But he promised to come see us."

Lies, lies, and more lies. Her heart twisted at what she'd become. She'd turned into someone who'd jeopardize the pregnancies of two very nice women who'd done nothing to deserve it, all for a massive amount of dough.

Someday, she'd send a letter of apology to Livy and DeeDee and hope they could forgive her. Someday.

Julius muscled an armchair through the van's yawning rear door as she neared, anchoring it against a sofa. "Is that it, then?" he asked, jumping to the ground.

She nodded, and he took the box from her. From the sparkle in his eye, he was enjoying every minute of his great escape. No doubt, he felt he'd gotten away with something big.

Amanda tapped her leg twice, then one more time, harder. "Mommy, can we ride with Aunt Jen and Hunter?"

"Of course, honey." She opened the Lexus's rear door where Hunter slept in his car seat. From the driver's seat, the metallic pop of Jennifer's Diet Coke cracked the silence.

Mandy set the toy bag on the car's floor and climbed into the larger car seat beside Hunter. "Strap me in, Mommy."

Crissy obliged, staring at the face that looked so much like Theo, Drew's best man at their wedding. Tears prickled her eyes and nose, and she sniffed. How could someone so precious result from such a meaningless tryst?

Her crying infected Mandy, who gaped at Crissy and wailed, frightened by her mother's unexpected reaction. Soon Hunter awoke and caught the crying fever.

Two wailing kids. One overdue escape, coming right up.

They were nearly free.

So why this feverish churning in her gut?

~~~

Crissy wouldn't have noticed the police car creep by if Julius hadn't pounded on the Lexus window. She flung open the door. "What?"

He elbowed her aside. "Hide me. Quick." He folded himself to the floor and crouched there.

The hairs on the back of her neck prickled. "What's going on?" Was his paranoia talking again?

Jennifer let out an exclamation. "A cop car just drove by. Real slow. Jule, is there something you're not telling me?"

"Don't want them getting suspicious." His muffled words emerged from the vicinity of his knees.

Chills swept over Crissy. "Why would they? We're not doing anything suspicious."

A coughing fit seized him, the kind of deep, unhealthy cough common in smokers.

Crissy eyed the cop car, which had stopped and was now backing up.

Directly to the curb outside their house.

She sat frozen as two male cops, one middle-aged, one young, emerged. One said something into his hand-held radio. Jennifer stared wide-eyed, for once struck with wordlessness, as the policemen approached the driver's door.

The tap of the older cop's knuckles on the window galvanized her to action. She rolled down the window.

"I'm looking for a Julius Brodie." He glanced around the car, his expression unreadable.

"Uncle Julius." Amanda grinned as though this was all a big game. "Why are you sitting on the floor?"

The cop perked up. "Is Mr. Brodie in the car?"

No one said anything for ten seconds.

Jennifer gripped the wheel, her knuckles ghostly white. "Can I ask what this is about?"

"We have some questions to ask him regarding an assault investigation."

"Assault?"

"Ma'am, please get out of the car. All of the occupants need to get out right away."

Crissy glanced at the intimidating holster on the cop's belt. Maybe if she cooperated, he'd go easy on her.

She hoisted Mandy from the car seat and got out, then stood beside Jennifer on trembling legs. "Wanna get down, Mommy," Mandy whined.

"Shush." Crissy clasped her daughter tighter, certain the cop could smell her guilty conscience.

"Mommy, who's that man?"

"Shush, I said."

The policeman ignored them and peered into the back seat. "Mister, get out of the car with your hands in the air."

Inch by inch, Julius appeared, arms raised. Curses spewed from him like toxic waste. "I have rights, man," he insisted.

The cop frisked him. "I need to see your ID, please."

"Why? I have the right to refuse."

"We can take you to the station, if you'd prefer."

The roll of Julius's eyes couldn't mask the fear in them. Keeping one hand raised, he retrieved his wallet and handed it over.

Amanda squirmed and whined while the policeman took his time thumbing through the wallet's contents. "Mandy, honey, you can get back in the car real soon. Make-believe you're having your picture taken, okay? Hold real still and smile."

Mandy complied for half a minute. Then, "Mommy, what that man doing?"

The cop handed back the wallet. "Mr. Brodie, we have a warrant to search your property. Please take a seat in the patrol car while we conduct our investigation."

"Can I see the warrant?"

The cop held out a clipboard, and Julius's eyes bugged. He shook his head as if he were hallucinating.

The younger cop grasped his arm, and Bro stumbled alongside him to the patrol car. Right before the cop half-shoved him into the back seat, he cast one wild-eyed glance over his shoulder at Crissy. She shuddered at the depth of misery there.

The older cop studied the moving van, then turned to Jennifer. "Where are you all moving to?"

Don't tell him, Jennifer.

"Vashon Island."

Foolish woman.

"Is this house empty?"

"Yes."

"We'll start with the van, then."

"What are you looking for, exactly?"

"We'll let you know if we find anything."

"May we get back in the car?"

"You may. Stay there until we're finished."

Crissy watched, her heart shuddering helplessly, as they started with the cab of the van. Five minutes later, the younger one pulled out a briefcase.

Dread sunk into Crissy's gut. She knew what they'd find there.

Jennifer clutched her heart. "Isn't that where Julius keeps his cash from the house sale?"

"Um, Jennifer, that's not really where the cash came from." Jen wasn't the sharpest bulb in the garden. Then again, neither was Julius.

Jennifer whirled. "What do you mean? Where'd it come from, then?"

"I think you need to ask your fiancé that question."

"It's from drugs, isn't it?" Jen chewed her nails. "I knew he was up to something. But he wouldn't tell me what." A sob broke through.

The cops returned to their car and got in. Jennifer

hopped out and hurried over as the engine roared to life. "Wait a minute." Her voice carried through the open car door. "Is he under arrest?"

Crissy tuned out when Mandy fussed again. Doing her best to calm her restless daughter, she watched Jennifer return to the car, watched the cop car carry Bro away. Her deep relief at being spared the same fate wrestled with guilt. She'd aided and abetted him, yet with no charges against her.

So this is it. His greatest fear happened. Her eyes stung. Despite his steep personality decline these last few weeks, he'd been a good brother to her for ten years. She couldn't reconcile that Bro with the Bro who would attempt murder against a beloved celebrity.

Somehow, she knew she wouldn't see Bro again this side of a prison cell.

Chapter Forty-Two

One month later

The hallway of Saffire School of Dance held a welcome quiet away from the din of the auction in Studio A. "Let me show you around." Howard held Mel's hand as he opened the door to the dark, empty Studio B and hit the light. "I don't think anyone will miss me right away."

Mel glanced around the suddenly bright studio lined with mirrors and barres. "You don't think anyone will notice the guest of honor is missing? It's your auction!"

"Let's just see how long until someone comes looking for me." He grinned at her and led her back to the corridor.

"Quite a nice little place your daughters have here." She swept a hand at the colorful walls. "I like the combination of crimson and yellow."

He steered her to the photos arranged mosaic-like on the back wall. "This here is m—Luna Tunes you've heard so much about." Mel probably wouldn't appreciate his lifelong habit of calling his late wife "my Luna Tunes."

He studied the ten photos of Luna captured midpose in various moves. Then his gaze drifted to the woman beside him. He needed to get used to "my Melodie."

"I remember that album," she said. "LunaTunes. At the time, I didn't realize you named it after your wife. I just thought it was a clever play on words." Melodie, transfixed on the photos, pulled her glasses down from atop her head. "She was very beautiful."

"Yes, she was." His arm snaked around Mel's waist. He no longer saw Luna. "But so are you, my love."

She turned then, with that indescribable smile on her face. He thanked God every morning for bringing love back in his life, the kind of love he and Luna had.

With the kind of woman he felt safe confiding in. "By the way, I attended my assaulter's preliminary hearing today."

"Did you learn anything new?"

"One of the detectives testified that they traced the cash in Bro's possession back to me." He tightened his grip on her hand when shouts from the auction reached him. He wasn't ready to go back in. "From the first poorly written email my extorter sent, I knew right away he wasn't too bright. At our second meeting, he told me to bring unmarked bills. But I wrote my initials on one of the bottom stacks of hundreds in fluorescent marker, and Luna's initials on another."

"You clever man."

"There'd be no way for him to see it in ordinary light. Plus, I figured he was most likely to spend the top bills first. So if he were ever caught before he spent it all, I could prove it was mine."

"Ha. Way to be proactive."

"More like protective."

"You're good at that too, my love."

They shared a smile filled with mutual delight. She broke the spell first.

"Thanks for the update, love. Shall we go see how the auction is coming along?"

Back in Studio A, the din of voices amped up, nearly drowning out the background soundtrack of all his hit songs. Strange faces, and a few familiar ones, turned to watch him enter hand-in-hand with Mel. He nodded at each one and pumped hands all around, then gave slaps on the back to his former bandmates, all prepped for a little show later on.

His heart twinged at his old memorabilia laid out for all to see. And purchase. To handle and paw through. "This is harder than I thought."

"What is?"

"Auctioning off all my stuff. I didn't realize how attached I was."

"But I bet you'll recoup your funds."

"Lord willing." With Mel at his side, he beelined over to Nick, who manned the pay station, and DeeDee beside him, cradling tiny Xena. Baby Kane wriggled and fussed in his carrier while Livy rocked him and tried to get him to take his binky, but he spit it out each time. His mini fist pawed at his eye as if he couldn't make up his mind whether to sleep or awaken.

What healthy, beautiful babies. He gazed upon his precious grandchildren, thanking God for the ten thousandth time they'd weathered the scary weeks of no growth, and here they were just a few weeks old, thriving and gaining weight.

"Couple of good-looking specimens right there," he said to Mel, who smiled and cooed at Xena.

"Hey, Dad." DeeDee tossed them a smile. "You're raking in the bucks."

Nick nodded. "Nearly halfway to your goal."

"Really?" The floor-to-ceiling mirror reflected the guitar collection leaning against it—a golden Gibson, shiny as LL Cool J's head—a gleaming old Fender Strat once owned by Jimi Hendrix, a bargain at five grand—and so many others he collected over the years that he'd forgotten their origins. At the opposite wall, Gus and two friends stared awestruck at the five amps, large, small, and in-between. Over at the keyboards display, Scott anchored Kinzie as she pretended to plunk out a tune on Howard's Yamaha synthesizer.

Mel released his hand when her phone buzzed. "Excuse me a minute," she told him and stepped away to read the text. A flash of surprise crossed her face, and she tossed a quick, almost furtive glance at DeeDee and Livy.

He forced himself to smile and nod at the autograph seeker nearing him while Mel showed the twins her screen. Even from here, he heard DeeDee's guttural oath of protest, saw Livy's face freeze with shock. He scribbled on the woman's scratched copy of his first album and thrust it back into her outstretched hand. Curious, he edged closer to the women.

"You tell her if she shows her face here" — DeeDee's words, though whispered, carried unmistakable venom — "Nick and I will make her sorry."

~~~

DeeDee clutched Xena closer to her as if to protect her from unseen threats. Like Psycho Woman. She met Livy's distressed gaze, seeking support. Needing answers. "What do we do now?"

Livy shrugged her free shoulder, her other hand rocking Kane with quicker, jerkier motions. "I don't need this right now. Why don't you go deal with her? You're much better at confrontation."

DeeDee glanced up at her baby's proud, glowing Grandpa. Ha. Perfect. She stood. "Dad? Would you like to hold Xena for a few while I steal Mel from you?" She didn't wait for his response, merely reached out and placed her baby in his arms. The perfect spot. He'd had plenty of practice holding her.

"What's going on?" he said between kisses on Xena's head.

"No time to explain." She grabbed Mel's arm and hustled to the lobby, then spun Mel to face her. "Did she say when she'd be here?"

"She's on her way."

"She's actually going to show her face here after what she did?"

"She doesn't realize you know."

"I can't believe you haven't ghosted her yet."

"Like I told you, I talk to her as little as I can these days." Mel wrung her hands as she marched her long legs toward the entrance and DeeDee hastened to follow. "Which is fortunate because I'm not very good at hiding my feelings. She'd know right away something was up."

"Hmmph." DeeDee crossed her arms and lurched to a stop at the front door. "How did she find out about the auction?"

"I suppose the same way everyone else did. You know what a huge fan she was of your dad's."

DeeDee tapped her foot, never taking her eyes from the tall windows flanking the sapphire-blue front door. The first step Psycho Woman took inside this door would be her last. That old rage DeeDee thought she'd conquered after she got saved boiled inside her. "She should've been arrested along with her brother. Livy and I should press charges against her."

No answer. She snuck a peek at her friend. Mel's face was a mask of sorrow. Her wide eyes, staring straight ahead, held a misty sheen.

"What?"

Mel turned a searching gaze on DeeDee. "What would Jesus do?"

"Oh, please. Don't go all Jesus-y on me." As soon as the words left her lips, her heart gave a mighty twinge. She knew that feeling. She'd grieved the Lord. "Sorry, forget I said that. Jesus would, I'm quite sure, forgive *Psycho Woman*." She spat the last two words.

"Look at your beautiful, thriving baby girl. God didn't allow the enemy's scheme to succeed."

DeeDee, shamed, had no answer. The door opened, and a couple of graying baby boomer men entered, their heavy partying history etched into leathery skin.

Still no Cr...Psycho Woman.

Suddenly, there she was.

The witch was actually smiling. DeeDee's fists balled, but at her sudden lurch forward, Mel stepped in front of her. "Crissy!" she exclaimed. "Long time no see." Mel shifted each time DeeDee tried to move around her, as if she had eyes in the back of her head. Mel actually embraced her former friend, like she were your everyday normal nonpsycho.

Lord, help me not punch Crissy. If she couldn't yet forgive her, at least she could refrain from assault, even though Crissy deserved it.

She stepped forward before Mel could stop her. Crissy tossed her a wobbly smile. "DeeDee! I heard you and Livy had your babies."

DeeDee's nostrils flared. "We did." She lowered her brows, and Crissy's smile vanished. "Now, I suggest you leave and never come back."

Crissy cast a bewildered look at Mel, then DeeDee. "Is something wrong?"

DeeDee took another step toward her, but Mel was quicker. She grasped Crissy's arm and ushered her outside. DeeDee started to follow, but something stopped her. A check in her spirit.

Vengeance is Mine. I will repay. And stop calling her Psycho Woman.

Okay, God. Fine. I trust You'll see to it that Crissy gets what's coming to her?

She imagined what Mel must be telling Crissy and how shocked Crissy must be that she was found out. She moved closer to the window to watch the two women. With a jolt of something like satisfaction, she noted the tears streaking Crissy's face, Mel's intense gestures, then Crissy turning to leave.

Mel burst in moments later. "Not to worry. She's gone for good."

"What did you tell her?"

"Just that you and Livy found out that her tea was responsible for the babies' growth issues. I told her both babies were born premature and had to spend time in NICU. She started crying."

"Did she admit it was deliberate?"

"No, she just said to tell you both she was very sorry and she was glad your babies were healthy."

"Wait till we sue the pants off her."

But somehow, that solution left her with no peace in her spirit.

Mel nudged her and pointed to the wall clock. "We'd better get back. Your dad is about to play, and he still has Xena."

DeeDee allowed Mel to coax her back to the auction. Like Scarlett O'Hara, she'd think about this later. She retrieved her daughter and went to stand beside her twin. "Rock out, Dad," she said just before he summoned his bandmates to Studio C where their gear stood ready to entertain guests. "Livy and I will spread the word."

After the guests surged to the other studio, DeeDee locked Studio A behind them and followed the crowd.

Dad and the band stood at one end warming up. She spotted Nick at the soundboard, but she hung back near the door with Livy and hoped the band would keep the volume down. Xena still slept peacefully, and she needed to stay that way. Kane had finally settled down and now sucked his binky on Livy's shoulder, his half-open eyes flitting to and fro.

DeeDee glanced around at the crowd, about half of them involved in the local music scene. Over there, the owner of Emerald City Guitars, his red hair and beard conspicuous in the muted lighting. Near him, some new acquaintances of Dad's, the lead singer of a Christian rock band and his backup band. Two or three worship pastors from suburban megachurches, here to see if the rumors were true: Declan Decker found God.

The musicians stopped, and Dad stepped to the mic. "Hello, everyone."

A few people clapped. Then applause rang out.

"Declan Decker is back, meaner than ever." He cracked a grin. "Not really. In fact, when you hear what I have to tell you, you're going to think you're dreaming. Or that I'm crazy." He paused while the room quieted. "As you can see"—he gestured down at himself—"I've almost fully recovered from my fall, thanks to the superb medical pros who tended me and especially thanks to one very special lady." He beckoned to Mel, a few feet in front of him. "C'mon up here, sweetie. Let me introduce you to all my friends."

A bashful Mel went to his side, and he draped his arm around her. "This beautiful lady, Melodie Lansing, stood by me during my long weeks of recovery and didn't give up trying to lead me to Jesus, my Lord and Savior."

Murmurs resounded. DeeDee could imagine what they must be saying. What an impact Dad's testimony could have.

"Yes, I know you're all shocked. Not nearly as shocked as I when I came to the end of myself. But then I looked up, and there was the Cross. I tell you, people, it's the best feeling in the world, knowing your sins are forgiven and you're right with God. If any of you want to know how to have that peace, come see me afterward.

"And now, I want to sing for you a song I wrote last week, with Mel's help." His face turned pensive, his gaze leveled on his Gibson guitar. Soft strums emanated as he leaned closer to the mic and opened his mouth.

" 'Thought I didn't need You, God, I knew what I was doing.… But You had other plans, oh Lord, and that was my undoing.…' " His voice, still the same raspy baritone that made him famous, exerted emotion.

Something stirred in DeeDee's heart as he sang his testimony. Along with everyone else in the room, she was hearing it for the first time.

A tear slipped down her cheek, and she saw the misty sheen in Dad's eyes reflected in Mel's. She felt Livy's hand softly grasp hers and squeeze. They shared teary grins.

He ended the song accompanied by enthusiastic applause and whistles, and DeeDee whooped.

"Bravo, Dad," she shouted over the din. She'd clap too if not for Xena snuggled in her arms. She caught Nick's eye from across the room, and he tossed her a wink.

She could see in his face what he was thinking. Same thing she was thinking.

Declan Decker was back.

Better than ever.

Epilogue

Two weeks later:

A pair of shrill infant squeals knifed through the room. Livy jumped up from the sunroom sofa, DeeDee close behind, and hurried to the lemon-yellow bassinet their babies were sharing. They lay together like yin and yang, as though they were true siblings instead of first cousins. Livy's heart squeezed with acute tenderness at the sight of her son's plump arms waving helplessly and his pink mouth open wide like a tiny cavern. At moments like these, she could easily forget the sleep deprivation, the feeling that she was no longer her own person. She could forget the hard days when she felt like a machine designed for the sole purpose of keeping her baby alive.

She snatched Kane up at once. She couldn't take her eyes off him as he lay like a warm scented bundle in her arms, wrapped in sweetness so intense it brought tears to her eyes. She cooed at him, and he regarded her with his deep blue eyes, the most beautiful eyes she'd ever seen, locked on hers as if he were memorizing each line and plane of her face. He poked a foot out of his gingham blanket, and she lifted him to her shoulder. Tiny puffs of baby breaths tickled her neck. His head felt soft as velvet beneath her lips, his eyelashes impossibly long against his smooth cheek. She ran her hand along his bottom. Dry.

"Precious baby boy just needed Mommy-lovin'," Livy whispered.

She and DeeDee returned to the rocking sofa Nick had bought. DeeDee made faces at Xena, who opened her mouth wide in an infant version of a smile. The sisters' cherished morning ritual of hanging together with their babies, either at Livy's or at DeeDee's, was the best part of the day. This particular Saturday, DeeDee's house was quiet. Their husbands had left together for a shopping trip at Home Depot, and even the pets were subdued as if they sensed the sacredness of the moment.

Then the doorbell rang.

Livy jumped. "Who could that be?"

"Probably someone selling something." DeeDee slowly rose and flip-flopped to the door in her sweats.

Mel's voice carried clearly from the foyer. Why would she pop by unannounced?

Had something happened to Mel and Dad?

She didn't have to wait long. DeeDee poked her head in. "Livs, Mel has something for us. We'll be at the kitchen table."

Livy carried Kane to the pool of sunlight bathing the kitchenette. Mel sat there with an envelope in her hand. DeeDee, cradling Xena, took the seat across from Mel.

Oh no. Was this a break-up letter from Dad? She'd give him a tongue-lashing if he'd hurt sweet Mel. She searched her friend's face for a clue. "What's wrong?"

Mel, her face revealing nothing, handed over the envelope she'd been kneading in her fingers. "A couple days ago, I got this in the mail. It's from Crissy. She asked me to give it to the two of you."

"Who even writes letters anymore?" DeeDee glanced at the envelope. "It was mailed from New York." She removed two sheets of notebook paper and smoothed them on the table with her free hand while Xena slept on her shoulder. " 'Dear DeeDee and Livy,' " she read from the handwritten sheet. Livy leaned forward to follow along.

> By the time you get this, I'll be long gone. I hope Mel told you how sorry I am about the tea. I want to explain to you what happened. Not saying there's any excuse for what I did, but at least, you'll know why I did it.

> Growing up in Brooklyn, I never knew my half-brother, Julius, my father's son from a previous relationship. My mother raised me as if I were an only child. It always bothered me that, after the divorce, she wouldn't let me know my relatives on my father's side. As soon as I turned eighteen, I contacted my father, who was more than happy to pay my way to Seattle. He let me live with him until I got established, and I connected with Julius for the first time since I was little. Even though he was about ten years older than me, we hit it off right away. Julius and his girlfriend, Jennifer, welcomed me in and made me part of the family again. Soon I met Drew, and you know the rest.

> But before long, I found out some things about my new family that dismayed me. My father was an alcoholic, and he hated Declan Decker with a passion. He infected Julius with the same hate. According to

Dad, Declan Decker stole away the girl he loved, and then, years later, Decker refused to promote Dad's band. Dad always felt his band might have been successful if Decker had given them a chance.

It might seem random that I happened to cross paths with you two and with Mel. But it wasn't. After Dad died of liver failure, Julius kept tabs on your father on social media, trying to find a way to get in contact with him. He had some sort of scheme up his sleeve, but he wouldn't tell me what. He tried to get me to "friend" Decker's followers, said there'd be something in it for me. Which surprised me, 'cause I didn't think he had anything to give. Dad hadn't left us anything but a falling-down house.

Drew and I had been struggling for so long. I was so weary of it, so I went along with him. Before long, I noticed Mel was a frequent commenter on your dad's pages, as well as you two. She seemed to know you, and, being the Decker fan that I was, I saw a chance to eventually meet him. So I reached out to Mel, and we became friends. When I told Julius, he was so jazzed. He kept saying, if I could somehow meet Decker's daughters, I might someday get to meet him. Then Julius could see to it that the injustice was rectified.

When your dad announced he was moving home from LA, Julius said, "Here's our chance." After your first appointment with Dani, he persuaded me to get your dad's address from your emergency contact information. I totally wish I'd never done it. Honestly, I had no idea what he really had in mind.

As it turns out, karma got him big time, in more ways than one. According to Jennifer, he was so severely assaulted in prison that he had to be hospitalized. Apparently, the guys who beat him up were two of your dad's biggest fans. They told Julius that Declan Decker entertained them in jail (I never knew your dad went to jail!) a long time ago, before he got famous. He brought a spark of life to that awful place. And they never forgot him. When they heard why Julius was there, they decided to give him a big taste of his own medicine.

Eventually, my brother will heal. But I doubt he'll ever be safe anywhere, once people find out his crime.

I want you to know that the tea swap, the extortion, all of it was his idea. I'm not making excuses. I could've refused to help him, but I didn't. I can't express how sorry I am. I hope you'll find it in your heart to forgive me someday.

If there's a God, He totally watched over

your dad and your little ones. I'm so
thankful they're all okay.

Crissy.

Tears fell from Livy's eyes to the page and smeared
the ink forming Crissy's signature. She touched the wet
spot, unsure what moved her more—the terrible justice
inflicted on Bro, or Crissy's guilt and regret?

"Looks like he got what was coming to him," DeeDee
said in a flat tone. "In the sweetest possible way." She
jabbed her finger on the pages. "She talks like she didn't
commit any crimes herself. What about *her* karma? When
will *she* have to pay?"

Her lips trembling, Mel sat frozen, staring at the
letter. "She used me."

Male voices at the door alerted them that Scott and
Nick had returned. The men came in to find Livy in tears,
DeeDee hard-faced and muttering under her breath.

Scott dropped a kiss on Livy's cheek, then stood back
and ran his finger along her face. "You're crying. Bad
news?"

"It's Crissy." Livy pointed to the two sheets of paper.
"Read this."

The men read as the silence stretched for endless
minutes. Livy patted Kane, light rapid pat-pats on his
back to give her agitated hands something to do. Mel sat
with elbows on the table, face hidden in her hands.
DeeDee rocked Xena back and forth, brows drawn into a
frown.

Once finished, Nick massaged DeeDee's hunched
shoulder. "He was asking for it. But what about justice for
her?"

DeeDee thrust her outstretched palm in Nick's
direction. "What Mr. Deeds said."

Scott dabbed the moisture from Livy's face. "It's all over, sweetheart. They're both in God's hands now."

Drooping with sudden exhaustion, Livy planted her left hand on the table. "I need to go lie down." She tottered to the mint-green and lemon-yellow nursery and lay on the daybed with Kane snuggled to her chest and pulled a blanket over herself. He began to root, and she lifted her shirt to nurse him.

DeeDee followed her in and sat on the edge of the bed.

"Where's Xena?"

"Nick has her. So what's up with the crying? He got what he deserved. And so will she, someday."

"I could tell she was conflicted. She got pressured into doing something she probably wouldn't have dreamed of doing otherwise."

"Hmmph."

"Hmmph yourself. Look what Jesus has done in our lives, Deeds. Our babies are healthy, despite Crissy's sabotage. Dad is on the mend and has found true love again. The Lord's purposes are so much more powerful than the enemy's."

DeeDee shook her head, a reluctant grin twitching the corners of her mouth. "You're so Christlike, you make me feel like a total douche."

Despite the charged atmosphere, Livy laughed. And suddenly, it was over. DeeDee snorted with laughter, and it escalated, each feeding off the other. Kane's mouth slackened as he gazed at Livy.

"What's so funny?"

Nick's voice at the door interrupted their shared amusement. Laughter turned to giggles. Scott and Nick stood there with bemused smiles.

"Oh, nothing." DeeDee waved a dismissive hand.

"We're just counting our blessings."

"Our precious babies." Livy kissed Kane's head.

"An awesome dad."

She eyed DeeDee, reading her mind. "And the world's best husbands!" they said, in unison.

THE END

Dear Reader

The adventures of Livy, DeeDee, and Declan Decker have come to an end. I hope you're as sorry to bid them farewell as I am. After three books, I've come to know them almost as well as I know myself!

This trilogy began back in 2015 when I published my first book, the novelette *When Lyric Met Limerick*. It tells the story of the twins' parents' romance, and it was quite a shortie of a story, only six chapters. While I got some positive reviews, several reviewers wished it were longer, or suggested I make a full-length book out of it so they could find out what happened to Howard and Luna.

Thank you readers who suggested I make the novelette into a full-length novel...this book is for you. Howard and Luna's story has been woven into this book as excerpts. I hope you enjoyed the full-meal deal!

And what better place to set an attempted murder than Freeway Park, Seattle's Murder Central. On a recent visit with a friend, I was struck by the spooky vibe of the place. I wouldn't have even ventured there if I'd been alone, even in broad daylight. Interesting tidbit — there really was a blanket submerged in the pond, which gave me a germ of an idea. If someone would throw a blanket in the pond, why not a mattress, too? From there, the assault scene fully unfolded in my mind.

This project could not have come to fruition without the faithful community of fellow authors. To my OCW critique group, your feedback, both positive and negative, was priceless. Thanks to Jen L, beta reader, for honestly pointing out what didn't work, and suggesting a better way. To Deirdre, my editor, who pushed me to dig deeper—what a rock star. I couldn't have done it without her. And to Cheryl H, retired nurse, I owe a big thank you for reviewing the medical scenes. Any errors are strictly my own.

If you enjoyed this book, would you be so kind as to share your thoughts with the reading community?

Blessings abundant,

~~DVC~~

About the author

Dawn V. Cahill, an indie author from the land of microbrews and coffee snobs, published her first book, When Lyric Met Limerick, in 2015. She published her first full-length novel, Sapphire Secrets, in January of 2016. "The characters in my stories face situations that would have been unthinkable even 20 years ago. We live in a vastly different world than our parents did, and that's the world I write about."

Seeing an unfilled niche in the Christian market for edgier fiction, Ms Cahill came up with the concept of Hot Topic Fiction (HTF) at an intensive four-day writers conference. HTF isn't afraid to explore the question, how does God want us Christians to live out our faith in this not-so-brave new world? Without insulting the reader by offering pat or easy answers — because there aren't any — HTF tells stories of ordinary Christians following hard after Christ in a world of terror and violence, of upside-down morality, of hostility to Judeo-Christian values.

She has written several newspaper articles and more limericks than she can count. Email her at dawn@dawnvcahill.com, or find her on Facebook, Twitter, and her website. She is a member of American Christian Fiction Writers (ACFW).

(If you enjoyed this novel, would you be so kind as to hop over to Goodreads and let the world know what you thought of it?)

Other books by Dawn V. Cahill

SEATTLE TRILOGY
When Lyric Met Limerick – Prequel
Sapphire Secrets – Book I
Moonstone Secrets – Book II

GOLDEN STATE TRILOGY
Paint the Storm – Book I
Paint the Desert – Book II